Índigo

a novel by
Tim Adams

This is a work of fiction. With a single exception described in the Afterword, the names, characters, businesses, places, events and incidents in this novel are either the products of the author's imagination or used in a fictitious manner. Any other resemblance to actual persons, living or dead, or actual events is purely coincidental.

First printing 2025

Book cover art based on *The Great Wave off Kanagawa*, 1831, by Katsushika Hokusai.

ISBN 978-0-9896203-2-1

PART I

CHAPTER ONE

She called the suicide hotline for the first time at 7:34 p.m.; exactly then, on September 9, 1974; hotline volunteers had to log call details in the office record book. Mark took the call on the second ring, leaning away from the desk so his bushy Klondike beard wouldn't drip sweat onto the log. The thermometer had hit 98 Fahrenheit that afternoon, and the office A/C was broken.

He was slightly stoned, still felt the effects of the weed he'd smoked a few hours earlier. Later he would wonder if that was why he'd missed any clue of what he'd eventually see as a perfect Rhaytana moment. The contact would change his life, change it profoundly, but the only unusual element he noticed at first was that she spoke so formally.

"Hello," she said. "I would like to speak to someone about a personal problem, please."

Her voice was stiff, strained, with careful enunciation and pauses between the words. She could have been a shy librarian reading a petition aloud at a town hall.

"You can talk to me. Go ahead."

She started to say something, then seemed to catch her breath. Behind him Toby's chair squeaked. Mark motioned for his trainer to sit still and tightened his sweaty fingers on the receiver, pressed it so hard on his ear that it hurt. The office line quality was atrocious. He could barely hear her.

"I need to talk to someone about a problem with my husband."

"Please go ahead."

"My husband is being ..." Her voice trailed off. Mark heard her swallow. "I'm sorry. I've never made a phone call like this before. I don't know what to say."

"Anything you say is fine."

"I'm not suicidal. If there is another service I should call, please tell me." She sounded embarrassed. "I don't have anyone else to talk to. I'm sorry. I don't want to take up your time."

"You can talk to me. What's happening with your husband?"

"He ... he's being very violent with me," she said. "Last night he punched me. He knocked me down. I ... I was bleeding."

She stopped. Mark pressed his right hand on his free ear to block out the traffic noise from the street, waited for her to continue. The silence continued.

"Please go ahead."

She started to cry. Mark ground the receiver onto his ear, felt a vague, growing panic penetrate the lingering marijuana haze as he listened to her quiet, helpless sobbing. He'd been on the hotline phones for six weeks now. Tonight was his last night of formal training. He hadn't yet dealt with a gun call, but already had listened to desperate people: a father weeping uncontrollably for his addicted prostitute daughter, a cancer-diagnosed, twenty-five year old newlywed; others.

Something about this woman's desolate, humiliated crying set off alarm bells. A hospital worker had once told him: some people call for blisters and hangnails, others call only after getting stabbed or shot. One had to know the difference.

"Please go ahead."

The line went dead.

CHAPTER TWO

"Lost her." Mark dumped the receiver disgustedly into the cradle.

"What was it about?" Toby asked.

"Violent husband."

Mark printed the words in the log, forgot to lean back far enough. A dime-sized blob of sweat fell from his beard onto the record book.

"Why didn't you tell her to hit him back?"

"Don't be gross."

He swung his chair to face Toby at the rickety poker table behind the call desk. His hotline trainer and mentor was chewing on a candy bar, his second of the shift, his tremendous gut quivering slightly under his stretched, sweat-soaked Grateful Dead t-shirt. Fresh peanut brittle crumbs were flecked on discarded cards from their last hand. He was supposed to be listening in, on Mark's final night of training, but had let Mark take calls solo for the last three sessions.

"What's the dif? You lost her. She can't hear me. She's probably stringing up a noose in her backyard right now."

"Cut it out."

Toby gathered the cards, shuffled and dealt. He was thirty, eight years older than Mark, parted his hippy-length black hair down the middle, so the bangs partially concealed his plump, pockmarked cheeks. Toby had volunteered longer than anyone else in the nonprofit. He was excellent on the phones, and spoke caustically afterward about most of the callers. One trainee had quit in horror.

Mark picked up his cards, then grimaced disgustedly as the walls shook with the vibration of a passing truck. The windows were wide open, had to be in the heat wave. Potential suicides heard honking taxis and accelerating Harleys.

"Tell me the truth," he said. "If you'd never volunteered in this dump, would you ever think a suicide hotline could be this bad?"

"Maybe in Bangladesh," Toby offered. "Or Dakar." He nodded at Mark's beard. "'Course, maybe if you cut about three inches off of that thing you'd be more comfortable. Even a sheepdog gets a summer trim."

Mark ignored the jibe, fingered a pair of tens together.

"This has to be the worst call center on the West Coast. Has to be. The A/Cs out. They won't fix the lines. I feel like I'm listening to people through a two foot straw. I could hardly hear her." Mark flicked three cards into the discard pile. "We shouldn't even be here. Couldn't they patch calls through to Sacramento, Santa Rosa? Or open a Northern California WATS line?"

"Somebody would have to pay for it."

No help for the pair of tens. Mark glowered at his cards, remembered the sound of her crying. And he couldn't do anything.

He pushed a single chip between them. Toby didn't respond.

"Shit," said Toby, "you look really bummed. Is this your first night here or what?"

"If you'd heard her, you'd be bummed, too."

"This marital crap." Toby waved a dismissive hand. "You get the big boo-hoo-hoo tonight, and tomorrow they're all lovey-dovey. You don't know anything about her."

"You're such an anus," Mark muttered.

Toby leered. "I go with our beautiful office."

•   •   •

A half-year before Mark had started with the hotline, Jennifer had watched Toby handle a gun call during Jennifer's first week of training. A bad, bad gun call. A prison guard with a .45, holding it on his wife and two small children. Threatening to kill everyone in the family. Jennifer had been listening in on the trainee line, heard everything.

Toby had awed her. A-w-e-d her. As rotten as their office was, as lax and incompetent as the nonprofit management was, she was sure that they'd had the best call center volunteer on Planet Earth that night.

The guard had blasted holes through his bedroom walls. The roar of the shots had hurt Jennifer's ears, even with their lousy lines, the roar and the hysterical shrieks and screams of his terrified wife and children. Jennifer had had to get off her line twice, even though she'd only had to listen. To compose herself; to not vomit; to remember how to breathe.

Toby hadn't missed a beat. The screams and the gun shots hadn't phased him. Maybe because he'd been in Vietnam. The call had lasted six nightmarish, excruciating, mind-numbing hours. Toby had stood through most of it, completely focused, listening and talking to that murderous, suicidal guard patiently, steadily, perfectly. Twice he'd pulled over a wastebasket to have something to piss in.

And Toby had brought the guard through it. After six hours, the guard put down the .45 and let the cops in.

"He saved the whole family," said Jennifer. She shook her head as she told Mark the story, eyes wide. "That woman and those children are *alive* because of Toby. Our fat fuck trainer. We're *doing* something in this dump."

•　　•　　•

A month later, the same Jennifer had taken Mark aside at the hotline's holiday party, and shared a sad confidence as they contemplated their obese, greasy-haired mentor sprawled in front of a TV, dully wielding a newfangled remote control to click through channels as the rest of the team socialized nearby.

"Don't you sometimes think," she asked, "that he should be calling us, instead of the other way around?

CHAPTER THREE

The next day — three hours before his first night alone at the hotline; three and a quarter hours before his second call from the woman with a violent husband — Mark smoked his afternoon bowl after his shift at the liquor store. He toked up in the cool storeroom, as he usually did; opening the door to the alley to let out the smoke and lighting up with his back to the rows of crates and pallets, to the bottles and cans offering varying potencies of alcohol.

It was pretty good weed. From Panama, supposedly. Reddish. Too many twigs in the baggie that Chas had sold him, but still: pretty good. Mark held in the smoke, hoping as always to get a real high out of the bowl, and knowing at the same time that it wouldn't happen. He'd been smoking too long, at least a bowl nearly every day for almost seven years. His body had long ago adapted, took THC consumption in stride. His high school glory days as a newbie stoner were long gone.

He finished the bowl, tucked his trusty pocket pipe into his jeans and crossed the alley into the sweltering heat of the main street. His stash was getting low. He'd hoof it over to Yanny's, a pinball and video game parlor a few blocks away. Maybe he'd find Chas there. Mark headed west, concealing the light effects of the marijuana through long practice as he shuffled past the liquor store entrance, a tall, undeservedly athletic-looking figure (as he never exercised) who could have been plucked out of a catalog of twenty-something males of that era in the Northern California suburbs, except for his dark blond, sternum-length grandfather beard.

Yanny's was dim, air-conditioned, almost empty. Chas wasn't around. Mark headed to his favorite pin ball game, Sea Ray, slipped a coin into the slot. For the next fifteen minutes he collected some mild effect from the marijuana: hunched over the machine with his fingers on the flippers, slack-jawed, eyes wide, tripping out on the flashing lights and the red and blue bumpers as the silver sphere ricocheted from lane to ramp to kick-out hole.

But only for fifteen minutes, because then a bunch of teenagers came in. They clustered around the machines to either side of Mark, laughing, joking, swapping insults, sliding sodas and pink fingers on the cabinet glass.

One tapped his shoulder. Mark turned, regarded unruly cowlicks over a pudgy, adolescent face speckled with pimples. He'd spoken to the youth before, but he couldn't remember when or where, or a name.

"You know where I can get some ..."

The youth pinched thumb and forefinger in front of his mouth to finish the sentence, mimicking the smoking of a joint.

Mark frowned, stared at the youth's pouty mouth and cherubic cheeks, then muttered a curt 'no' and turned back to his machine. He tried to get back into the game, the flashing lights and caroming ball and the *zziiinng* sound of the flippers, but the teenies made too much noise, and when one teenie brayed an insult that Mark hadn't heard since high school he abruptly walked out, with two balls left to play in the game, swearing under his breath as he hurried away from Yanny's.

He couldn't get a good stone anymore. There he'd been digging on Sea Ray, and then these dippy teenies had to come in and bum his trip. It weirded him out, that was all, being surrounded by teeny-boppers. He was twenty-two. An adult. It made him feel like he wasn't going anywhere in life.

* .　　•　　•

At 6:55 Mark opened the hotline office for his first shift alone on the phones. He opened the window and positioned the log book on the center of the desk in front of the phone and put his dog-eared, creased, coffee-stained copy of *Letters from Rhaytana* beside it, so he'd have something to read between calls. He started to chuck the newspaper Toby had left behind, but then saw the empty spool of the towel rack and with a muttered obscenity tore out a few newspaper pages to have something slapdash to mop up sweat in the roasting-hot office. **PRESIDENT FORD PARDONS NIXON**. That was the big headline, the big news on TV and on the radio. Even the boozers at the liquor store had talked about it.

At 6:59 he sat with his head tilted up to watch the second hand sweep around the dial on the wall clock, and when it reached 12 for 7:00 p.m. flicked the switch beside the phone to make the hotline go live. Then he opened *Letters* and waited for a call. There were seventeen letters in all, that Rhaytana had sent to his old roadie buddy Paul while wandering the southwest. Mark figured he'd re-read the Arizona letter about Calvin's daughter. The one with the suicide, that had inspired him to volunteer at the hotline.

The woman with the violent husband was the first caller, at 7:15. The phone line quality was so bad that at first he didn't recognize her. Then she apologized for having hung up the night before, and he knew who it was.

She began hesitantly, awkwardly, then gradually relaxed, and spoke steadily: still in the stiff, formal voice, with pauses between words and careful enunciation. She seemed to have prepared herself for the second call, seemed determined not to cry again.

Mark pressed the receiver on his sweaty ear, strove to block out the traffic noise from the window that couldn't be closed in the heat wave. Slowly, pleasurably, he felt himself entering — being transformed by, dissolving into — the role of a hotline volunteer. He knew he was good on the phones. Toby and Jennifer had both said so. He could even get into the vibe of communicating on such a bad line; he'd shut his eyes, hold his hand over his other ear, groove on focusing on every faint, tinny word that whispered through the receiver. He was a helper when he was on the phone, a benefactor, a complete, realized adult, reaching out to lost, suffering people from the other side of the chasm.

Someone like Rhaytana. Not like the person he really was.

Mark learned her story.

•   •   •

Mark could call her Greta. If he didn't mind. The hotline volunteers didn't use their real names. He wasn't really named 'Parker,' was he? She'd feel more comfortable if she didn't use her real name, either.

Greta's husband Phillip had lost his lower leg in Vietnam. One day on patrol he'd stepped into a punji stick trap. Five of the sharpened bamboo sticks in the trap had stabbed deep into his calf. The Viet Cong usually coated the sticks with feces or urine, to infect the wounds. Phillip had already had jungle rot sores on both legs. The calf had become badly infected, and the MedEvac helicopter hadn't come in time to save it. The surgeons had cut below the knee.

Sometimes now he tossed and turned for hours with burning, itching 'phantom pain' from the missing calf. He hated to use crutches, but the prosthetic leg chafed and itched, and he always had sores on the stump. He had migraines, too. He'd had these before the war, but now they were worse, much worse, had kept him in bed for days. Still: the injury and pain were only part of his problem. The dedicated Christian Phillip who had been drafted into the war, who had believed that Jesus had given him a low draft number for a reason, could have adapted to life as an amputee. The bitter, angry Phillip who had returned: no.

"He could control himself for the first months after he returned," Greta said. "It was like he knew he had to put up a front to return to civilian life, no matter how he felt inside. He was cold. He never wanted to make love. He told horrible jokes about 'gooks,' but could still pretend to laugh if I complained. He'd say I was just being German, that I had no sense of humor.

"Then all his anger started boiling out. He said abusive things to me. I thought at first that he'd apologize, but he never did. It was like he'd crossed a line, and wasn't going back."

The first time he'd been violent with her had been right after their move. They'd *had* to move; Phillip had gotten in a big argument about the war with a co-worker, and his company had transferred him out of the county. They were at a shopping center, looking for sheets for the new bed, and when they joined the check-out line Phillip saw a little girl in the next line wearing an anti-war t-shirt.

"A really *strong* anti-war shirt. Maybe her parents were militants. '1, 2, 3, 4, we don't want your blankety-blank war.' With the F word. There were asterisks for the 'U' and the 'C', but anyone could guess what it meant. And that girl couldn't have been older than ten.

"Phillip stared at her. Just openly staring, and then chuckling and shaking his head without hiding how angry and disgusted he felt. The little girl saw him. The other line was only a few feet away. She started to look frightened."

"Her mother stepped up. 'Why are you looking like that at my daughter?' 'What a patriotic shirt for a little girl,' Phillip said. And then gave a sarcastic little bow. 'Thank you. I'm glad you appreciate my service.'

"They started arguing. With other customers in both lines staring at us, and the cashier staring too. Phillip was yelling. His face was all twisted, he was so furious. 'What do *you* know about it?! Were you in Vietnam?' And then he called that little girl a horrible word, and said why didn't she ask her mommy to make a shirt with that word, too, so people would know what she was. And the little girl was crying.

"At least he let me push him out of there. I was so ashamed. We got in the car, and I said, 'Phillip, please, my God, don't you know what you're doing?!'

"That's when he struck me. Next to me in the front of the seat. He grabbed the front of my blouse and slapped me hard, three times, with his face all twisted up. '*Shut Up! Shut Up!*' And then he called me the same word he'd called that little girl."

Greta's voice broke. Mark twisted sweaty fingers on the receiver, listening to her quiet snuffles and gasps and sobs; restrained tonight, but as painful to listen to: defeated, hopeless, humiliated.

"You said that he punched you and knocked you down."

"Yes." Greta inhaled sharply, stopped crying. "I had blood in my mouth. But I ... that time was different. Really. It's a long story. I'm going to forget about that one." She seemed to freeze up, was silent for several seconds. And then: "To me the way he speaks to me and looks at me is almost as bad as him hitting me. I don't have my husband anymore. He's so angry and bottled up, I can't get through to him."

Mark heard an automobile horn in the background. Greta's voice quickened.

"That's his ride home. I have to hang up. Please, will you give me permission to call you back?"

Permission? Mark felt confused, didn't speak. The office was listed as a suicide hotline in the phone directory, but they didn't have any set rules about who could call, or how often. If they'd had rules, they couldn't have enforced them.

"Please." Greta sounded suddenly desperate. "We just moved here, I don't have anyone else to talk to. Please let me call again. Please."

"Of course you can."

"Do you mind if I talk to you again? I'd like to speak again just with you, if you don't mind."

No, he didn't mind, said Mark, and told her what days and hours he volunteered at the hotline.

CHAPTER FOUR

"She ought to get out of there," Jennifer said, when Mark told her about the call the next day. "That guy sounds like a menace."

"Is there some kind of center or organization in town that she could contact?"

Jennifer sighed. No, she said, not really. The only dedicated facility she'd heard of for women with violent partners was something called 'Haven House,' and that was in Southern California. They didn't have a NOW chapter in town. There was a Womyn's something-or-other south of downtown, but that sounded way too extreme for someone like Greta.

"She ought to see a therapist. At least. Or someone from her church.

"And fast," Jennifer added. "He's already gone from yelling to slapping her to punching her hard enough to knock her down and make her bleed. He could kill her."

•   •   •

After that Greta called almost every time that Mark was on shift. Sometimes the phone already was ringing when he opened the office and switched on the hotline. She spoke only with Mark. Other hotline volunteers reported more hang-up calls.

"Your Kraut girlfriend," Toby sneered.

Single-mindedly, obsessively, she talked about Phillip: had he smiled, frowned, yelled at her, ignored her, thanked her (even in a mumble, under his breath), touched her, threatened her? How were his migraines, the sores on his stump, the phantom pains from the cut-off-in-Vietnam calf? Had he slept, eaten all his food, gone to work on time, had any trouble on the job? What could she do to help him heal? No, she didn't want to leave her husband, as Mark had guessed. Vietnam had mutilated the Christian man of her dreams, physically and mentally, but she remembered the Phillip that the war had stolen and would martyr herself to make him whole again, to help him again become the loving man who would join her in building a family, in fathering her future children.

They were new in town; she'd only exchanged hellos with her minister, couldn't imagine talking to him about anything so intimate, not face to face. A professional therapist would be even worse.

The phone was different. The phone was anonymous. There was no charge for the calls; Phillip wouldn't find out. And she liked talking to Mark. If he would please, please, please let her keep calling him at the hotline. That was all she asked. She could keep the calls short, if she was using too much time.

Of course, she could keep calling, Mark said. Superfluously, even ridiculously; he liked talking to her, felt flattered; her calls were the high point of his shifts on the hotline. He lobbied Greta repeatedly for a move away from her violent husband or a call to a professional, but she wouldn't budge, and he guessed that he might lose her if he pressed. So he listened, with a helplessly growing sense of attachment and responsibility. What would he do if Phillip got worse?, he wondered, and then cringed.

Phillip *was* getting worse.

CHAPTER FIVE

One evening the conversation drifted to Phillip's appearance.

"Oh, Phillip's not handsome," Greta said, as if the suggestion amused her. "Not at all. With that round head, and those ears ..." She laughed. And then: "I'd never be serious about a really handsome guy. I might go out with him once, if I weren't married, but no more than that."

"Oh?"

"I'll tell you," said Greta.

Mark heard what could have been the clink of a coffee cup in the background, the sound of a chair squeaking. As if she were making herself comfortable. Phillip was at home, but had been in bed all day with a migraine. He was too ill to bother her. Greta sounded more relaxed.

"My *father* was that handsome. A 10 on the 1 to 10 scale. Women would stare at him." Greta chuckled. "And he was absolutely worthless. He walked out on my mother. No child support. She did everything. He usually showed up just to leech money.

"Well, one April when I was in second grade she got him to take me to a Walpurgisnacht festival ..."

"A what?"

"Walpurgisnacht. Walpurgis Night." She sounded apologetic. "I'm sorry. It's German, you wouldn't have heard of it. It's mostly pagan, but they'd adapted it to be completely Christian. A festival, with dances and presents, something for kids. Mom had helped me make a costume to look like Saint Walpurga. And then her boss told her that she had to work that night. I guess she thought, 'My ex, as worthless as he is, he can at least drive our seven year old daughter to a park twenty miles away for the festival, and then drive her home again.'"

Greta chuckled again, but with less humor.

"I smelled the alcohol on that louse as soon as I got in the car with him. But he got us there without crashing into anything, and then until dark I was all busy being little Miss Saint Walpurga in the park, walking in the kiddie parade and being on stage and so forth. I remember shouting, 'Look at me, Daddy, look at me!,' and he hardly noticed. He was standing next to a woman in a bikini top.

"Well, the festival ended. It was dark. Everybody started to leave. And where was my father?"

Mark pressed the receiver to his ear, struggled to focus. Her voice had changed. She sounded angry.

"He was off necking with Ms. Bikini Top. Another kid's parents found him for me. The reason *they* helped me is because I'd been running through the park screaming my little lungs out, I was so frightened.

"Then he tried to tell me, 'Oh, I forgot. I was about to come back for you.' No, he wouldn't have. That rotten snake. He would have left me there all night."

Mark heard the chair squeak, guessed that she had stood up, as if to finalize her story. She laughed.

"Listen to blabbermouth me, talking your ear off! I'm so rude."

"No! No, please ..."

"I might even have offended you. You might be a male model, for all I know!"

"No." Mark gripped the receiver, felt suddenly, inexplicably anxious that she not feel alienated from him. "I'm as ugly as they get."

And then felt guilty, as he'd just told her an outrageous lie.

CHAPTER SIX

Mark fielded three more calls that night. The first was from a Latino evangelical who thought God hated him for desiring men. The second was from a compulsive gambler who said he had sent a succession of lovers into bankruptcy, and couldn't think of a reason to remain alive. The third was from their serial crank caller, the Fishman.

A Fishman call was always the same. He said he owned some land on the coast, and thought that fish farming could help alleviate world hunger. He would promote this idea soberly and reasonably until the volunteer asked why he was sharing it with a suicide hotline. Fishman would then become irate, and insult the volunteer until the volunteer ended the call.

Tonight Mark listened for about ten minutes: aware that a genuinely desperate caller would get a busy signal while Fishman hogged the line, and guiltily grateful for the break, the comic relief. He didn't have to focus with Fishman, hardly had to listen. He'd already drawn a swimming fish in the call record book in lieu of a description, and noted irritably that Toby had doodled iron crosses and swastikas next to entries with Greta's name.

Eventually he hung up, amidst a torrent of Fishman's insults. His shift was ending. Mark rinsed out cups and the coffee machine, and at 11:00 locked up.

It was only as he reached the street that he remembered that he had to call his mother. She'd clogged up the kitchen sink again, for the fifth time that year, couldn't afford a plumber and didn't know how to open the U-shaped P-trap under the sink to fix the clog herself. He thought of calling from home, but didn't want his roomies to hear him on the phone with his mom, or to see how he sometimes looked when he talked with her.

So he could call from Drake's. There were a couple of payphones by the cash register.

He fished a quarter out of his jeans, turned from the sidewalk under the blinking yellow D! R! A! of the Drake's Family Restaurant neon sign. He'd almost made it to the phones when he heard his name hailed from one of the booths.

"Oh *look*, Karen, it's *Mark*! Oh, Ma-ark! Over here!"

Shannon and Karen, who remembered him from his teenage dreamboat days, before he grew the beard out. Already giggly and bright-eyed, waving at him from the booth.

Mark approached, resignedly, pasting on the expected smile, guessing what he was in for. The giddy, girlish coquetry — self-satirizing now, years after high school; an impromptu parody — the intrigue, as if there were still a status in proximity to a former heartthrob who (they both knew full well) hadn't amounted to anything.

"Look, Karen, I'm sitting next to *Mark*." Shannon mimicked a gasp, like a groupie next to a rock star. "If only I had my camera."

"What brings you here, Mark? Are you having an affair? Anyone we know?"

And soon, inevitably:

"Mark, why don't you shave off that ridiculous beard? Don't you want to be handsome?"

Mark played along; it was easier, nodded and smirked when they expected him to, waited a few minutes before making up a story: he was looking for a friend, thought the friend would be at Drake's but the friend wasn't so he'd better keep looking. Adios.

·   ·   ·

He wound up calling his mother from a gas station pay-phone two blocks away. Repeatedly having to interrupt to get her on track; trying to help straighten out her chaotic life without moving back in with her and feeling like more of a boy than he felt already. 'Mom, do not spend your money on that crap, you're never going to get caught up that way,' but he knew she wouldn't listen, just as she never remembered not to pour coffee grounds down the sink; that the moldy stacks of newspapers and magazines with cut-out coupons would grow ever larger in her tiny apartment (behind the couch, flanking the closet, beside her bed), that she would waste time and money sending in sweepstakes entries for cars, TVs, American Colonial dining room sets (although she didn't have a dining room), gala vacations in impossible, unimaginable places: London, England; Paris, France; Madrid, Spain.

Mark promised to visit soon to try to fix the sink, hung up, walked home.

He rented a room with two other potheads in a tract house near the town center. His roommates were watching *Kojak*, sprawled on the battered gray couch that Mark had helped them carry from the thrift store, their slack-jawed faces lit intermittently by the flickering TV. Stoned. Mark mumbled a greeting, shut his bedroom door behind him, deposited his stash and pocket pipe and the dog-eared *Letters* on the upturned cardbox box that served as a bed nightstand. Then he knelt beside the bed and lifted the side of his old mattress with one hand so he could push the other as far under it as he could reach, until his fingers touched the spiral curls of the notebook he hid there.

His diary. Or his almost diary, a diary that was more like a journal, as he didn't feel comfortable writing directly about his life as Mark. It made him antsy. He liked writing as if he were someone else. These days like Parker, as if he were Parker at the hotline.

. . .

He'd known that he was unusually good-looking by middle school. A thirtyish neighbor initiated him into sex at fifteen, practically under his scatter-brained mother's nose. After that there were many partners, more than the norm for his male friends, who openly envied him.

At eighteen he entered a real relationship, or at least became infatuated enough to want to see the object of his affection long-term. She moved to L.A. to pursue a connection in the music business, and he regularly hitchhiked south to see her, learned the ins and outs of travel by thumb on the California freeway grid, occasionally made the trip in a single day and learned to conceal his sleeping body in roadside landscaping shrubs when he couldn't, like an opossum. She only broke into one music group, and dragged him along on some gigs; he vaguely remembered banging a tambourine while stoned under stage lights on the Strip. Then when they had wearied of each other there had been many others: girlfriends, pick-ups, relationships-for-a-fortnight, for a season.

It had been with Paula at age twenty that he had first felt used. She was twenty-seven, a corporate attorney, was happy to let Mark stay for days in her swanky condo when she jetted off to L.A. or New York for work, as if he'd been a pet cat that didn't need a litter box. She liked him to keep his shirt off in the condo, was only interested in sex, made excuses if he suggested a restaurant or a movie.

One day he overheard her on the phone when she'd thought he was sleeping.

"I can't possibly take Mark to that party," Paula was saying. "Be serious. At the Transamerica with a high school dropout! You can put a monkey in a tuxedo, but what if people talk to him?"

Mark broke it off, insulted, went back to playing the field. But his personal last straw wouldn't be long in coming: the relationship with Emily, only a few months later. That was when he'd decided to grow the beard.

No one blamed him for what had happened to Emily. Everyone knew that she'd chased him, that he'd never pretended she was more than a fling.

But Emily hadn't seen it that way. She hadn't yelled at him, or stalked him, or tried to get revenge; no, she'd quietly disappeared and fallen apart in private. It was her brother who told him that she'd been hospitalized for depression. He hadn't been angry with Mark, either.

Enough, Mark had thought. He didn't know how he was supposed to relate to chicks, but knew for sure that he didn't want to keep going in the same direction. He'd get out of the scene for awhile. Mellow out. Take a breather.

The beard hadn't ruined his looks until it was long enough to hide his jawline. But then it did, and he'd never regretted it. It had ruined his hitchhiking luck, seemed to frighten away drivers when seen through a windshield, but that was the only downside. Life was more peaceful. Women didn't look at him. If he changed his mind, he knew how to find the barber.

•   •   •

Mark sat on the mattress with pillows bunched behind his back and opened the notebook on his lap. His last entry had been a fantasy about Parker fielding a call like the call that Toby had taken with the prison guard. It was unfinished. Most of the entries were unfinished, never got past the third paragraph.

Tonight he thought he'd write a real life entry, about Greta. Mark pressed the clicker button on the ball point, wrote:

> *Greta seemed like a super cool person. With this observation taken away, Parker also could tell that she was super stressed-out. Even on the hotline phone, which was totally, completely fucked up the ass.*

The pen paused. He crossed out the sentence about the phone, caught himself glancing up at his stash and pipe on the cardboard nightstand.

Why couldn't he give it a rest for the evening? He didn't need to toke up to fall asleep. He could read the Rhaytana letters, if the diary felt weird, or his underground comics collection, or a music magazine. His stash wasn't going to go anywhere. If he skipped a night, maybe he'd feel it more the next day.

Mark wrote:

> *Parker knew that Greta depended on him. Parker felt the alertness and readiness a man would feel for any emergency.*

That was as far as he got. Mark dropped the notebook and pen on the mattress and reached for his pipe, brushing fingers through the beard that kept him homely.

He could be homely, if that was what he wanted. He didn't have a problem with sex.

He had other problems.

CHAPTER SEVEN

4/3

Dear Paul,

You tempt me. Truly. Rich Jenkins: best sound engineer I ever worked with. Dawel Roberts: best light tech, except for never remembering how to pronounce his name. This is a dream roadie team you're waving under my nose, you crafty son of a bitch ... but you and I both know I'm not managing another tour. My twenty hour days of coddling rock prima donnas are behind me. Rhaytana has turned a new leaf.

As for your other issue: Craig Spiegel is an ass wart, but he pays, and pays on time. Better put up with him, at least for now. You have a mortgage.

4/4
CONTINUED NEXT AFTERNOON

Pressing question: where am I? Inquiring minds want to know.

In the Arizona middle-of-nowhere, south of the Hopi Reservation on Interstate 40. I am cook, waiter, handyman, janitor and shoulder-to-cry-on in the named-with-delirious-optimism Interstate Gourmet, a humble, twenty-two seat café that cringes in the shadow of its neighbor, the huge, utilitarian ALL USA TRUCK STOP. Travelers patronize our freeway exit for the truck stop or the

gas station, and those unwilling to coun-
tenance the culinary fare offered at these
places must turn to us. I'd call the relationship symbiotic, but know I don't cook
well enough to attract a customer who isn't
simply hungry. ALL USA's corporate chief-
tains likely see our café as a harmless
parasite.

I wandered in here, and have remained.
That's my vagabond life these days, Paul.
Owner Calvin asked if I can cook, and took
me on. We have become confederates since, as
I'll soon explain, if I ever get around to
finishing this letter.

I spend most of my working hours not with
Calvin, who is depressed, but with Ricky,
a nineteen year old local. Nothing about
rural Arizona appeals to Ricky: not the
spicy smell of sagebrush, not the brilliant
fossilized conifers of Arizona's Petrified
Forest, not even the Hopi Kachina. No: young
Ricky is obsessed with rock n' roll: the
Airplane. The Dead. The Stones. The Who.
The Allman Brothers. Sly. Jimi. Janis. He
scours *Rolling Stone* and *Creem* for tidbits
about his idols, shares them excitedly while
I sweep or scrape down the griddle. I present myself as a perfect ignoramus, express
a mild, detached curiosity, as if attending
to the competition stories of a former high
school breast stroke champion. From these
lips will slip no hint that I was once a
professional comrade of many of Ricky's rock
star heroes, knew some of them better than
I would have liked.

Hark! A customer! A customer! Pulling into a parking space. Tc be continued.

4/5
CONTINUED

Hey ya, Paul,

Have you ever heard of the Barringer Crater? I suggested a visit the other day to café owner Calvin in the vain hope of cheering him up. It is a roughly 4,000 foot wide hole in the ground, a memento left by a three hundred thousand ton meteorite that walloped the backside of the future state of Arizona some fifty thousand years ago, when the Sweetheart State still belonged to wandering mammoth and giant sloth.

4,000 feet comes to 3/4 of a mile. You may see the crater from the air if a gig ever takes you on a flight to Albuquerque. It is my favorite local attraction. A gentle reminder of our mortality.

Calvin knows everything about me, including the sordid details cf my life as a rock n' roll tour manager. Ricky won't hear a word of it; Calvin promised. We have become bosom buddies, soul mates. In my one month tenure at Interstate Gourmet, I have acquired keys to restaurant, storeroom, Calvin's home. Paul, it's a problem. The more he entrusts in me, the greater grows a helpless sense of responsibility. What can I do for the poor man when it's time to move on?

A few years ago, Calvin's twenty-two year old daughter jumped to her death from a Manhattan high rise. This is the source of his depression. She was wide-hipped, stout-thighed, about thirty pounds overweight, regarded by most as homely, and clung to dreams of an acting career. The New York thespian magnet pulled harder than the equivalent magnet from Hollywood. She headed east. She was nineteen.

Three years of slights, humiliation and disappointment followed. She contacted dad Calvin occasionally for money, was obviously unhappy, but adamantly tight-lipped about why.

At last, she reached her limit. She stepped out onto the fifteenth story ledge of an apartment rented by a Manhattan drug connection and entertained morbid voyeurs below by threatening suicide. The police came. The crowd grew. A few yelled, "Jump!" Perhaps she heard them, because she did.

Worst of all, the moment is immortalized in a photo. An eager beaver photographer had found a way to an equal-height story in a facing building, had talked his way into a living room facing the woman in peril. When she made her leap, he was ready.

I could only bear to look at the shot once. A shameless news sheet published the photo; no one can convince Calvin to throw it away. Would the photographer have hoisted his camera if he'd known how the image would affect her father? The jump was metaphor for the woman's life, a self-portrait: I am an ugly fat girl photographed in mid-air free fall doing a **cannonball** to my death, a swimming pool cannonball, with my knees and chunky thighs bent up, my cheeks puffed out, and yes, holding my nose. Pinching my nostrils shut as I plummet to be spattered to a oozing puddle of blood, tissue and splintered bone on the sidewalk, in the gutter. You who have mocked and ignored me shall get your last, sick treat in how ridiculous I look in my leave taking.

That's enough for tonight. I try to cheer up Calvin, and now I have depressed myself.

4/6
CONTINUED

Paul, old Paul,

If I don't wrap this up, I'll need an extra stamp for postage. I should buy onionskin paper, if I'm going to be so long-winded.

I thought unseriously of suicide after Abby's death. (You might remember a few of my desperate phone calls. Thank you, Paul; I haven't forgotten your patience.) One day I asked myself to write an argument to remain among the living: not a canonical, ol'-Jehoshaphat-is-a-gonna-fry-your-bacon-but-good-if-you-make-an-early-exit, but a sober, defensible argument for a staunch atheist. The result is so humble that I fear it would convince some fence-sitters to reach for the razor or sleeping pills. I wonder if I would have shared it with Calvin's daughter.

But for me, it worked, because I accepted it as true; not superficially, but deep, deep down. I saw I wasn't BSing myself. I suppose I might consider suicide again in case of terminal illness, but the case for kicking off would have to be a lot stronger.

I want to remain alive because I may be only a meat machine, and can demonstrate no verifiable alternative to what I think, feel and experience as such a machine. I may be more, but certainly am a meat machine, at the very least. Human meat machine-hood endows me with consciousness, and in the greater scheme of things this consciousness may be inexpressibly, unimaginably rare.

An MIT scientist may get credit or blame for coining the expression 'meat machine' a couple of years ago. It offends. *I* am offended by it. Here we have Martin Luther King, Jr., marching on Washington: a meat machine. Isadora Duncan, arms aloft in *Dance of the Furies*: meat machine, a robot assembled with slithery red parts from the butcher's shop! Beethoven, Cervantes, Einstein: meat machines all, beep boop beep, obscenely dismissed by a callous academic as automatons, robots. Have you no soul, sir? Are you one who would fart in the bathtub and play with the bubbles while calling your dying mother to offer solace on her death bed? A cad is what you are!

But Paul, the expression appraises as true.

Consider our eyes, which refract light through cornea and lens to retina, that encode fantastically detailed messages sent through the optic nerve to our brain's occipital lobe. You yawn over my immortal prose because this machinery in your thinker is working. Or the meat-machinery of our ears, so often tormented by our clients in professional life: sound waves reaching ear drum, transmitted through three tiny bones to the pea-sized cochlea, where thousands of tiny hairs vibrate to different frequencies to transmit also encoded signals to the auditory cortex in our noggin's temporal lobe.

The architect, the engineer: evolution. T-rex and triceratops could see and hear, too, but were stupid, lizard-like. Big ugly dummies. Evolution has bequeathed humans with a super-duper dee-luxe premium advanced brain, frontal cortex included!, that can feel, reflect, concentrate, deduce. Further: we have opposable thumbs, so we can grab stuff (like the pen I'm holding), build what we think about.

But we still measure up as machines. Everything that I think, feel, remember, want, regret, everything that I think of as me, my memories, my sense of my own life, arises from electrochemical signals zipping around in the kilo-and-a-quarter of soggy tissue between my ears.

Religion fuzzes up the picture by introducing shovelfuls of indemonstrable speculation in the mix. 'When I die, I will be reunited with my loved ones. God will take my soul to another plane.' Or, 'God will judge me in the afterlife, and choose my next incarnation accordingly.' Or, 'God will send me to heaven or hell.'

All speculation. Show me real evidence for a soul, or an afterlife, or reincarnation. But I can produce plenty of evidence that I'm a meat machine.

And if that's what I am, the preservation of my conscious, feeling, fragile meat machine-hood becomes incredibly important. If an axe busts open my head bone and those electrochemical signals stop zipping around in that soggy tissue, I simply stop, end, like a smushed bug. Maybe, sure, *maybe* a superior-to-human intelligence might have other plans for ol' Rhaytana, might have some way of transporting immaterial me elsewhere. Pure speculation. What evidence suggests is that with death I become rotting meat, categorizable with dirt and kitchen slop, lose the colossal privilege of conscious human thought.

Die and the universe ends.

Die and the universe never was.

She was twenty-two when she jumped off that ledge. If she could have just made it through that tough, tough stretch, called for help, joined a program, lived one day at a time, she'd likely still be with us now, in the universe, on the evolutionary timeline, thinking, conscious, intelligent.

And her meat machine dad wouldn't be such a basket case.

   My goodness, can I drone on! You's a-lucky you ain't on tour with a windbag like me, Paul. I'd talk your ear off. L8R, brother.

Rhay

CHAPTER EIGHT

Greta decided that she had to get Phillip to return to church.

She thought he was getting better. Yes, in the past week he had been violent once, in the kitchen he'd shoved her, shoved her hard when she'd tried to talk about his drinking and she'd fallen, hit her cheek on the edge of the counter and had to tell people at work the next day that she'd gotten the bruise from a door. And no, she hadn't talked about it before on the hotline. But that had been the only time in a whole week.

If she could just get him to come to church. They were new in town, she didn't know the minister or the congregation, but he had been such a dedicated Christian before Vietnam, they had gone to services practically every week. If he could sit in a pew in a house of God and feel Jesus come into his poor suffering injured soul and help him heal.

She brainstormed, wanted Mark's advice on how to convince him.

"Well, are there any special services coming up?" Mark asked. "Do they publish a calendar? Or is there anything special coming up in your family?"

"Yes!" cried Greta. "Yes! Oh, my lord!" Their wedding anniversary! How could she have not thought of using that? That was perfect. Perfect!

•   •   •

The next night she called an hour into his shift. A good sign, Mark had decided. On bad days she usually called as soon as he switched on the hotline.

It had worked! She had given him a little gift, as Mark had suggested, a new wallet, and hadn't said anything about him forgetting their anniversary, and then as sweetly as she could had said that she already knew the perfect gift that he could give her in exchange.

"'Phillip, will you please come with me to Sunday service?'

"For a second I thought I'd gone too too far. He gave me that awful frown of his. But then I said how I missed our church Sundays, and asked if he couldn't try it again this once.

"And he said yes! This Sunday!"

She talked to Mark about how to prepare. Phillip hadn't worn his church clothes since Vietnam. She'd take everything to a dry cleaner. And she agreed with Mark, it would be good to try to talk to the minister beforehand. Not to be too personal, but to tell him that her husband was a Vietnam vet and that she wanted him to start going to services again.

"He's coming around. If someone has an ugly wound, you don't just look at the wound and think that's what he looks like all the time. He can heal. I'm going to get my husband back."

Before she signed off, she asked if she could ask him an unrelated question.

"Do you have a paid therapy practice, too? As a professional?"

Mark felt bewildered. Greta explained. She'd read somewhere that some professionals volunteered in their off-hours. Like doctors in free clinics, or lawyers taking clients with no charge. She wondered if Mark was a professional psychiatrist or psychologist volunteering at the hotline.

Mark was shocked, momentarily speechless. Then he remembered the hotline rules, and told Greta that he couldn't tell her anything personal about himself.

Greta said that she'd only wanted to see if she could afford to see him in person.

• • •

She didn't call the next two nights. On Sunday Mark didn't work or have a shift at the hotline. He'd planned to trip on LSD and hit a free concert at Sherman Park, but the supposed acid he'd scored from his roomies was a dud, and he realized as he milled with the shirtless, tie-died, braless, bearded, pony-tailed others in front of the concert stage that he felt almost completely sober.

Mark thought of Greta, guessed that at that moment she was either in church with Phillip or preparing to escort him there.

What did she look like? He had a vague image of her as blonde, although he knew that 'blond German' was a stereotype, that she was as likely to be brown or black-haired. He pictured a tall Aryan in a knee-length dress and conservative heels, hair styled in a Doris Day hairdo, walking stiffly beside her abusive, battle-scarred husband as she escorted him to his first church service since Vietnam.

Maybe it would work out. She'd said that he was coming around. Mark didn't believe he was, but hoped he was wrong. Maybe he'd helped her get through the worst of it.

Mark looked down, appraised himself, staring past his Klondike beard and tattered cut-offs at the big toe protruding through the beat-up sneakers he'd worn to the concert. How would Greta have reacted in meeting him face-to-face? Mark imagined the tall Aryan recoiling in horror, smiled with sad humor.

She'd thought he was a professional therapist. Him. Mark imagined a return trip to Paula's swanky condo, just to tell her. A professional *psychiatrist*. Him.

But the phone already was ringing when Mark switched on the hotline on Monday evening. Greta was crying.

.   .   .

The service had been a disaster.

"I don't see how anyone that insensitive can be a minister. Maybe it's that he's so young. I'd talked to him, too, during the week, to tell him about Phillip. He'd smiled at me and said he wouldn't forget.

"Well, he sure didn't forget. He stepped up to the pulpit and scanned the congregation, and for a second his eyes locked on Phillip and me in our pew. Right off he turned his sermon to Vietnam. I thought, 'Okay, that's putting us in the limelight, but maybe he's got something special to say to make my poor husband feel comfortable.'

"How can anyone so thoughtless call himself a man of God? He didn't say anything about how men like Phillip had been drafted against their will, how they'd suffered and how hard it was to cope back home. No, the sermon was all about the *sins* soldiers had committed in Vietnam. Like all the draftees had been rapists and murderers at My Lai, that they had to seek God's forgiveness for what they'd done there."

"I couldn't believe what I was hearing. I was frozen. I looked at Phillip, and then I knew how bad it was going to be. He was shaking with anger. Just shaking.

"Finally he stood up, in the middle of the sermon. Everyone was staring at us. The minister stopped talking. Phillip pushed his way out of the pew and started to walk out. But with his prosthetic ... you don't just strap it on after an amputation and walk like you used to. There are things he has to remember when he walks, and if he gets upset ...

"He was limping up the aisle, all jerky and strained. And I swear, it was like a thought balloon went around that church, 'This man lost his leg in Vietnam, he must be the kind of dirty war criminal our minister is preaching about, and now he's walking out because he won't atone for his sins.'

"Phillip lost his balance and toppled into one of the pews. With everyone staring, and the woman he tumbled into looked disgusted and pushed him away. Like she'd been touched by a child molester."

Greta took a deep, rasping breath, seemed to shudder as she exhaled into the receiver. Mark imagined the mysterious woman on the other end of the line, sitting alone in her kitchen or bedroom, fighting to control herself.

"In the car I tried so hard to say, 'Phillip, I'm sorry, this turned out all wrong, please, please, I'm sorry.' He wouldn't even look at me. He just sat and stared out the windshield with that stiff, bitter, angry look he gets. And I already knew: if he won't even yell now, it's going to be really bad later.

"Late that night, he called me into the living room. He was drunk by then, he'd been drinking all evening. He was sitting in the dark with his bottle, not even watching TV. I walked up, God, I could smell his breath. His eyes were all glassy. He looked crazy.

"'Sit down, sit down,' he said. Friendly-like.

"I sat on the ottoman in front of him. He leaned forward and took my wrist. He was smiling, but oh, God, that was the most horrible smile I ever saw.

"'You planned that today, didn't you?' he said.

"*Planned* it?! *Planned* it?! Then he told me what he thought. That I was having a sexual affair with that minister, that the two of us wanted to drive Phillip into a breakdown so I'd get his VA benefits.

"Just the craziest ideas you can imagine, and he's telling it all matter-of-fact with that bitter, hateful smile, like now he could relax and be calm because he'd figured out the big scheme. And digging his fingernails into my wrist until I thought I'd bleed.

"I had to practically rip my arm away from him. Then he started shouting, and by then I was shouting, too. And then ..."

Greta broke down, almost as she had on her first call to the hotline, cried pathetically, uncontrollably. Mark winced, braced himself for bad news. For once he felt grateful for the bad phone lines. It would have been tougher to hear her clearly.

"That night I woke up, maybe three in the morning. I couldn't breathe.

"Phillip was on top of me in bed. He had his fingers on my throat. Choking me.

"'Admit you planned it!' Yelling into my face, crazy and drunk. Calling me horrible names. 'Tell me the truth!'

"I couldn't breathe, I swear, I thought he was going to kill me. Finally I got him off me. Maybe he'd realized he'd gone too far, that he was about to be a murderer.

"I slept in the back seat of our car in the driveway, with the door locked. I don't know what our neighbors thought, if they saw me getting out the next morning in my bathrobe. At breakfast he didn't look at me or say anything."

"What are you going to do?"

Greta managed a weak laugh. "Well, I'm going to have to put some make-up on my neck. The marks show."

She was going to watch and wait, she said. This had to be the bottom; Phillip couldn't get any worse. And as bad as it had been, she had to put the choking in a special category.

Because it had been partly her fault, hadn't it? She'd provoked him.

CHAPTER NINE

"She thinks she *provoked* him," said Jennifer, when Mark told her about the call. She was studying for a master's degree in psychology. "He almost choked her to death, and she thinks it's her *fault.*"

"How about if she calls the cops on him?"

Jennifer snorted. "Sure, if he's beating her head in with a hammer on the front lawn when they get there. Otherwise, forget it. Arrests in family disputes are a last resort. You ever heard of Ruth Bunnell?"

Mark hadn't. Bunnell, Jennifer explained, had made over twenty calls to the San Jose police before her husband murdered her in 1972.

"Your Greta's got to get out of there."

• • •

The next day at lunch Mark hitched a ride to Womyn's World south of downtown.

The storefront window was plastered with feminist posters: raised fists, Venus symbols, photos of Germaine Greer, Angela Davis, Betty Friedan. Mark entered, found a slender thirtyish woman with buzz cut black hair sitting alone behind a desk. She regarded him suspiciously.

"I can hear you from there," she said, when he was five steps from the desk. Her hand rested conspicuously on an open top desk drawer.

Her expression softened as he described Greta and explained why he'd come.

"Well, she's welcome to come here," the woman said. "You probably already knew that. But she doesn't sound like the type."

Mark asked if she could think of an alternative. The woman folded her hands behind her head, cast reflective eyes at the ceiling, thought in silence for over a half-minute. Then:

"Is she seriously Christian? Like, hardcore, with Bible study, a pocket Bible in the purse, the whole shebang?"

"I think so."

"Then she could try Saint Catherine's. It's a Christian women's group. They do support, counseling. I think they have housing."

The woman rubbed her thumb and forefingers together.

"They're well-funded. Beaucoup bucks." She looked sympathetic. "But it's super private, and strictly women only."

She took her hand from the drawer to rummage through folders in a file cabinet. She found what she sought, and stood up to walk around the desk and hand him a flier.

"The address is at the bottom," she said.

•   •   •

"Do you understand how committed I am to my husband in my faith?" asked Greta. "Even if you don't agree? Do you understand that I remember a better man, and that I still love my husband in spite of what he's done to me?"

Mark decided to change the subject. "How is he now?"

Greta sighed. Mark thought he heard a glass clink, guessed that she was calling from the kitchen, that Phillip was still at work. She'd become more fatalistic and matter-of-fact since the choking episode, had stopped insisting that Phillip was improving.

The phone line hadn't improved, but at least now he could hear without pressing his right palm over his free ear. The days were shorter and cooler in late October; he could keep the office window closed. The only sound competing with Greta's voice was the hum of the space heater.

"His supervisor called me today," she said. "Called *me*. That's bad. They can't cut Phillip much more slack. With his mood issues, all the days he's missing. They thought it was time to let me know.

"And oh dear God, if he loses his job. At least now he's got a reason to get up in the morning."

He was drinking more and more, Greta said. He'd tried to keep it in check, but he was in constant pain, from the migraines and his leg. He was losing the battle. He *knew* he was losing it.

"He sits up in the living room until four in the morning. Sometimes he watches TV, but a lot of time he sits in the dark with his liquor and his service medals. He says nobody can take those medals away from him.

"He's got his favorite chair backed into the corner of the living room, with the TV in front of it. So no one can sneak in and *get* him. That's what he said. He knows two cops in the local P.D. from the service, the cops could tell him how crazy that is. Get him. Sneak in and attack him from behind in our living room.

"Maybe he means me," Greta sighed. "The other day he asked me if I have any gook blood. If I'm part Vietnamese."

.　　.　　.

The address for Saint Catherine's turned out to be a high-end office building downtown. Mark again hitchhiked there on his lunch break, but wished this time that he hadn't worn a t-shirt. The uniformed security agent at the lobby desk regarded him coldly, and wouldn't let him take the elevator to the floor corresponding with "St. Catherine's" in the lobby directory.

"You can call up for permission," the agent said, and nodded to the phone on his desk.

A woman answered. Polite, distant, cold.

Saint Catherine's, she said, was a Pentecostal women's organization that had helped Christian women in need for more than a half century. She was sure that the central office in Dallas would be happy to send literature. Greta was free to contact them for information or help. As for Mark: they had no services for men, and only male Saint Catherine's staff were permitted in the office.

.　　.　　.

"But it's Pentecostal," protested Greta, when Mark described Saint Catherine's. She hadn't called for a couple of days. "They roll on the floor sometimes, speak in tongues. That's not me at all."

"Will you copy the address, at least? For me? Please."

Greta put down the phone to get a pen, wrote as Mark dictated the address.

"How is Phillip?"

Greta didn't answer immediately, sighed deeply, resignedly. Mark felt a cold foreboding.

"Bad. I didn't know ... that's why I haven't called. He got fired. Finally. He got into a big argument with someone at work. About nothing. Last straw. So now ..." She took a deep breath, let it out slowly. Controlling herself. "Now he doesn't have a reason to be sober. He can drink all day in front of the TV. Yelling at the news announcers. I mean, yelling, at the top of his lungs. Our neighbor complained to me." She laughed, humorlessly. "Maybe there'll be help that way. If she calls the police and they arrest him. At least if one of his service buddies doesn't get the call."

"What are you going to do?"

"I don't know," Greta said, and added matter-of-factly that she wasn't sure that she'd come through alive.

•   •   •

His next night on shift was chilly, wet. Mark turned up the space heater another notch, watched the rain pelt lightly against the window.

Greta called at 7:00 sharp. The distant voice sounded thicker, slightly slurred. Something was different.

"Where is Phillip?"

"In bed. Migraines. I'm alone."

"How is he?"

Greta chuckled sadly. "Well, he didn't hit me today. How's that? Or say I'm poisoning the food, or that I'm doing blankety-blank with that minister. That's pretty good, isn't it?"

Mark didn't answer. Greta took a deep breath, coughed as she exhaled.

"I'm sorry," she said. "I'm all woozy. I think I'm coming down with something."

"That's all right."

"I slept in the back seat of the car again. I tried to sleep in the bed, but since he choked me ..." Her voice trailed off. "I didn't feel safe. So I went out to the car for a couple of hours. I was shivering. Maybe that's why I feel sick."

Mark heard her swallow, then a faint sound like a glass banging on a table. Could she be drinking, too? Greta drinking, after what she'd said about Phillip and her father?

"Parker, do you ever think about me when you're not on the hotline?"

Mark tensed, tightened his fingers around the receiver. What was he supposed to say?

"Greta, I think I told you, the hotline has rules ..."

"You have rules, you have rules." She sounded amused. "Can't you even tell me that?"

What was he supposed to say? Mark found himself wishing deliriously that this was her first-ever call. He could have been detached then, bing bang boom, talk inside guidelines and that was that. But now ...

"Well, of ... of course I think about you, Greta. Just as I think of other ..."

"Well, I don't think about you-oo," interrupted Greta, almost in a sing-song. "I don't think about you more than ... oh ... eight hours a day. Absolutely no more."

Mark winced, didn't speak. He felt sick. He imagined Toby hard-timing him, pounding the table: 'That's what you get for tromping over boundaries with this Kraut chick. Why do you think we have rules?'

"Greta, I don't think ..."

But she interrupted a second time. She sounded defensive.

"Well, what did you expect? Really? I hardly know anyone here, my husband is beating me, he's going crazy, and there's one man I can talk to on the phone, I don't know if he's a therapist or a priest or a college professor or what, he's gentler and more understanding with me than any other man I know. Am I supposed to just think about you like a treadmill or whirlpool I'd use for physical therapy?"

A *priest*. She thought he was ...

Mark didn't speak. He clutched the receiver and now sat rigidly upright in front of the desk, as if correcting his posture would help him fathom how to answer.

Seconds passed. Greta sighed wearily.

"I'm sorry, Parker. I shouldn't talk that way to you."

Mark said that was all right. She shouldn't have called him when she was almost out on her feet. She'd recover. She still had some fight in her.

"Please don't give up on me," she said.

CHAPTER TEN

In his diary, Mark wrote:

> The great Parker knew that he wasn't the sharpest can opener in the kitchen, or the most sober, but he still knew that his concerns for serial caller Greta had spiralled totally out of the solar system of acceptable hotline attitudes. He was only a volunteer. No caller could expect a red carpet WATS line to Sigmund Freud. Hotline service was strictly economy class. Some callers would not survive.

> But what was he supposed to do? His admitted volunteer amateurishness meant that expecting him to be some kind of freeze-dried Dr. Spock about this shit was a totally moot point.

> He hoped Toby didn't catch on to how obsessed he was and yank him off the phones.

·   ·   ·

The office door was ajar when Mark arrived the next evening for his shift at the hotline. Toby was at the card table, playing solitaire. Mark felt a quick surge of worry.

"Shit, where's your book?" asked Toby in greeting, and nodded at Mark's empty hands. Mark had felt distracted enough about Greta to leave *Letters* in his bedroom. "How're you going to field calls without your book?"

"Not tonight." Mark glanced reflexively at the clock. He'd switch on the hotline in three minutes. "What's up, boss man?"

"I had to do some paperwork." He looked at Mark levelly. "Also, I wanted to rap with you a little bit."

"Oh?" Mark sat at the hotline desk, tried to look nonchalant. "What about?"

"Do you know how many hangup calls we usually log in a month?"

"No idea."

"Five," said Toby. "And can you guess how many we logged last month?"

"More than usual?"

"Nineteen." Toby dealt a solitaire hand. "Now, I don't know that it's your Kraut girlfriend, but that's my educated guess."

"No foolin'."

Mark tried to look thoughtful, only mildly interested, as if Toby had described a broken window in a neighboring building.

"Sorry, man. She knows my hours. I've told her she can talk with other people here."

Toby looked mildly put out. "Well, can you tell her again when you're on shift? Please? Maybe ask her to write it down? These hang-up calls ..." Toby nodded at the record book open by the hotline. "The stats in there get written up in a chart. If the hang-up calls shoot up, someone who cuts checks might wonder why."

7:00 p.m. Mark flicked the desk switch, activated the hotline.

"I'll tell her. Is that all you wanted to rap about?"

"That's all."

Mark feigned a small yawn, concealing relief. Toby wasn't going to pull him off the phones.

Minutes passed. The hotline didn't ring. Mark watched his mentor play solitaire.

Toby didn't look good. His eyes were puffy, red; his clothes looked like he'd slept in them. All the volunteers knew that their mentor dealt with his private demons. Jennifer had seen him once nodding out drunk in a bar at 1:30 in the morning. He'd looked so completely alone, she said, like he didn't have anyone. Once she'd even asked Mark if he thought they should do an intervention. But not seriously; how could they do an intervention with their trainer?

Toby had been in Vietnam. Mark thought of Phillip, wondered if Toby could offer feedback.

"As long as we've been talking about Greta," he said, "maybe you've got an idea."

"Shoot."

With a deliberately light, disinterested tone, Mark told what he knew about Phillip. Toby grimaced when he mentioned the punji sticks and the amputation, but otherwise listened impassively, as if hearing a variation of a story he'd already heard many times before.

"Remember, I didn't see combat," he said, when Mark finished. "Ol' Toby is a mechanic. Don't forget. I boned up on anything a mechanic might work on over there and made damn sure the military knew what I knew. Soldiers with my MOS number usually didn't get shot at."

He dealt a hand of solitaire, shrugged indifferently, sadly.

"Phillip got screwed," he said. "That's all. We all were. Think about it. The word 'draft.' Conscription. We were 'drafted' into military service. What's that mean?" He looked at Mark cynically. "It means slavery. The U.S. government enslaved over a million young men, sent the slaves to Vietnam.

"This Phillip can't process it. Me, I had a relatively light time, I can look back and say, 'well, the United States screwed me. Next question.' But Phillip's never going to get his lower leg back. He's probably going to be in pain for the rest of his life. He's trying to convince himself that this huge, huge loss was for a good cause, but it wasn't. He got screwed. No way he gets a pass for hitting his wife, but do you think he would've sunk this low if he hadn't been in 'Nam?"

Toby stared grimly at the card table, turned over cards. Mark looked at a pasty ketchup stain on Toby's t-shirt, at the dark circles under Toby's eyes. No, Toby didn't look good.

"Hey, have you seen *Parallax View*?" Mark asked.

"What's that?"

"*Parallax View*. The new flick with Warren Beatty? About a secret group that trains political assassins."

"Oh."

"My roomie said it's good." Mark rapped knuckles on the card table. "My treat, boss man. You come with me, I'll pay for the tickets and buy you a round of popcorn. That ought to hook you."

Toby leered, shuffled the cards, didn't look at him. "Naw. I've got popcorn at home."

"Come on, don't be a drip. We can hang out. You can get on my case for everything I'm doing wrong on the phones."

The hotline rang. Mark turned the chair back to the desk, picked up the line. It wasn't Greta. A minute later he heard Toby shut the door behind him.

CHAPTER ELEVEN

"No matter how this turns out, I'm going to be grateful to you," Greta said. "You have no idea how much you've helped me. Even if I don't make it through this alive."

"Please don't talk like that."

"Can I tell you how I picture you?"

Mark bit his lip, twisted his fingers on the receiver.

"I know you can't tell me," Greta laughed. "But can I tell you? Just for fun."

Mark said nothing. How she *pictured* him.

"You're about fifty years old." Greta chuckled softly, not flirtatiously, like a grade schooler playing a guessing game. "You're ... let's see ... you have gray hair at your temples, and you wear tweed coats and a sweater, and sit late at night with books in your home library in a big plush Victorian armchair in a gold lounging robe. Your wife is a professional too, and you have two children and they're ... let's see ... they're in college now." Greta laughed. "How'd I do?"

Mark forced up a weak chuckle, stared unseeing at the lines of volunteers' scribbles in the log book. Reading in his home library in a Victorian armchair in a gold lounging robe. Him.

•   •   •

Phillip deteriorated. His headaches were more frequent, excruciating, kept him in bed for days. At least then Greta could talk more freely. He couldn't hear her from the phone in the kitchen.

"I can't cook for him anymore. He thinks I'm poisoning the food. He eats from the cans and jars in the living room. I can only pick up when he's not there. I feel like a zoo keeper.

"He talks to himself all the time. Or yells to himself. All about gooks and slopes, and how he married a gook.

"He keeps saying I'm really Vietnamese. It's like if he keeps saying it he can believe it's true, and then I'll be a pure enemy, like the Viet Cong.

"He said if he finds out I've been sexually intimate with the minister, he'll kill me. He said he'll fix it up with his service buddies on the police force."

She chuckled softly, sadly. Without emotion, resigned.

"I don't think this can go on much longer."

•   •   •

Jennifer sounded antsy. "I don't know, Mark. This feels weird."

"But it's for a good cause," Mark insisted. Jennifer was female; Saint Catherine's would talk to her. She could find out if they'd put a woman up with same day lodging in an emergency. Then he could tell Greta.

"Tell them you're Foursquare or Assemblies of God. And you're having a big spiritual crisis."

Jennifer finally agreed, called Mark back a half-hour later.

"They're bucks up, all right," she said. Yes, they could provide emergency housing. With all of four hours notice.

•   •   •

Greta's last call to Mark at the hotline was from a payphone.

"I spent most of the night in the park," she said.

A chorus of accelerating vehicles sounded in the background; the phone booth likely was near a crosswalk. Mark thought immediately of the cold. It was mid-November now; Thanksgiving was coming up. Mark had passed turkey and pumpkin lawn displays on the morning walk to the liquor store. At least today it was dry.

"What did Phillip do?"

Greta told the story, matter-of-factly, almost as if telling an ambulance driver about an accident she'd witnessed. She rarely cried on the phone now. The crying and the emotion had been for the first weeks, when she had believed that Phillip would recover. Now she seemed resigned to living a nightmare.

Her sin had been to see Phillip crying.

"I can't get to the bathroom without passing the living room. He sits there in the dark, like I told you, with his medals and his alcohol. I try to walk by fast, because that's when he's most dangerous."

She'd just returned from an evening shopping trip. She left the bags in the kitchen, stocked the refrigerator, but then she'd had to put the toothpaste and toilet paper in the bathroom.

On the way toward the bathroom, she saw Phillip weeping.

"Parker, I loved that man," said Greta, adamantly, defensively. "I know you must think I'm the craziest woman in Northern California, but I loved the man I married. I wanted to bear his children. And to see him crying alone in the dark ..."

So she had stopped, with the toothpaste and toilet paper in her hand, to look at him, to show concern, to hope once more that there might be a breakthrough, a way to get through to him. But it had been a mistake. Phillip's expression had hardened as their eyes met, become angry, menacing, even indignant that his wife had stared at him in a vulnerable moment.

"So I went on to the bathroom without saying anything and dropped off the things, and then I decided to go out for awhile. Without saying anything, just to leave him alone, give him his space. I felt so suffocated there."

She put on a light coat and walked a couple of blocks to the baseball diamonds. Did he know where that was in town? Two baseball diamonds, with metal bleachers for spectators. High schoolers were playing a night game under the floodlights.

She slid onto one of the benches and hugged herself in the chill, and then for the next several hours got lost in the game. It felt good to be there. She could have been the big sister or cousin of one of the players. To feel normal. She thought of Phillip before Vietnam, watching him play, the funny faces he'd made at her when he'd struck out.

When the game ended, she walked home.

"But I should have thought of how long I'd been gone.

"When I walked in ... I had to go to the bathroom ... he was sitting bolt upright in that chair, scowling at me, and I should have paid way more attention: he was wearing his prosthetic. He should have had it off, if he's just sitting in the living room. He hadn't had it on when I'd left.

"But I didn't think.

"I sat on the toilet, I urinated, and then Phillip started hammering on the door. 'Open up!' I said, 'okay, just a second,' I was pulling up my underwear and the door burst open. Phillip looked insane. With his fists balled up. 'Where were you?!' And then all this horrible stuff about how that minister had picked me up in his car and driven me somewhere for sex.

"Then he attacked me. And this time ..."

Greta's voice broke, at last, into a long, defeated shudder.

Mark realized he was trembling with anger. Enough. Phillip had hit her, choked her, left her with bruises and cuts that she lied about at work, and now she couldn't go home. Enough. He clutched the receiver, forced himself to wait in silence. He knew she'd continue.

"He's never attacked me like that before. Even when he choked me. I swear, I thought he was trying to kill me. With his fists, with all his strength.

"I kicked at his prosthetic. That's the only reason I got away, because I've helped him with it so many times and I know how it's attached. He fell, and I kept kicking and pulling the prosthetic until it was nearly off and he couldn't walk with it. Then I had time to get away."

Enough.

Mark stood up. Trembling.

"Tomorrow I can ..."

"Greta, please listen to me now!!"

Greta stopped, surprised by his tone. Mark clutched the receiver, jaw rigid, staring at the wall with wild, unseeing eyes. Whatever image she had of him as some smooth fifty year old in a lounging robe was likely about to go out the window. He was through trying to give airy detached hotline feedback. Phillip wasn't going to hit her again.

"Do you have your pocket Bible with you?"

The question obviously startled her, but yes, she had it. Mark felt reckless, furious. Enough.

Mark told her to take it out, put it on the tray under the payphone, put her hand on it and vow to him and to God that she would call Saint Catherine's tomorrow, not once, but until she got through to a live human being, and that she would then tell that live human being that she needed emergency housing immediately. Immediately.

"They have the housing, Greta. They can take you tomorrow. We have been talking for months, Greta. For months. I have a right to care what happens to you. I don't want to read about you in the newspaper. I'm not asking politely. I'm insisting."

Greta still seemed surprised by his tone, but said mildly that, of course, she would do what she had just vowed to do.

"What are you going to do tonight?" Mark asked.

Well, she had enough cash for a motel, and some food. But she only had cash, and only enough for one night.

"And you'll call me here tomorrow," said Mark. "At seven."

"But you're not on shift tomorrow."

"I'll switch shifts," said Mark. "I'll be here."

CHAPTER TWELVE

Scheduled for the next evening's hotline rotation was an undergraduate psychology student who had only finished training a month before. Mark called to say that he either wanted to switch shifts or take calls for the first hour, felt relieved that the student accepted the shift change without explanation. Confessing the real reason would have been the same as telling Toby to take him off the phones.

Mark tried to write in his diary about what 'the great Parker' would do, but gave up. He didn't know what Parker would do. He thumbed through Rhaytana for a letter he hadn't read recently, gave that up, too. He turned off the light and lay in bed staring up at the ceiling, occasionally glancing at the fluorescent hands of his alarm clock to check the hour, to acknowledge how much sleep he was losing over Greta.

If she'd gotten into Saint Catherine's, fine. Problem solved, at least temporarily. But if she hadn't gotten into Saint Catherine's, for whatever reason, then he decided that he was going to arrange to meet her in person. Mark hadn't saved copies of the paperwork he'd signed with the hotline nonprofit, supposed he could even get in legal trouble for so grossly violating the rules. It didn't matter, he didn't care. She'd be in for a shock when he showed up without his gold lounging robe, but that didn't matter either. Sleeping on his scroungy mattress in his dumpy bedroom would beat sleeping in the park. Mark could sleep on the couch or on the kitchen floor with the cockroaches.

It didn't matter, he didn't care. The hotline had booked a volunteer. He wasn't a veteran police dispatcher who could arrange his thoughts into professional life versus personal life compartments after hearing people getting raped, stabbed, shot, killed. 'I thought he was trying to kill me.' Well, no. Sorry. He wasn't going to learn what Greta looked like when the evening news showed her photo in a story about her murder. His mind was made up, and with the awareness of his own resolution Mark finally drifted into a sound sleep.

But the next afternoon Jennifer called him at the liquor store. Mark picked up the receiver as he was finishing a check-out, felt a quick surge of dread and bewilderment as he recognized her voice. No one from the hotline had ever called him at work.

Jennifer was upset.

"Mark, don't go into the hotline today."

"Why not?"

"The cops are all over the place. Toby blew his brains out in there."

CHAPTER THIRTEEN

Mark learned the details of Toby's death on the evening news. Tobias Cartwright had been his legal name; the broadcast showed a military service photo of a slimmer, younger, short-haired Toby over the news anchor's spray-dried coiffure, as Mark had so long feared seeing a photo of Greta. Toby had been a native of San Bernardino, the news anchor said, and a high school bowling champion. Mark had never known.

Toby had been alone in the office. The news anchor said that he had used a high-caliber revolver, and seemed to tip-toe around the observation that the team leader of a suicide hotline had killed himself at the hotline's call desk. As if he could anticipate the heartless, sneering jokes that soon would be told about Toby in bars, offices and living rooms all over the state, but wouldn't risk any public acknowledgment of the grim irony.

Mark watched the broadcast while squeezed between his roommates on the living room couch, grimly offered one-syllable replies to their pruriently curious questions. Occasionally he glanced at the clock, watched the inevitable progress of the hour and minute hand toward 7:00 p.m.

Soon Greta would call. She'd hear the recording that volunteers switched off when they went on shift, would try again at 7:01, and 7:02. When would she give up? Mark imagined the desperate, frightened, absolutely alone Greta continuing to feed coins into the slot at 7:15, 7:30, 8:00, unable to understand how the volunteer she imagined as a psychiatrist or a priest or a professor hadn't kept his word.

God damn you, Toby, Mark thought. Toby, you bastard, you son of a bitch. Why'd you have to kill yourself there?

•   •   •

"I talked to one of the cops," Jennifer said the next day. "He shot himself with a .44 Magnum. That's like the biggest revolver you can buy. An elephant gun, practically."

Jennifer was in her mid-twenties, an "anti-Zionist Jew," whatever that meant, said her family had been part of a wave of Jewish leftists that had emigrated to Northern California at the turn of the century. She wore a hippyish peasant blouse, wire rim glasses and a headband, and now regarded Mark dejectedly as she slouched on her side of the booth. They were in the McDonalds near the liquor store, had agreed to meet there during Mark's lunch hour. He'd thought of taking the whole day off, but needed the bread. Duke had told him that the liquor store wasn't breaking even; he was about to be out of a job.

"He must have offed himself there on purpose," Jennifer said. "I mean, don't get me wrong, *they* didn't kill him, okay?, we all knew how messed up he was, but still. He was team leader, he had to talk every week with those cruds in the nonprofit office. He hated them. He even talked to a lawyer about some kind of ... I don't know ..."

Her voice trailed off. She shrugged, managed a sad chuckle. "So I guess he figured, his time had come, he was going to go out with a protest. Like that monk who set himself on fire in Saigon."

They were silent for nearly a minute. Mark felt dazed, shell-shocked. He had slept only two hours the night before, had lain in bed in the dark staring up at his ceiling as he grimly considered scenarios, trying to convince himself that Greta had surely, surely, surely gone to Saint Catherine's, after her promise, her vow, even while afraid that she hadn't, that she was still in the park, or worse, had even returned to her murderous husband. He'd been afraid to sleep, afraid that he might dream about her.

"When are they going to open the hotline again?" he asked, finally.

"Probably never."

"What?!" Mark sat up, stared at her incredulously. "But don't they ... they have to open ..."

"No, they don't," Jennifer interrupted. She looked disgusted. "They're total assholes. All they ever cared about was the funding." She held up a hand, angrily counted off negatives on her fingers. "No A/C in the summer. Never fixed. Horrible phone lines. I once had to ask a woman who was threatening to slice her wrists to *repeat* herself. That place was a joke."

Jennifer threw up her hands. "And now the non-profit's got a big, fat scandal, the team leader offs himself at the call desk. Do you think they're going to face up to it? Oh, no-o-o-o-o. Not them. If Toby thought he was going to change anything, well, forget it. 'Closed indefinitely.' That's what the announcement's going to be tomorrow, but what it means is 'closed, period.'"

"But there has to some way to ..."

"No, there isn't! There isn't! We don't have a gig in there anymore, Mark. That simple."

She stared broodily at the table top. Another long silence ensued.

"Did you know Toby was that messed up?" she asked, finally.

"Not *that* messed up," Mark said, and described Toby's appearance in their last chat, the spurned invitation to the movie. He realized as he spoke that Jennifer was watching him intently, as if she'd perceived something in his expression or tone that wasn't in his spoken words.

"I'm going to tell you something," she said. "Maybe I shouldn't say it now, and maybe you're going to hate me for it, but for you, there's a silver lining in this. It was time for you to get off the phones."

Mark stared at her.

"You are way, way, I mean, waaaaaay too strung out on that chick who's been calling you. Don't think I can't tell, because I can. I'll bet you've been thinking about her non-stop since I called you yesterday. What'd she call herself? Helga? Olga?"

"Greta," said Mark softly. He lowered his eyes, nodded slightly.

CHAPTER FOURTEEN

Mark had Thanksgiving dinner with his mother. He arrived with pumpkin pie and cranberry bread, and these wound up serving as the base for their Thanksgiving meal, along with soda and still-edible potato salad scavenged from the back of the refrigerator. His mother had forgotten how to defrost a turkey properly. The bird had been raw, inedible.

She apologized in her scattered, defenseless, vaguely masochistic way: whisper-cooing little "oh, no!"s as she shook her head twitchily from side to side, and stared at the raw, red meat as a student would regard an unanticipated 'F' on a term paper. Through Mark's boyhood she had offered similar apologies for forgotten appointments, shut-off utilities, collection agency visits, and for a steady parade of useless, handsome men who consumed money and alcohol before disappearing. Mark occasionally wondered which hunk-of-the-month had been his dad.

This year, at least, her anarchic life was a welcome distraction. She took his mind off Greta.

●　　●　　●

He was smoking more weed, had started hitting the pipe harder after his meeting with Jennifer, when he realized that the hotline wouldn't open again and that he no longer had a reason to be at all clear-headed in the evening. Jennifer had probably smelled the pot on his clothes when they met. He expected no pleasure from smoking more, and thus wasn't disappointed; he only felt duller, thick-headed, more out of it. He had gone to a couple of movies, passed the bong with his roomies, flirted unseriously on the phone with Shirley, a high school fling who had told him repeatedly that he sounded loaded. He avoided writing in his diary, didn't want to confess how Parker was behaving.

He left his mom's on Thanksgiving at 8:00, and at home decided on impulse to get seriously stoned. His roomies were gone, out with their families. He smoked twice his usual ration, and for a half-hour stared with open-mouthed incomprehension at a *Dragnet* re-run, faintly aware that he was so out of it that he could have passed for a psychotic medicated with Haldol in a mental institution.

The show ended, Joe Friday got his man. Mark weaved into the kitchen to fetch a beer, switched on the light, and jumped back in alarm as a quartet of cockroaches fled under the refrigerator.

What high he had felt immediately went bad, degenerated into anxiety, paranoia. Cockroaches; he imagined scuzzy brown cockroaches with their antennae and hairy legs scuttling all over the house, creeping under his clothes. He turned on the light in his bedroom so he wouldn't see any roaches, curled on the bed in a fetal position with the blanket pulled over his head. Gradually he drifted into a half-asleep state, and in this state imagined himself with Greta. She was in this reverie tall, blonde, a woman at once Aryan and strong-jawed but obviously vulnerable, and there was Mark beside her, escorting her along an indeterminate walkway, path, sidewalk, a gentle arm draped around her shoulder, his chin tilted toward her ear as he spoke to her gently, reassuringly, as he had spoken to her on the hotline, as the psychiatrist or priest might have spoken to her. Her protector.

But this he was not, was he? The hotline had closed.

Mark twisted the blanket over his head, yielded helplessly to thoughts he didn't want to have while so stoned, like a criminal confessing in a courtroom: that Jennifer had been wrong, as he had known all along; that they *could* have done something, weren't as helpless as she'd said. They could have contacted the press. They could have picketed the hotline *and* contacted the press.

But such action belonged to the domain of vital, clear-headed, courageous adult actors in the real world, didn't it? Loadies didn't do such things. *He* wouldn't. He wouldn't get off the pipe. Life had given him a test that he hadn't even tried to pass. He didn't deserve to see himself as Greta's protector, and Mark knew at some level that he wasn't being reasonable, that he was guilt-tripping because of the weed, even as he wholeheartedly and sincerely despised himself.

. . .

Two days later, Mark happened to glance at the mini-television on one side of the counter while he was ringing up a six pack at the liquor store. He didn't know why. Duke liked having the set there, squeezed next to the chewing gum rack and snuff tins. Mark usually ignored it, sometimes read *Letters* when he didn't have customers, accepted the set's drone and burble as background noise, like the sound of traffic.

A local news anchor was reporting a husband's arrest for the Thanksgiving murder of his wife. The victim's face flashed on the screen: blonde, mid-twenties. Beaten to death by her husband in their living room.

Mark thought he would vomit, felt so sick that he could hardly stand at the cash register. The customer glowered at him as Mark shoved the change roughly across the counter, offering no apology when coins clattered to the floor. 'No, oh, God, oh, please, oh, no,' he thought, and then said these words like a mantra as he paced dismally behind the counter whenever a customer wasn't in the store, wringing his fingers, banging his fist on the counter. 'Oh, please, oh, God, oh, please, oh no.'

His torment ended only with the eleven p.m. local newscast, when Mark finally learned enough about the murder to be sure that Greta hadn't been the victim.

· · ·

That night he prayed. He'd smoked his good-night bowl only fifteen minutes earlier, would later use the fact of this intoxication as an excuse to himself for having prayed at all. He didn't believe in God; at least that was how he thought he felt, how he had described himself to others. He hadn't prayed since early elementary school.

Yet now he knelt beside his bed, clasped his hands on the sheets, whispered his desperate, embarrassed prayer on his fingers.

If she could just be okay, God. If he could just please please know what happened to her.

CHAPTER FIFTEEN

The next evening, Sunday, Mark caught a ride across town with his roomies to buy weed. A friend of a friend was selling off lids from four kilos of pot from Maui. Mark hoped he could afford it. Duke had just told him that the liquor store was closing for sure in a couple of weeks. He could quit when he wanted or stick it out to the end. He'd need a new gig, and soon.

A few other stoners already were lounging in the living room when Mark arrived, passing a bong across a low coffee table littered with green marijuana flecks. Mark dropped onto a fresh cushion on one side of the couch, next to an easy chair supporting a thick-set thirty year old.

The thirty year old looked so much like an undercover cop that Mark decided he couldn't be one. He looked like he'd come from work, wore a polyester sport coat and business slacks, even had white socks. He was short-haired, sported a trim mustache between pudgy cheeks, held a roach smoldering in an alligator clip.

Mark soon realized that the stranger was staring intently at his beard.

"Anything I can help you with?" said Mark with mild sarcasm, when the staring began to bother him.

"Sorry. Didn't mean to gawk at you." The stranger sat up, proffered a hand. "Name's Bill. Pleasure to meet you."

"Mark," muttered Mark uncertainly, and shook hands. Such greetings weren't typical at pot parties. Bill now admired his beard openly.

"That's one hell of a set of whiskers," he said. "How long did it take you to grow it out like that?"

"As long as it is now? More than a half-year."

"Are you looking for a job, by any chance?"

A *job*. Mark stared, curled an amused lip.

"As a matter of fact, I am, but I wasn't expecting to find one here."

"'Cause with that beard," said Bill, "ten to one I can get you hired as mall Santa at Knockers."

Knockers was a new mall complex flanking the old Coopers Pond in North Town. The developer had spruced up the pond with landscaping and covered walkways, built two huge, round, three level mall pavilions to either side of it, each with dozens of stores. The mall's official name was something like 'Great Heritage Mall of the Golden State,' but everyone referred to the two round pavilion buildings as Knockers. Some employees spoke of working in 'West Tit' or 'East Tit.'

"Me?" Mark tapped his chest. "Christmas Santa at the mall?"

"With that beard, sure bet."

Mark chuckled, told Bill that he had to be smoking some truly righteous pot to imagine Mark as Santa, and ambled into the kitchen. Here he found cans of lukewarm soda, and the friend of a friend and one of his roommates fingering buds from a kilo split open on the counter. Neither paid any attention to him.

After awhile, with nothing to do, Mark drifted back to the living room. The only free seat was the one he'd left, beside Bill. Bill didn't seem offended.

"Have they got any other gigs out there besides Santa?" Mark asked.

Bill shook his head. "Not 'til January. If then."

Bill, it turned out, was one of the mall managers. And he'd been serious about the Santa offer. The mall's big Christmas push was only a couple of days away, and corporate brass was especially eager for a clean roll-out, partly to compensate for the fact that they were going to get by in '74 with a single Papa Noel, instead of a Santa for each pavilion. The PD had just chucked their main squeeze Santa in the calaboose for slugging a bartender. Knockers needed a replacement, needed one badly, and fast. Mommy and Daddy would spend their discretionary dollars elsewhere if Junior couldn't recite his Christmas 'gimme gimme' list while sitting on Santa's knee at Knockers.

"Forgive me for dreaming," said Bill, and waved the roach at him. "If you don't want to do it, you don't want to do it. But with that beard, if you were to dye that sucker white — and assuming you don't have any felony convictions, you understand — well, holy moley. We'd be superstars. You'd be top Santa in NorCal, maybe in the whole state. And we pay top dollar, too."

Mark said he couldn't see himself as Santa, and asked Bill about life as a mall manager to change the subject. It wasn't bad,

Bill answered. And even if people made jokes about the nick-name, Knockers was one of the best malls on the West Coast.

"We've got Zorr's Seafood in the food court. That's a pre-mium eatery, man. We were the only mall they'd look at."

Mark nodded politely, beginning to feel bored. Bill opened the alligator clip to drop the now-tiny roach into the ashtray.

"And our conference rooms," he said. "We didn't cut corners. If we're going to have conference rooms, meeting rooms, they're going to be the best. Toastmasters, everything they do in town is with us. The Lions are coming.

"Now, I'm not saying we haven't made mistakes. This Saint Catherine's shit ..."

Bill offered an exasperated look to the ceiling, didn't notice that Mark was now sitting up straight and staring at him intently.

"Letting them in was my *predecessor's* decision," said Bill, with contemptuous emphasis. 'My *predecessor* thought it would be appropriate to open our conference rooms to ding-dong Pen-tecostals who speak in tongues and roll on floors." Bill rolled his eyes.

"But," he added, "Saint Catherine's took the problem out of my hands. End of the year the whole kit and kaboodle of crazies is packing up ship and moving to L.A. They'll never come back on my watch."

"Isn't Saint Catherine's some kind of women's group?" asked Mark.

Bill nodded. An affluent, well-funded Christian group, which was why his *predecessor* had been impressed that the women's group would want to use Knockers for all their area meetings.

"Maybe he didn't know how they carry on," Bill said.

"When does this mall Santa gig start?" Mark asked. He was trembling.

PART II

CHAPTER SIXTEEN

Five days later, Mark was a star on the local TV news. He watched the evening broadcast with his snickering roommates, holding the bong in front of his now nearly white-dyed beard, wincing as the camera showed his near-stumble in the baggy Santa pants while trying to step out of the helicopter onto the Knockers parking lot. He was now a Santa professionally, would be through Christmas Eve.

Mall staff had been nice, but had treated him at times like a poodle to be groomed for a magazine photo. "Christmas prep" was a familiar ritual, like yearly inventory and fire drills. Santa was another item on the 'to do' checklist, like prepping Santa's throne, the tree, the fake presents. At least this year they could deal with only one Santa, instead of two.

His hair had been first. Bill had given him a voucher for a mall beauty salon, where Mark had lobbied successfully for the "golden platinum" dye for his hair and beard, rather than the "white" or "platinum" dye, so he would look marginally less conspicuous in off-work hours. Next: a rack of holiday clothes in a storage room, where a yawning mall worker had fitted him with a cumbersome Santa pillow-belt and the expected red-and-white Santa suit.

Then: the helicopter.

"You never mentioned anything about a helicopter ride when you told me about this gig."

Bill had rolled his eyes, offered a martyred look. He wore a wide orange tie with the polyester suit, looked to Mark as if he could have been pitching miracle support underwear on an infomercial.

"Ten minutes in the air, tops. Your whirlybird takes off from West Tit ... from West Pavilion, then touches down in the East Pavilion parking lot. Santa steps out — namely, you — and is greeted by adoring kiddies, parents, and press. What's to mention?"

And this was what had happened. The helicopter pilot had looked like a walk-on from *Twelve O'Clock High*, complete with mirror sunglasses and leather bomber jacket. Mark would remember the roar of the helicopter blades, his sight from the air of the crowd waiting below on the cleared East Tit parking lot, and the surrealistic awareness that the minions below were waiting for him. The helicopter had touched down. Mark had jumped out, nearly stumbling in the baggy red pants, toting a sack of Christmas trinkets.

"This way, Santa! Over here, Santa!" "Wave for the camera, Santa!" Mark had staggered through the phalanx of broadcast cameras, popping flash guns, the white puff of his Santa cap bouncing on his cheek as he waved, pulled trinkets out of the bag to be tossed to the pudgy grasping fingers of the squealing children. "*Ho! Ho! Ho!*" he called out, and tried to smile jollily, and wondered briefly if a marijuana fleck might be caught between his teeth. He felt like a star on the Oscars red carpet.

But for less than two minutes, as the crowd and reporters vanished when he entered East Pavilion. He had a job, and, with it, a chance to find Greta.

•   •   •

The 830 bus took twenty minutes to trundle from a stop near Mark's home to the mall. Mark caught it the next morning, and soon recognized and fell into chat with a young security guard who had helped block off crowds from Santa's helicopter the day before. The guard's name was Carl.

Carl had bad news: the meeting rooms that Mark said he was idly curious about were in West Tit. Santa's throne was in East Tit.

"It's a real hike between titties, too," said Carl. He was trim, black, short-haired. "I do it every day. The pond's more than a half-mile around."

Mark asked why the mall had only one Santa for 1974. Carl leered, rubbed his thumb and forefingers together.

"'Cause the West Tittie retailers didn't pay up." He looked at Mark confidentially. "Now, what I heard, they might still be negotiating. If West Tit sees their business drop off, they'll cough up the bread and get their own Santa in a week."

Carl gestured as they approached the mall bus stop, started to stand, then seemed to remember something.

"Anybody told you about the harpies yet?"

"Harpies?"

"Watch out for them," Carl said, and explained: the Knockers' corporate owners employed two women to roam the mall grounds and look for anything that wasn't up to standard. Anything: an unscrubbed window, a dusty handrail, a security guard like Carl who hadn't pressed his uniform trousers. The harpies didn't socialize with other staff, were supervised and paid separately.

"Their job is to be mean," said Carl, as they walked to the mall entrance. "There's a black chick and a white chick. Both in the official corporate colors, maroon and yellow. Watch out for them. You're going to see more of 'em in East Tit, too. They've got their office there."

. . .

Santa's red-and-gold throne was on a glittery red carpet on the ground floor of the East Tit atrium, surrounded by waist-high stuffed reindeer and shiny-wrapped boxes with huge bows. Behind the throne towered a huge, bauble-and-bead-bedecked fir tree, towering to the pavilion's second level. The mall's biggest toy store was close-by; a nearby rack of tear-off coupons offered a five percent discount.

Mark adapted. The first hour on the throne was the strangest: belly-laughing the *Ho! Ho! Ho!*; helping to hoist children to his knee, or greeting the children deposited on his knee by parents; deepening his voice to an imagined Santa register to ask questions. Had they been naughty or nice? Did they think it was snowing at the North Pole? What did they want for Christmas?

An "elf maiden" steered the waiting-to-see-Santa line and offered to take instant camera photos for two dollars a pop. She turned out to be a substitute, told Mark that he'd meet the regular elf-maiden Cindy in a couple of days. She was a mall veteran, though, and knew where he could find a conference room schedule posted in East Tit: there was one by the janitor's closet in the store room near the bathrooms.

. . .

Hours later at the end of his shift, still dressed in his Santa costume, Mark ran his finger down the conference room schedule mask-taped on the storage room wall. Toastmasters, Podiatrists Association, Investors Club ...

His finger stopped on Saint Catherine's. Mark studied the schedule, suppressed disappointment. Most of the Saint Catherine's meetings coincided with his shift as Santa. He couldn't swing by, not while stationed in East Pavilion.

Most, but not all: Mark spotted an exception, a Saint Catherine's afternoon meeting booked for next Monday, his day off. He could return then, in two days, out of uniform.

Mark memorized the time and meeting room number, turned to leave, found himself in his first face-to-face encounter with a harpy.

"What are you doing here?" she asked coldly.

Mark brushed the droopy top of his red Santa cap away from his cheek, looked at the maroon skirt and starched yellow blouse of the young woman who now regarded him coldly. "Ms. Bane" (according to her name tag) was a pasty-faced, pug-nosed thirty-something with a bouffant hairdo that looked like it had been frozen stiff with liquid nitrogen. Mark already pictured her writing parking tickets and jury summons on her day off.

"I wanted to see the conference room schedule."

"Why?"

Mark repeated the same line he had used with the elk-maiden: that he was interested in public speaking, knew that the Toastmasters met at the mall, wanted to find out when he could go.

"You know perfectly well that you could have found that out by calling Toastmasters," said Ms. Bane snarkily.

"Sure, but ..." Mark shrugged. "I work here now, so I thought it would be easier to step in here than call."

Ms. Bane turned on her heel without replying and walked out. Mark copied the Saint Catherine's schedule on the back of a mall flier.

CHAPTER SEVENTEEN

The mall's meeting rooms turned out to be on the western-most end of the top floor of West Pavilion, at least fifteen minutes in a fast walk from Santa's throne. There were three rooms, side by side, with waist-height-to-ceiling windows fronting the walkway.

One was occupied when Mark arrived on Monday, twenty minutes before the scheduled 11:30 start of the Saint Catherine's meeting. Mark allowed himself a quick glance through the windows as he passed, spotted a dozen businessman types listening to a speaker. Their meeting room and the other two were ritzy and sterile, with long, wood laminate tables, plush leatherette chairs, little else.

Now all he had to do was wait.

The business group meeting ended. Middle-aged men in suits filed out, alone or while chatting in groups of two, avoided looking at Mark or glanced at his t-shirt and beard with faint unfriendliness.

Ten minutes to go now before the start of Saint Catherine's. Mark rested elbows on the walkway's railing, gazed down at the West Tit foot traffic on the atrium floor two stories below. How was he supposed to act, so the women in the group wouldn't wonder why he was standing there?

He'd act as if he were waiting for someone, Mark decided. Waiting impatiently.

The first two Saint Catherine's participants arrived: thirty-somethings, unremarkable, indistinguishable from other mall visitors. One opened the meeting room door; Mark watched her hand turned the knob, noticed that she didn't need a key.

Mark began to pace the walkway a safe distance from the meeting room entrance, glancing occasionally at his wristwatch as he looked for an imaginary, tardy friend. He bit his lip, tried to look anxious, irritated.

More women began to arrive: in trios, singles, quartets, as young as eighteen and as old as sixty-five, of all races. Mark avoided looking at any directly, pretended to swear, paced the walkway, and stole another glance at the meeting room.

A young, German-looking blonde was approaching.

Mark stopped pacing, let himself look openly. Already his pulse had quickened. Intuition; a sixth sense.

The woman was alone. She was square-jawed, average-looking, had tied her blonde hair into a modest bun, looked like Mark's image of a church-going Bavarian homemaker. The sturdy lines of her strong jaw were belied by an expression of unexpected vulnerability, shyness.

Faint red marks showed on the right side of her face. They could have been birthmarks; he wasn't close enough to make a good guess. She could have bumped into a door.

They also could have been marks that Phillip had left in a fight, with time to fade.

The woman saw him staring. She looked at him, right at him, for a full second. She didn't seem bothered by his staring. She looked as if she had sensed something in his face, too, triggered by the same intuition.

Then she was gone, had disappeared into the conference room. Mark silently whispered two syllables:

"Greta."

.   .   .

Twenty minutes later he fought to slow his racing thoughts while sitting with a coffee in the West Tit food court.

He didn't know. First and foremost, that fact: he didn't know. He wanted to see Greta. The woman had looked like the image he'd formed of Greta. She'd had the marks on her face, and Mark knew that Phillip had attacked Greta on the night before her last call to the hotline. But Greta had never talked about her appearance, or her age. And he didn't know for a fact that she'd kept her promise to contact Saint Catherine's.

But when in his life had he ever felt such a strong intuition?

Mark glanced at his watch. The Saint Catherine's meeting would end in a little over an hour.

He'd follow her. Try to talk to her. Perhaps in the parking lot, away from the crowd in the mall. What harm was there in that?

Because if she *was* Greta, he could shrug off the invisible weight he'd carried since the hotline had closed. Even if she curled a contemptuous lip at his beard and t-shirt, and wanted nothing to do with him. He'd still be happy, relieved, vindicated. To know that Greta was okay, that Phillip hadn't killed her.

· · ·

When the Saint Catherine's meeting was due to end, Mark stood at a spot on the ground floor that allowed him to look up two stories through the atrium to the meeting room doors. He'd follow her when the meeting ended; discreetly, from below, watching her head and shoulders as she approached the escalators. Then on the ground floor he could walk up, could speak to her ... in the parking lot, if he wanted to wait, but really, any time.

Easy.

12:58. 12:59. 1:00 p.m. Mark gazed up, locked eyes on the door.

1:01 p.m. 1:02 p.m. Nothing.

1:03 p.m. The door opened.

The first woman who exited was so short that Mark only could see the top of her head. Then two others followed, and then came the German-looking blonde. She turned east, walking behind the other women but obviously by herself. Mark watched her shoulders sway lightly under her hair bun as she headed along the walkway to the escalator.

He followed. Easy. But he was moving among ground floor shoppers now, had to watch where he was going. Mark weaved around a mustachioed elder with a cane, darted between two oblivious teenagers, eyes darting constantly between the steadily moving hair bun of the blonde above and the human obstacle course ahead of him.

She reached the escalator; Mark stopped, waited, watching; stared at her hand resting on the black handrail as she descended to the second floor. He had to be extra careful now. He assumed — expected, wanted, had almost taken for granted — that she'd continue to the next elevator, would join him on the ground floor. But on the second floor she also could turn in several other directions. He could lose her.

She reached the second floor. Mark started to move again.

A merrily squealing three year old darted suddenly away from his mother, scampered into Mark's path. Mark braked sharply, almost tipped over, had to swivel his arms to keep his balance and avoid a collision. The mother winced apologetically.

Mark looked up again as quickly as he could. Too late; the blonde had disappeared.

• • •

Another event was underway in the meeting rooms. Mark glanced through the window as he returned, spotted a woman in a pantsuit orating behind a table stacked with plasticware.

The room that had hosted Saint Catherine's was still empty.

Mark touched the door knob, twisted.

Unlocked. Open.

Mark glanced behind him. No one was watching. He opened the door, stepped inside.

Against the far wall of the dark room was a large cabinet, with labeled drawers. Mark stepped close to read the words. "Northern California Drywall Professionals" "Positivists Association" "West Coast Beverage Retailers" A storage space for each group.

Mark saw the drawer labeled "Saint Catherine's," tried the pull. It didn't open.

Did he still have his hobby lock pick set from high school?

• • •

He did have it.

At 8:00 p.m. that evening, an hour before the mall closed, a nervous, determined Mark returned with the tools and a pen flashlight.

It was time to take a chance. He'd be back in the Santa throne tomorrow, wouldn't be able to get out of his costume and hustle over to West Tit with any time to spare before closing for the rest of the week. Knockers would prosecute if they caught him jimmying the cabinet, but how likely was it that they'd send security on rounds to check conference rooms that they didn't even bother to lock, that contained nothing worth stealing?

The cabinet lock was dinky, a cinch. It was worth the risk. He needed the bread, but wasn't at Knockers because he'd dreamed of being a mall Santa. He'd already written that afternoon in his diary about this latest escapade of the great Parker, to psyche himself up.

The meeting rooms were dark; no events were in session. Far behind him on the walkway a stooped seventy-something with coiffed gray hair was squinting at the window display of a closed gift shop. No one else was in sight, on a Monday an hour before closing time.

As naturally and quickly as possible, Mark stepped into the dark conference room and closed the door behind him.

There was plenty of light from the walkway and atrium to allow Mark to see the lock; unfortunately, there was also plenty of light for a passerby to see him. He was vulnerable now, couldn't if caught explain away his presence by saying that he'd forgotten something, left something behind; not that late, not while standing in the dark.

Mark fit the tension wrench into the bottom of the lock, turned, then slipped in the dimpled Bogota rake. There was no point now in checking over his shoulder; if seen, he was sunk. Mark moved the skinny, three-pointed tool rapidly, see-sawing as he pushed the rake in and out.

The lock didn't give. Mark felt a cold surge of fear, pulled out his Snake rake, tried that instead.

The lock turned.

Inside the drawer were papers, notebooks, two binders. Mark pulled out the whole stack, then stepped back to the conference room door. He deposited the pile on the floor and sat cross-legged on the floor beside it. He was relatively safe now, with his head under window level, using only the pen light in the dark, with at least twenty minutes before the loudspeakers would announce the 9:00 p.m. closing. He could take his time.

Mark flicked on the pen light, started to flip through papers in the stack.

●　　●　　●

He found what he was looking for in one of the binders, after ten minutes of leafing through meeting scripts, attendance lists, sermons. It was white, three ring, contained more than thirty pages of member profiles: one page per member, each page with a paper-clipped snapshot and, beneath it, a lined table of personal information.

The information was limited. Mark guessed that other women in the group had security concerns. The members were listed as Sara L., Marsha B.; no last names. Most of the table was dedicated to answers to Christian discussion questions: 'What is your favorite Bible passage?' 'How have you felt the Holy Spirit in your life?'

But each profile also showed the date of the member's admission to Saint Catherine's.

Mark flipped quickly through the pages, aware of the time, aware that he had to finish before the loudspeaker announcement; glancing at each photo and then homing in on the admission date. If Greta had followed through, she would have been admitted before Thanksgiving. If the binder was out-of-date, of course, he was sunk ... but, that's what he was looking for.

The profile page for the woman with the blonde bun was the next to last in the binder. Maybe it had just been added. She was smiling, but again looked vulnerable, shy. Mark felt that she was staring right at him: through the lens, through the film, as if she or something in the universe had somehow known when it was snapped that he would eventually see it. The bruises on her face were more prominent, looked more like bruises left by a blow.

Mark looked at the admission date.

November 25, 1974.

Which was off by a few days. She would have been admitted earlier, if she'd called Saint Catherine's the day after her last call. Or maybe 'admission date' was the date they'd entered her name in their books. Mark counted backwards, remember that November had thirty days. The twenty-fifth had been a Monday, then. A logical enough day to do admission paperwork.

No other profile page showed a date within a half-year of November.

Mark looked for the blonde's name. Greta had told him that she was using a false name. Maybe she'd chosen a name close to her real name, as he had with Parker, so it would be easier to remember.

Grace. That was the blonde's name. Not Greta. Grace C.

Mark flicked off the pen light, shut the binder and carried the stack back to the cabinet drawer. He was trembling, felt giddy with triumph, relief. He closed the drawer, checked the lock, and as he stepped across the dark conference room to the door again voiced aloud the syllables he had spoken upon first seeing the blonde that morning.

But more loudly now, because he was almost sure. Not as sure as he wanted to be, but almost.

"Greta."

CHAPTER EIGHTEEN

Now he only had to know for sure. Because the dates didn't quite line up, because the name 'Grace' could be a coincidence. He felt like a distance runner with a half-mile to go in a marathon. To be face to face with her at least once, to ask, to hear her answer. To know.

If he could just work out of the west pavilion. The conference rooms would be close by. She'd probably walk by a West Tit Santa throne on her way to meetings. If he stayed in East Tit, he'd likely never see her again.

•   •   •

The next morning on the bus Mark asked Carl the security guard if he'd heard anything about opening a second Santa in West Tit. Carl looked at him knowingly.

"Those harpies are getting on your case, huh?"

"Not yet."

"They will." Carl swung his hand from side to side, as if playing table tennis. "Negotiating. Big business, man. Back and forth, back and forth. It could go either way."

•   •   •

Mark finally saw the second harpy when he entered East Tit ten minutes later. She was trim, black, about his age, with the expected maroon-and-yellow uniform and straight, collarbone-length hair. She was looking at the shiny-wrapped boxes arranged next to Santa's throne and marking something on a clipboard. A freckled, unhappy-looking teenager in an elf-maiden uniform stood beside her. This had to be Cindy, the elf-maiden regular.

Mark was still wearing street clothes, and wasn't surprised that neither looked at him. When he returned in his Santa suit, Cindy looked irritated.

"She is such a major, total, flaming spazz," Cindy said.

"Who?"

Cindy looked at him with wide-eyed incredulity. She had worn sparkly green eye shadow and green lipstick to complement her elf-maiden uniform.

"Ms. Runsen. Who else? Well, duh!"

Ms. Runsen, the second harpy, had just warned Cindy about not dusting and cleaning the bow-wrapped boxes next to the Santa throne.

"That is for janitorial. Okay? I am here to sell photos. How completely anal. Ms. Runsen needs, like, an emergency enema. In an ambulance."

Mark sat on the Santa throne, fluffed up his pillow belt under the red jacket. His first customer soon waddled up, a towheaded six year old bearing a hand-scrawled list smeared with jam. His mother stood by, beamed proudly as the boy laboriously read the list aloud. Mark only had to help with two words.

By then other children had arrived. Cindy herded them ably into a line next to the stuffed reindeer, talking up the two dollar photos to their parents, pausing when necessary to snap a photo of a child on Santa's knee. She soon reminded Mark faintly of Toby, in that she referred privately to customers as 'dorks' and 'retards' while publicly doing her job well. She was a much better photographer than the substitute, had a knack for getting children to smile.

Mark already felt like a veteran. His *Ho! Ho! Ho!* was better. He'd developed a technique for deftly deflecting sticky, candy-smudged fingers, when children wanted to touch or pull his beard. Children believed in him, he had realized by then, either as the one and only Santa or as a VIP Santa's helper. Most looked shyly away when sitting on his knee, and recited their 'gimme, gimme' lists as if spelling out words in a class spelling bee. Later in the morning, a mean-spirited older boy walked by braying "San-ta is fa-ake, Santa is fa-ake." The parents glowered at him, but the children seemed little affected. Their faith was still unshakable.

Rhaytana had written about children. He'd said that every child concealed a camouflaged future adult in a cute, wide-eyed exterior, that in kindergarten the young Adolf Hitler had likely been as cute as the five year old Mahatma Gandhi. Mark tried, but couldn't see the future adults in the kids who perched on his knee. He wondered what he'd been like at age five, if he'd ever sat on a mall Santa's knee for Christmas.

Late in the morning, they had an unexpected break when a proud parent insisted on seating a reluctant three year old on Mark's knee. A few other unwilling kids had cried, but this one bellowed so lustily that he frightened away the others in line.

Cindy took advantage of the moment to step up to chat. She wanted to show Mark a photo she'd snapped with the Santa camera of her boyfriend's Chevelle.

"It's an SS 454," Cindy said. "See the grille? It's so-ooo bitchin'."

Mark asked if she'd heard anything about a possible second Santa in West Tit. Cindy rolled her eyes.

"God, I want to go if they do. Get away from the harpies. They are strictly barf patrol."

•   •   •

Bill arrived unexpectedly at noon the next day, all smiles, escorting a thirtyish Latino toting a professional camera. Cindy looked intimidated.

"This year our Santa has a real beard," said Bill proudly. "How long did you say that sucker took to grow, Mark?"

"More than six months."

"Undoubtedly grown because you knew you'd be Santa at our mall some day." He winked, gestured expansively to the photographer. "And now you're about to get some well-deserved attention in the press. This is going to be in the *Life & Town* section, isn't it, Dave?"

The photographer nodded. He asked Mark to comb his beard, then piqued Cindy's interest by adjusting the lights facing the Santa throne. He took shots from different angles, some while kneeling, others while holding the camera vertically; offered Bill a thumbs-up sign, and left.

Bill watched him walk away, then turned to regard Mark with a playfully simpering expression.

"Young man, how would you like to make a clean *breast* of your work here?"

Mark blinked bewilderedly. "What'd I do?"

"To a clean new breast of our *mall*." Bill looked impatient. "To West Tit."

"Is it *opening*?!?!" Cindy squealed. Bill held out a staying hand, waited for Mark's reaction. Mark tried to look poker-faced.

"Same hours, same pay," said Bill, "but you'll go to the Santa throne in West Tit instead of here." Bill shrugged. "Or you can stay here. Your call."

"*Can I go*?!?!" Cindy cried.

Mark felt his pulse pick up, told himself to look calm.

"Sure," he said. "Why not? A change of scenery. I'll go."

Bill nodded. "Wednesday the 18th will be your start date. The West Titters only want to pay for a week's worth of mall Santa."

"*Can I go with him*?!?!"

"We'll see," said Bill, with a skeptical glance at Cindy. He left.

Cindy grabbed Mark's arm, began lobbying for his help to convince Bill. The harpies were such epic barfers, even seeing them ten percent less would be a relief. Spazz patrol Ms. Runsen had only given her two write-ups, that was absolutely *not* enough to keep her chained to East Tit so the harpies could sniff her butt all day, Mark absolutely *had* to convince Bill or she'd go up to the second floor to grab a humongous boning knife from Wally's BBQ supply and do hara-kiri and bleed to death on the Santa throne.

Mark hardly heard her. He felt triumphant, vindicated. Saint Catherine's had meetings next week. From a West Tit base he'd have at least three clear shots to see Grace/Greta. She'd probably walk right by his Santa throne on her way to the conference rooms.

He'd talk to her. Maybe she wasn't Greta, but he'd find out, hear it from her face to face. It was fated to be. Destiny. He couldn't miss.

•   •   •

For his first two days at the mall he'd forced himself to go in sober, without smoking anything in the morning. He never noticed the smell of pot on anyone's clothes or breath or hair, but he knew other people did. He couldn't take the risk.

But he felt so antsy and fidgety and weird when he didn't smoke. Like his skin didn't fit on his body anymore. So on the third mall day, after he'd had trouble sleeping and had awakened two hours early, he had thought: what was the harm?, and on impulse smoked a bowl in his bedroom. In the nude, so the smell wouldn't get in his clothes. Then he'd showered, washed his hair, washed his beard, eaten an apple, brushed his teeth, gargled with mouthwash and thanks to the weed had felt way better all day. Like he'd taken his medicine, like his skin fit on his body again.

No one had noticed, no one had said anything. Not even Cindy, who was around him all day. (Although Cindy said she had sinus problems.) The harpies didn't hassle Mark. Cindy griped about them, but that was because they wanted her to tidy up the gift boxes and reindeer statue and other stuff around the throne. Once Ms. Bane had given Mark a dirty look from a distance and tapped her chest, and he'd figured out that she'd wanted him to straighten his Santa coat. That had been his only warning from them.

So the next day after toking up he took a shorter shower, and skipped the apple and mouthwash before brushing his teeth, and felt better again — sane, whole, like himself, like he'd taken his medicine; people had smoked marijuana for thousands of years, this was one point he didn't really agree with Rhaytana on — and no one noticed. Mark knew he could have dug up a pot brownie recipe, that would have been safest, but he was all thumbs in the kitchen, he'd only tried to make pot brownies once and they'd been a total failure. It wasn't necessary. He was being vigilant for nothing. People looked at Santa. They didn't smell him.

Did they?

CHAPTER NINETEEN

On Friday he woke up late. The alarm sounded, but he hit the snooze button and maybe hit it twice without realizing it, and in any case when he rolled out of bed he had almost a half-hour less time than usual to get ready for work.

The smart thing to do would have been to skip the good morning bowl. But it was Friday the 13th, and even though he didn't think of himself as superstitious it weirded him out, and he couldn't see being cold stone sober and feeling weird about the 13th all day at the mall.

So he smoked his morning bowl and felt better, but as soon as he left his room he heard the shower running, and there in the hall was his second roomie with a towel around his waist. Mark quickly felt sick, in spite of the weed, the dread and fear overpowering whatever high he felt, ruining it. They almost never got up so early. He didn't have time to wait for the first roomie to finish, let alone the second. He was screwed.

In the kitchen he brushed his teeth and thought of washing his hair, but the sink and counter were piled high with dirty dishes, there wasn't space or time to make room and he would have had to use the green dishwashing soap. Mark improvised, found a vial of patchouli oil in his dresser, stuffed it in his pocket and rushed to the 830 stop. At the stop he rubbed the oil into his beard and hair and then when the bus came opened the window and in spite of the cold held his hand on the sill to direct air onto his beard.

Maybe it wouldn't be so bad, he thought, maybe he'd get away with it, but knew even as he offered himself these assurances that he didn't believe them, that he was taking a big, big chance and what was the date? Friday the 13th. It had to be, just had to be, Friday the 13th.

Cindy was already in the throne area, straightening the glossy bow on one of the presents. Mark offered a big, dishonest grin, and felt relieved when she launched into a typically Cindy tirade about a disgusting parent who had let her barfy child stick gum on one of the reindeer. She didn't smell the weed. But he noticed that she was snuffling, too. Maybe her sinuses were worse than usual. Maybe she couldn't smell anything.

Mark sat on the throne, adjusted his Santa pillow, shut his eyes, and deliberately and consciously crossed his index and middle fingers on the Santa trousers. Hope; he could hope.

In the next two hours he only had one obvious bad moment. "You smell FUNNY, Santa!" cried one little boy, and made a face while holding his nose. But the boy's mother laughed naturally, easily, and Mark quickly parried, said that the reindeer had flown the sleigh into a jungle by mistake. No harm. But there were two other worrisome moments, nearly identical: oddly hostile frowns offered by two mothers as they stepped close enough to deposit their children on Santa's knee. Maybe they didn't mean anything, Mark thought. Maybe the women were just like that, or irritated by something else. And the shift was well underway. Maybe, just maybe ...

•   •   •

At 1:30, Ms. Runsen approached to say something to Cindy about the dispenser for the toy store discount coupons.

Cindy groaned and rolled her eyes, but Ms. Runsen showed no reaction, continued as if Cindy had smiled at her. She was much more aloof and professional than the openly malicious Ms. Bane, could have been a judge in a dog show, matter-of-factly reciting reasons for subtracting points.

How, he had wondered, had a black woman become a harpy? The community was almost all-white. He remembered only about a dozen black kids in high school. He didn't think locals were racists; they hardly had anyone to feel racist about.

A six year old on Mark's knee was assuring him that she'd been a good little girl all year.

When the girl slid off, Mark noticed that Ms. Runsen was looking at him.

Don't look back at her, Mark commanded himself; don't look back. Cindy was still at Ms. Runsen's side, so Mark assumed line-steering duties, motioned to the mother accompanying the next child. This was a husky older boy in the twilight of his believe-in-Santa years. He looked slightly embarrassed, but still recited his 'gimme, gimme' list. Mark ho-ho-ho'd, kept his eyes steadily on the boy's face, and hoped that Ms. Runsen would no longer be in sight when the boy finished.

But she was in sight. She had, in fact, stepped closer, far closer than she had ever been to the throne before, at least when Mark was sitting in it. She stood to one side, not interfering with the line or blocking shoppers' view of Santa, inspecting one of the brightly-wrapped boxes near the throne.

Or pretending to inspect it, to have an excuse for stepping closer to him.

The next child was a spectacularly freckled redhead who had brought a numbered 'gimme' list. Mark invited the boy onto his knee, belly-laughed his now-expert *Ho! Ho! Ho!*. He felt sick.

Ms. Runsen remained by the boxes. She was too close now not to notice. She was watching him.

The boy finished.

Before Mark could nod to the next child, Ms. Runsen stepped in front of him and motioned for the line to hold. Mark grinned at the children, shrugged his shoulders theatrically, as if to say that Santa didn't know what was going on, either. He felt like an idiot.

Ms. Runsen now stood directly in front of him, no more than two feet away. Mark met her eyes. She looked at him coldly.

•   •   •

"You know, my ass is in a sling for this, too," said Bill, hours later. "I'm the one who recruited you."

He rocked in the swivel chair behind his office desk, looked at Mark irritably. Mark grimaced, said nothing. He was in street clothes.

"Doesn't the word 'maintain' mean anything to you, dickhead? You get stoned at home. *I* get stoned at home. You don't hit the pipe right before your shift as a shopping mall Santa and then try to cover it up with ... what's that shit you put in your beard, anyway?"

Mark took out the vial of patchouli oil, slid it across the desk. Bill picked up the vial, waved it at Mark disgustedly.

"Like this is going to fool anyone. You were out of your frigging gourd to think you could get away with this. And I get to explain why I recommended you."

"Okay," said Mark. He frowned at the top of the desk, embarrassed. "I messed up. I'm sorry."

Bill leaned back in the chair, glowered moodily at the sticky note-decorated wall calendar. They were silent for nearly a half-minute.

"The only reason you're not out on your ass right now is because of that *Life & Town* photo." Bill shook his head at the calendar, as if still hardly able to believe Mark's recklessness. "I had to argue for one solid hour: Mark's in the media, it's not in the mall's interest to get rid of him now, even if Mark is an unmitigated idiot." He shot Mark another irritated look. "One solid hour. And I have other things to do today."

"I'm sorry."

"Will you vow ... vow, I said ... that you will not consume weed in the morning before you come to work here? Will you?"

"Yes." Mark nodded, then looked at Bill beseechingly. "Look, I know I screwed up, but in five more days I'm going to be in West Tit ..."

"West Tit?!" Bill looked at him incredulously. "West Tit?! Are you serious? You're not going to West Tit now."

Mark stared at him, speechless.

"Do you really think, seriously believe, that Ms. Runsen's going to let you transfer to a pavilion *farther* from the harpies' office, where she'll see you *less*, after today? Seriously? You're going to have harpies in your hair like flies on shit until Christmas."

Mark's expression must have communicated his horror. Bill threw up his hands, looked briefly sympathetic.

"Bub, they don't work for me. Corporate chain of command. The harpies' bosses are over my head. If Ms. Runsen says you stay put, you stay put."

•   •   •

So he was ruined, Mark thought, as he left Bill's office. He wanted to quit, even if he needed the money, but knew he still had a slim, slim chance of running into Grace/Greta if he stayed. If he quit he'd have none.

Bill hadn't said anything about a parent complaint. For all he knew, Ms. Runsen had nailed him personally, single-handedly, just to be a goody-goody, maroon-fannied, yellow-titted corporate bitch. Just couldn't leave well enough alone, couldn't keep her nose out of it. And now shot to hell, his whole reason for hiring on as a Santa Claus ...

Mark saw that the object of his loathing was now walking directly toward him. En route to Bill's office, Mark guessed, likely to finalize the our-Santa-was-naughty paperwork. They'd docked him the day's pay.

"Thank you very much!" said Mark, as he was about to pass.

Ms. Runsen looked at him, matter-of-factly, as if he were a sheepdog she'd just kicked out of the dog show. Mark saw large brown eyes, a wide, smallish nose, the full African lips, medium-brown skin, unhappily admitted that he couldn't regard Ms. Runsen as ugly, medusa or witch-like, as much as he wanted to.

"You're welcome," she said.

CHAPTER TWENTY

Thereafter Ms. Runsen visited the Santa throne at least every three hours. She made no effort to conceal her purpose, was there to see if Mark looked stoned or smelled of marijuana. She would step close to the throne, inspect the white-and-red Santa suit while inhaling. Mark could see her nostrils open and her breasts rise under the yellow blouse. If she arrived when he had a child on his knee, she might smile brightly and make a diplomatic joke to the parent. ("I'm one of Santa's helpers!") If she arrived when Mark was alone, she regarded him with cool, remote emptiness, as if she had to complete a review of the ejected sheepdog.

·   ·   ·

"This is totally your fault," a bitter Cindy said to Mark, during a lull in the shift.

Mark grimaced, looked away.

"Every time she's here, she's got to check out everything." The elf-maiden screwed up her face to imitate Ms. Runsen. "'Cindy, the reindeer's antlers looked droopy.' 'Cindy, the icicles are touching the teardrops.' I am sure! Oh, barf. When all she cares about is if you reek."

She looked at Mark without friendliness. "You totally *have* to get Bill to transfer me to the new Santa at West Tit. The *day* it opens. She is driving me out of my gourd."

·   ·   ·

Mark had kept his promise to Bill, now hit the pipe only after his shift at Knockers. He went in sober, as he had on his first two days at the mall, stayed sober all day. Ms. Runsen had nothing to smell.

He hated it; felt antsy, nervous, high-strung; dealt with surges of irritation or anxiety that he was sure he wouldn't have felt if properly medicated. A part of him knew that the symptoms were partly in his head, that he felt panicked by the prospect of so many consecutive days of sobriety, but this didn't make him feel any better.

He thought that Ms. Runsen looked uglier every time he saw her. Her prissy walk, in the shiny, boring black shoes; the now monotonous, never-changing color contrast of her sepia skin with the maroon and yellow uniform and ever-present clipboard, that reminded him of indeterminate blobs he might see floating in a bilious stew; her conked hair (or whatever blacks did to straighten their hair; Mark had no idea); and, especially, her prudish, goody-goody, namby-pamby manner. He imagined a Ms. Runsen who saluted the flag whenever she had an impure thought, or perhaps reported herself to the police. Picking on Mark had to be the highlight of her day.

•   •   •

At first Mark suffered the visits in silence, ignoring Ms. Runsen if busy with a child or staring stonily into space if she approached when he was alone.

Then one morning she caught him in an unusually bad mood.

"Hey, why don't you just get a sniffer dog," he said, as she leaned over him. "Wouldn't that be easier?"

Ms. Runsen stood straight, looked down at him. She seemed slightly surprised that he had spoken.

"You can get the dog to trot over here, sniff my beard, bark up a ruckus if I smell like a doobie. Then you won't have to tramp all over the mall in those stiff shoes."

Ms. Runsen studied him before answering. She stood with her hands folded over the clipboard at her waist, regarding him with the familiar cool, controlled expression, in which changes of feeling seemed to register only as faint hints. But the hints could be interpreted. Mark felt surprised: she seemed to dislike him at least as much as he disliked her.

"Police dogs are expensive," she said. "It's cheaper to have me check on you. Besides, it might bite you. It might think you deserve it."

•   •   •

Bill managed to finagle a brief announcement in the local press about the second Santa at West Tit. Mark never saw his peer in person, came no closer to him than the small photo on newsprint.

Cindy's transfer came through, liberating her from Ms. Runsen. Mark was again paired with Martha, the nondescript, apologetic elf-maiden he'd worked with on his first day. Martha still took lousy photos, and discreetly avoided private chat with Mark when they didn't have kids in line. She'd likely heard mall gossip about him.

Mark continued to hope that he'd look up one day and see Grace/Greta walking past the Santa throne. Maybe she'd need something from one of the East Tit stores, or feel like exploring after a walk around Coopers Pond. It wasn't impossible.

But it wasn't likely, either. He'd lost, basically; he was screwed. Because of Friday the 13th, and because of Ms. Runsen. At least the pay was good.

.   .   .

"Did one of the parents snitch me off?"

Mark asked the question abruptly, without thinking, as Ms. Runsen leaned over yet again for an afternoon inspection. A second later he wondered why. He wouldn't get an honest answer.

Ms. Runsen straightened, looked at him in her cool, unfriendly way.

"I mean, forgive me for being curious. But I am. Did one of the parents say something to you, or did you just think I looked zonked while you were talking to Cindy?"

"Did you think I'd tell you?"

Mark curled an exasperated lip, looked away. Ms. Runsen jotted something on her clipboard.

"If a parent did tell me," she said, as she wrote, "I might put that parent in danger by telling you. You might guess which parent I mean." She stopped writing, offered an unfriendly, pearly-white smile. "So I'm delighted to take full credit, Santa. I snitched you off all by myself."

· · ·

Mark's dislike of Ms. Runsen grew steadily. He knew that the fault for his failed Grace/Greta plan was his own, but it was more comfortable to channel his resentment toward the black harpy who had managed to become so stiff, prissy and stuck-up well-before her twenty-fifth birthday. What kind of child had she been in her own sitting-on-Santa's-knee years? Mark imagined an insufferable teacher's pet, eagerly tattling on classmates who smuggled candy or copied homework.

Was there something he could say to get back at her, to get a dig in?

Maybe if he turned the tables.

"You ought to be more careful with the lipstick, Ms. Runsen," said Mark in a solicitous tone, as if trying to be helpful. He gestured to his lower lip. "There's a smudge right about here. Do you think I should mention it to Bill?"

Ms. Runsen replied that he should take any complaint to her colleague Ms. Bane, that Bill wasn't her supervisor. She said this calmly, but Mark also noticed that she was even more nitpicky than usual about his Santa uniform, and guessed that he had successfully irritated her. A weakness!, he thought, but then decided almost immediately not to bother her that way. He didn't get kicks from being mean. She was his cross to bear. He'd brought it on himself, would tolerate her.

· · ·

Ironically, it was when he'd lost interest in provoking her that he accidentally succeeded in doing just that.

Mark had merely asked why he hadn't been visited by Ms. Bane.

"There are two of you, aren't there? Doesn't Ms. Bane ever feel like trotting over here for a little sniff sniff? Just for variety. She might get off on the smell."

"We decided that I'd be harder to fool."

"Harder to fool how?"

Ms. Runsen hesitated conspicuously before answering. She looked as if she regretted saying as much as she had.

"Someone close to me had a drug problem," she said, finally. "I know the smell of marijuana."

Mark grinned. "Your daddy was a dealer, huh? Maybe if you give me his phone number, I can score some good toke for Christmas."

He said this lightly, unmaliciously, half-expecting her to manage a slight smile, to take it as a joke. But as soon as the words were out of his mouth he knew that they'd gotten to her. Ms. Runsen pursed her lips, shut her eyes for a long count of five. Trying to control herself. When she opened them he saw that she'd failed. The harpy was furious.

"So that's your little quip for the day," she said. "How funny."

Mark watched her, didn't answer, wondered what about the remark could have bothered her so much. Ms. Runsen kept glowering at him, jaws set. She pressed her clipboard to her blouse and started to go, then stopped and turned back to him. As if she were telling herself to quit, but couldn't, because she was so angry.

"Mark, what do you think of the people in this mall?" she asked.

"What do I think of ..." Mark shrugged. "Customers. People. Shoppers."

"They're our neighbors." Ms. Runsen looked around the atrium, at the anonymous mall-goers walking or hurrying from store to store. "All these little lives we'll never know anything about. Mommy and Daddy with their family problems, maybe barely making the mortgage, hardly able to cope with the stress of being parents, but you know what? They still find time to come here to let their kids visit Santa, because that's what their parents did for them and their grandparents did, and their kids are still young enough to believe that the likes of you could be Santa."

'The likes of you.' Mark sat up, started to answer, but stopped himself. What had he *said*?! Ms. Runsen was livid.

"But you know what? Last week some of them didn't get a very good visit, because the mall Santa couldn't be bothered to come to work sober. And maybe the kids didn't mind, but some of the mommies and daddies recognized the smell, and worried, and wondered about putting down stakes here and the homes with those big mortgages, because what kind of neighborhood would hire a shopping mall Santa who stinks of marijuana? And then left with one more thing to worry about, on top of their marriages and mortgages and their children."

Ms. Runsen bent toward him, her face on level with his, only a foot away. Mark felt stunned; she as much as hated him.

"And you know something? I don't think I should be sympathetic, Mark. Not really. I don't think you came here stinking of pot because you're careless, or because you have a drug problem, although you do, or a low self-image. I think you did it because you're a despicable, self-centered little boy who can't be bothered to feel a sense of responsibility for families in his own town."

. . .

Bill puffed up his cheeks, exhaled slowly, wearily. He slouched in his office swivel chair, stared across his desk at Mark with unconcealed amusement.

"You want me to write her up for calling you despicable."

Mark nodded defiantly.

"You're serious?"

"Yes. That's like an epithet. 'A despicable, self-centered little boy.' That's what she said. She filed a complaint on me, I want to file one on her."

Bill snorted, looked around the office, as if wishing for a witness to appreciate the joke. "Santa comes to work stoned. Santa get busted by the harpy. And then Santa wants to file a formal complaint because the harpy calls him despicable. I'll tell you, man, some of the top brass are going to get a real boot out of this. You might get a visit from the CEO. I ought to send this to *National Lampoon*."

Mark dug in heels. "You said I can file a complaint. I want to file it. She did me, I'm going to do her."

Bill shrugged, pulled a stack of pink forms out of his desk, started to write.

. . .

Mark had a shy five year old on his knee the next morning when Ms. Runsen made her first daily approach to the throne.

He glanced at her, knew immediately that she'd heard about the complaint. She looked defensive.

Ms. Runsen didn't speak to or look at him. Her breasts rose as she stood close and inhaled through her nose. A harpy doing a dog's job, thought Mark; what would she do if she had sinus problems, like Cindy?

"You're welcome," Mark said emphatically, over the child's head. Ms. Runsen walked away.

.   .   .

Christmas Eve was his last day at the mall. Saint Catherine's final meeting had been the previous Friday. The non-profit was now officially off the mall's client list, bound for Los Angeles, wouldn't return.

He felt lousy. Ms. Runsen's lecture grated on him. How was a kindergartner going to know he'd hit the pipe before coming to the mall? "You smell FUNNY, Santa!" That was what the kid had said. So what? Was it such a federal case if a couple of parents recognized the smell? What exactly did they expect from a mall Santa?

But: the whole thing bothered him. And he shouldn't have ratted her off to Bill. He'd regretted it almost as soon as he left Bill's office, but was he really supposed to apologize to someone who'd snitched *him* off, and was an impossible goody-goody prig, and had insulted him? Seriously? Wouldn't *she* have reported *him* for insulting her? In two seconds.

But: it felt lousy.

At least now he could be almost sure that Greta was okay. Mark tried to remind himself of that, to cheer himself up: the moment when Grace/Greta had met his eyes, the close-to-Greta name and admission date on the profile page. And the pay had been good. He'd leave with a fat wallet. So the mall hadn't been a total failure, even if it felt that way.

At 4:00 p.m. on Christmas Eve, Mark told the wide-eyed toddler on his knee that Santa had to leave for the North Pole. The mall beauty salon was open until 5:00; Bill had given him another voucher, so he could get his hair died back to a shade close to its natural color. The stylist introduced him to a snickering colleague as 'our stoned Santa,' asked while working on his hair if he knew where she could get some good hash. Mark did, but pretended ignorance; she didn't seem discreet.

An hour later he caught the 830, his life as Santa Claus concluded.

PART III

Chapter Twenty-One

11/3

Paul, please:

I did not state or suggest that you would like working with Craig Spiegel. Few have or do. I merely wrote that this work would be the best, practical, responsible adult solution to what I shall diplomatically refer to as your cash flow issues. Those who endure Craig Spiegel for six days can anticipate a reliably remitted paycheck on the seventh.

Incidentally: I assume that your mid-October letter that unjustly scapegoats me for your Spiegel miseries was the last you sent. Yes? No? It arrived after I pulled up stakes in Tucson, but my Tucson landlady was gracious enough to read it to me on the phone.

My new address is below. I may be here for awhile.

CONTINUED 11/4

Yes, Albuquerque, New Mexico! That's where I am. We gigged here, three times, I think, always at the Civic. Do you remember Hendrix, Steppenwolf, Three Dog Night? The Civic's acoustic issues? Carlos' miseries in trying to accommodate them?

The address belongs to a rented-by-the-week backyard in-law unit of an angular ranch house north of downtown. For now, I remain gainfully unemployed, devote my time to long walks, Alcoholics Anonymous meetings and the companionship of Zeke, my AA sponsee.

Zeke is why I'm in Albuquerque. He met me at a Tucson AA meeting while in town on business, recruited me as a sponsor, and thereafter called me every night from his hotel. The nightly calls continued after his return to Q.

Zeke knows that I am wandering my way through my mid-life crisis, convinced me that I might as well wander up to Albuquerque to help him stay sober. I live like Mary Worth these days, Paul, am recruited hither and yon as a listener, an empathizer, sometimes a shoulder to cry on. I don't mind. I'm flattered. Why not try to help, if I think I can?

But you don't know what a "sponsor" is, do you?

CONTINUED 11/5

Excuse the coffee stain. I plod forward with this missive in a restaurant near Zeke's favorite AA meeting. Several participants adjourned here for a social hour 'fellowship' afterward, have since left me alone in the booth.

In Alcoholics Anonymous, a "sponsor" is a fellow meeting goer recruited by a struggling drunk as a volunteer helpmate. Sponsors may answer questions about navigating AA's twelve steps, may help the drunk resist temptation to return to the bottle.

Now you know.

My sponsee Zeke is about thirty, tall, broad-shouldered, was once a star athlete at a local high school. He is handsome, friendly, extroverted. He also is — or was; read on — well-off, thanks to inherited stakes in an auto dealership and several local franchises.

Ten years ago, Zeke believed that God brought the ideal partner into his life: Tammy, met at a church service. Zeke is a Christian, but his faith is of a materialistic, worldly sort: he was unabashedly attracted to Tammy for beauty and body and, soon, for her zeal in bed. Even today he proudly describes his trophy partner with pornographic details: her fanny, how her gait spurred an irresistible twitch n' jiggle of bum cheeks in a mini-skirt; her succulent thighs, her breasts, with faintly visible nipple contour showing through blouse and bra; a face combining the most alluring features of Marilyn, Raquel, Liz, framed by a lioness' mane of buttery blonde hair.

Etcetera. And so forth. Male eyes devoured Tammy head to toe when the couple entered clubs, restaurants. Three friends, Zeke says — no, Zeke *brags* — confessed that they had fantasized about Tammy while masturbating. What man-to-man accolade could offer more real-world prestige?

Zeke's mostly-carnal bliss with Tammy lasted about six months. She then became pregnant; as pregnancy developed to childbirth and motherhood, her manner and appearance changed. She gained more than fifty pounds, and showed no interest in postpartum dieting; the fifty pounds, in fact, became sixty, then seventy. Tammy's taste for whiskey sours didn't help.

Her manner changed more dramatically still. Coquettish giggles became snaps, snarls. The "hottest fuck" in Q became, according to Zeke, Q's "biggest asshole."

Mind you, Paul: I have never met Tammy, have only Zeke's account to go on. I'd be amazed if he didn't play a much bigger role in the break-up than he now believes. Still, the divorce terms suggest that Tammy dealt with formidable inner demons: Zeke wound up with both sole legal *and* physical custody of their son, Wilson. Tammy, however, wound up with one lollapalooza of a financial settlement. As noted, Zeke is well-off no longer.

And now, a confession, that I can share freely in a letter that Zeke won't see:

I like my sponsee, but wouldn't stick in Albuquerque only for his benefit. My main concern is for their now eight year old son, Wilson.

Zeke loves him, but the love is poisoned by resentment. Wilson looks too much like Tammy, is a daily reminder of how Zeke believes life screwed him over. A parent's duties are legion, but Zeke fulfills many haphazardly or tardily. He gripes too loudly and quickly at an eight year old's inevitable mistakes: left-behind messes, forever untied sneakers.

If he goes off the wagon, his slipshod care of Wilson would be worse still. Far worse. A trusted elderly neighbor assists, minds the boy when Zeke is at AA or tending to other necessities, but is uninterested in the role of surrogate grandmother. Zeke is the main caregiver.

How can I convey the weight of his responsibility for a fragile, evolving human life? No, you didn't want it to happen this way, Zeke, but it did, and now this life that you brought into the world depends on you.

We go back and forth. I as much as stalk our conversations, look for angles, opportunities to woo him into a greater commitment to parenting. The balance is delicate. I don't trust his sobriety, not after only eight months in program. I fear kindling a resentment that could lead to a slip, a binge.

The waitress just offered a meaningful look at the lone Rhaytana lingering so long in the booth. Time to make myself scarce.

CONTINUED 11/7 ...

... on an Indian summer of an afternoon in Albuquerque's Roosevelt Park. I scribble on a bench in the generous shade of an elm tree, clipboard braced more-or-less comfortably on my knee. A nice place to hang out. Zeke is busy with business chores. Wilson is at school. Time I have plenty of.

You and I both know that Zeke's doomed romance with Tammy is but one variation of a sad, sad tale lived not millions, but billions of times on our globe's every continent, that the sufferers are at least as frequently women as men and that the essentials of the story likely would have been familiar to Hammurabi. A big part of the problem, me thinks, is that we credulous humans grossly underestimate the role in life of camouflage, deception. I wonder if the young might pair up less tragically if they knew deep down how little they should trust their desires.

I like little Wilson, but also understand that his third grade adorability is something of a fraud. Evolution has made kids cute, evokers of compassionate feeling; if they weren't, how motivated would adults be to tolerate those inevitable mistakes, to feed, clothe and shelter unproductive progeny? The growing eight year old conceals a future, full-grown adult, who will chart his own path, as we did, be his own individual.

Have you ever seen that famous photo of the one year old Adolf Hitler? What an adorable little lad he was, sitting with pursed lips, white booties and wide, wondering puppy eyes! Nature heartlessly and obliviously camouflaged the mass-murderer-to-be,

introduced the marauder to civilization as
a huggable Trojan Horse. In kindergarten he
likely was still as cute as the five year old
Mahatma Gandhi.

Nature lies like a bastard, Paul! Nature
can be to its individual members what a skel-
eton key or a jimmy are to a burglar or car
thief: I, duplicitous nature, help YOU, you
rotten crook, and the rest of humanity gets
to rely on its own adaptations and guile
to fend for itself. The nature that shows
a polar bear how to stalk a tasty seal's
ice breathing hole doesn't give a rat's ass
about the seal that the bear wants to kill,
murder, eat. The seal gets to find its own
help from nature to dodge that hungry bear
and survive.

Crafty, scheming nature even conceals the
purpose of the sexual act itself. What randy
young man thinks that he sports a stiffy
to father offspring? He wants to screw! to
fuck! to shoot his load! Delusion, delusion!
The aching putz he regards only with a smut
flick backdrop bears a reproductive payload
of sperm, that can enter ovum, fertilize
egg, make another Wilson. Nature won't even
tell the poor schmuck why he's horny.

And a schmuck he may be, interested only
in flesh, but it is also in his slobbery
rutting that he wields the power of a god.
Yes. A god. For he may create conscious
intelligent human life from nothing, even
while possessing no more awareness of the
evolutionary purpose of his hunger than a
salmon has of its drive to swim upstream to
spawn.

A mountainous German Shepherd is now trying to seduce *me*, Paul. It doesn't know me from Adam, but repeatedly deposits a saliva-coated red ball at my feet, urges me to ignore you and give it a heave, to play fetch. The Shepherd's owner leers at me knowingly, confident that I'll give in. He's got my number: I will. See ya, buster.

CONTINUED 11/8

I was about to stuff this overdue dispatch into the envelope when I realized that I failed to mention the kicker to the Zeke/ Tammy story:

What do you think Zeke's hobby is, Paul? Please, don't read on yet, cover the paragraph below. Try to guess.

Did you try?

Zeke is a hunter. It seems that New Mexico includes many spots where a murderously-inclined rifle toter can kill elk, and Zeke is familiar with most of them. My God, the man's got different camouflage-pattern outfits for different seasons, different hunting grounds, all so he can blend into the foliage while sneaking up on that unlucky elk to take a shot. He's even experimenting with turkey calls.

Turkey calls! I kid you not. He got the idea from another hunter, believes himself to be on a vanguard. Little dealie he sticks in his mouth to make a sound like a cow elk in heat. 'Ee-yaww, ee-yaww, oh-hoo, I'm so horny, you big bull elk, you, come screw the living daylights out of me, I can't wait, ee-yaww, ee-yaww' ... and the lust-crazed bull comes a-running, discovers too late that this mistake will be his last.

My sponsee Zeke, ruined by a Tammy-in-camouflage, swaddles himself in camouflage as a hunter.

No, I haven't pointed out the similarity. He hasn't seen it himself, and I don't want to be cruel.

CHAPTER TWENTY-TWO

Rhaytana's real name was Daniel Velasco Santos. He was originally from Spain, from some place called 'Asturias.' Mark thought this might be a Spanish town, but wasn't sure. In the 1930s in Spain there'd been some kind of war — or battles, at least; fighting — and Rhaytana's parents had fled the fighting and emigrated with their young son to the United States. They lived in New York City, then Atlanta, then Las Vegas. Rhaytana spoke Spanish at home, but wrote that he grew up as a thoroughly American teenager.

In his middle-twenties, he drifted into the music business. His high school friend Paul worked as a roadie, brought Rhaytana onboard as a last-minute fill-in for a stagehand. He never lacked work thereafter. A promoter compared him favorably to a ship anchor. The hull might rupture, the engine might fail, but the anchor wouldn't break. Jobs assigned to Rhaytana got done; a harried producer could stop worrying about them. Further, he was likeable, worked well with performers, and was sober when it mattered.

By his early thirties, he was an in-demand, steadily-employed tour manager, already on a first-name basis with many of the biggest names in rock and roll. Rhaytana bought a house on Los Angeles' Westside, but was hardly ever there: gigs kept him on the road most of the year. He worked sixteen hour days, drank, popped pills, smoked pot, described himself as a successfully practicing addict.

In his late thirties, he drifted again, in a different way: into a long-term relationship with Abby, a doe-eyed, painfully vulnerable groupie. Her guilelessness touched him; he felt like a father figure, a protector. Rhaytana installed her in the Westside home, returned to his road schedule, convinced himself that a stable home and financial security were all that Abby needed. But they weren't. Abby needed him as a partner. She wanted him to spend most of his time in L.A.

They bickered about his marathon schedule, then fought about it. Rhaytana inevitably got his way. He didn't see Abby as an equal; worse, neither did she. He was a fast lane, Porsche-driving, top-of-the-ladder music professional; she was still unemployed and dependent; he sometimes treated her like a household pet. He slept with other women on the road, returned to infect her with gonorrhea, shrugged off her complaints. These were inevitably expressed quietly, meekly. Abby didn't stand up for herself.

Her drug use increased. Rhaytana noticed, griped, but did little more. He suspected that she was being passive-aggressive, play-acting a problem she didn't really have to win his sympathy, induce guilt. Fine, he thought; he didn't have time for such antics. He wasn't going to give up his career because she didn't know how lucky she was.

One night in the first week of a tour, Rhaytana called her from his hotel room in Philadelphia. Abby said that she wasn't doing well and needed to be with him. Something in her voice stood out. She'd never before spoken quite that way.

Rhaytana told her she could see a therapist, that he'd pay for it, but that he couldn't possibly drop everything and go back to L.A. He thought of offering to fly her to Philadelphia, but decided not to. He knew Abby. She'd just be in the way.

Abby said she understood, and hung up.

She died of an overdose less than a week later. The autopsy showed that she'd been two months pregnant with what would have been Rhaytana's first child.

Rhaytana finished the tour. He was too much of a professional not to, but for the first time despised himself for his own professionalism. He had committed to a second tour, and completed this, too. His word was his bond; anchors didn't splinter apart and let ships go adrift. Yet inside he knew he was a ruined man. He hated himself. He hated to shave, to look at himself in the mirror, to slide the razor across the cheek of a man he now saw as heartless, soulless slime; a material world success who had let his only child die in the womb of a partner who always had needed much more than his money.

The second tour would be his last. Rhaytana spread the word that he needed time to cope with his partner's death. In practice, 'coping' meant a months-long, grief-fueled binge of drugs and alcohol. One night he drank enough to black out in his back yard in his underwear, and took himself to an Alcoholics Anonymous 'newcomers' meeting the next day.

Rhaytana stayed sober, refused new gigs, lived quietly while working the AA program. He became a bookworm in sobriety, developed an intellectual streak. After a year, he decided to sell house, Porsche and other possessions and hit the road. The anchor would pull itself off the sea bed, set itself free; he could wander, drift, be guided by whim. If he wished, he could cushion his nest egg by taking odd jobs. He'd never been status conscious, was happy to do most anything. A pick-up job also could be a way of meeting people.

His first stop was Kansas City. The AA program's ninth step stipulated amend-making to those one had wronged; Rhaytana had long wanted to apologize to a hotelier, stiffed and ignored after a teenie band trashed adjoining suites. In KC he rented a room at the Y, worked briefly as a dishwasher, then followed his muse to visit distant Spanish relatives in St. Louis. It was from the Lou that he sent his first letter to Paul, chronicling his reflections and experiences while traveling. In the next years he would write many more.

Paul liked the letters, asked in the middle paragraph of one response if Rhaytana would mind if he sent them to an editor friend at *White Rhino*, a fledgling rock music magazine. 'Why not?' responded Rhaytana, without thinking. As fate would have it, the letters' serialization in monthly editions coincided with *White Rhino*'s rapid growth into a second tier national music magazine. A horrified Rhaytana saw his prose in print while thumbing through *White Rhino* at a supermarket, learned that he was developing a small personal fan base.

In his seventeenth and last letter, Rhaytana wrote about the value of sobriety; that it was the evolved, intelligent human brain that separated homo sapiens from other mammals, that it was obscene to distort the perceptions of this evolutionary treasure purely for the sake of recreational intoxication. He also whimsically compared some rock stars to malicious pied pipers, as so many had led their fans astray and died ruinously of overdoses.

Many speculated that the publicity-adverse Rhaytana crafted this letter to get rid of *White Rhino*. If so, the strategy worked; they ended the serialization without comment, never printed his name again. Letters one through sixteen and the never-before-published seventeenth appeared in a slender paperback. Rhaytana had a tiny coterie of fans, whether he wanted them or not.

. . .

Fans like Mark.

Mark couldn't explain why he'd latched on as he had. He didn't understand everything in the letters. He avoided re-reading the letter about sobriety, even as he felt vaguely virtuous for daring to like a writer who had written it.

Being a fan made him feel like he belonged in a special club. That was part of it. Everybody and his kid brother had a Stones or Sly or Led Zeppelin record. There wasn't anything unusual about liking them. Rhaytana was different. Sometimes a stranger would chat him up if he saw Mark with the book. Not often, but occasionally.

Mark wanted to meet him. He'd never shared that with anyone, felt embarrassed that it was at least partly because he'd never had a father. If he could just ... ask Rhaytana some questions. About life, where he was going. What he was supposed to do. Rhaytana was honest, at least. He wasn't trying to sell anything.

Not that there was much chance of meeting him. A fan named Fielder had started a tiny 'zine to report news about Rhaytana, but the 'zine had folded; there *wasn't* any news. Rhaytana had disappeared.

CHAPTER TWENTY-THREE

Mark spent Christmas with his mother. They exchanged gifts (a TV guide subscription for her; for Mark, a Stevie Wonder album), ate. The apartment felt unusually quiet, and Mark finally realized why: they were alone. Boyhood Christmases usually had been joined by Mom's boyfriend *du jour*: inevitably handsome, frequently unemployed, at least civil with the 4 or 9 or 13 year old only child, and always temporary.

His mom was forty-one now. Her face had changed. She was a maniac about dieting, fussed over make-up and skin creams, but still: she wasn't a hottie anymore, wasn't being chased by useless boyfriends.

After they ate she wanted help with the refrigerator. The ice build-up in the freezer was so thick that she could hardly close the compartment door. Could Mark use a chisel? 'Well, no, Mom, that wasn't how you did it,' and then it was as he matter-of-factly described defrosting that something got to her. Upset her.

No, she didn't want to defrost, the plug was behind the fridge, she wasn't strong enough to move it, she didn't want him to have to come over to help her or have melting ice all over everything, and who knew what was behind the refrigerator anyway? There might be bugs. Why couldn't she get a nice new refrigerator and let the Sears installers clean out everything when they put it in?

Which Mark said was crazy, and that was when she started to cry. Quietly, steadily, helplessly, slapping her hand repeatedly on the dining table, like a student cringing in shame before a not-cruel, not-unfriendly teacher flabbergasted by her denseness. She couldn't do anything right. Not cook, not clean, not manage her life, not be a good mom. She knew she hadn't been any kind of adult example to him. She'd only been good at being pretty, and now she wasn't even that anymore.

·   ·   ·

The next day Shirley called. He'd continued to flirt with her occasionally on the phone, never seriously, but this time she said she was sick of being alone and having to masturbate when she felt so horny. Mark thought of the turkey-caller-for-the-moose paragraph in Rhaytana's Albuquerque letter, but still: it had been awhile, his luck with women was a lot worse with the beard, and so this time he asked Shirley when she wanted to get together. How about tomorrow night, Mark? Fine. Friday. She said she could hardly wait.

Well, he should have known. At least he didn't get blasted with a .338 Winchester like the stupid moose. She wrapped her arms around his neck and gave him a hot kiss at her door, but then wriggled away when he slid his hands to her ass, and asked with hurt indignation if that was all he wanted, if he'd only come to use her.

They went to Patricio's, a ritzy Mexican bar near downtown. Shirley held his eye while she slid her tongue suggestively around the rim of the margarita glass to lick off the salt, but then spent the next hour complaining about past boyfriends and men in general, and asked Mark repeatedly why he wouldn't shave off that ridiculous, ugly, scraggly caveman beard, did he think she liked going out with a date who looked like a hillbilly or feeling bristles on her mouth when they kissed? How repulsive.

. . .

Maybe it was time to get out of town. Like Rhaytana, when he'd sold all his stuff and moved to K.C. If he couldn't close the chapter on Greta, he at least could close it on NorCal.

He didn't like being anywhere near the hotline office. He'd passed it on errands, and felt bummed: gazing up from the sidewalk at the window he'd looked through while taking calls, remembering how it had felt to volunteer there. Or thinking of Toby, of playing cards with him, of their last conversation. Of how Toby must have looked in the last seconds of his life, sitting in the same chair at the call desk that Mark had sat on, with the barrel of that big revolver in his mouth.

One morning on impulse he splurged on a long-distance call to Saint Catherine's headquarters in Dallas. Mark tried to sound like a bored office flunky, said he needed to send files to the new site in Los Angeles.

"To the office or to the shelter?" the secretary asked. Mark thought fast, said he'd better get the information for both, came away with two street addresses in the Valley. So, yes, he could go down there, L.A. was familiar turf, but how much of an obsessed nutcase did he want to be? Did he want to act like stalkers who picked on chicks? It was over. He was never going to know for sure if Grace was Greta. Chapter closed.

But thoughts of Greta still returned, especially if he had to walk within blocks of the hotline office.

So maybe it was time to leave. Portland, maybe. Seattle.

. . .

A couple of days later, Mark received a hand-lettered envelope with a Las Vegas postmark. He recognized the handwriting: it was from Fielder, the sole writer, researcher, editor and publisher of the tiny defunct Rhaytana 'zine. Mark had sent in ten dollars to subscribe, but had only received two "issues"— stapled, mimeographed pages — before the 'zine had folded.

'Some kind of sales pitch,' guessed Mark, as he opened the envelope. But it wasn't. Inside was a flier for a series of interfaith concerts in the Los Angeles area. Different religious groups were participating: churches, mosques, synagogues, temples. Mark looked at the dates, didn't recognize any of the bands. The venues looked small: a community center auditorium in the San Fernando Valley, a church near Long Beach, a Westside recreation center.

Fielder had drawn a big oval around one name in the crew list, and had written exclamation points around the oval:

PRODUCTION MANAGER
D. VELASCO SANTOS

Mark stared at the flier for more than a half-hour.

It clicked. "D. Velasco Santos" was the name that Rhaytana had used professionally as a tour manager. Someone else with that name might conceivably drift onboard as a roadie, but managing a whole show — lighting, sound, everything — took know-how, experience. Mark had never heard of another "D. Velasco Santos" at that level. And an interfaith concert was just the sort of project that Rhaytana would take on now, probably for free. Way, way below the venues he'd worked at befcre, but for a good cause.

There was nothing else in the envelope. Fielder had just wanted to be a good guy, had spent his own money to mail his old 'zine subscribers a hot tip.

Rhaytana was managing the shows, would be in the listed venues on the scheduled dates. Mark could meet him. And if he was in L.A., would it really be so weird to check out Saint Catherine's while he was there?

Maybe it was fate. He didn't have just one reason to head south. Fate had given him two.

CHAPTER TWENTY-FOUR

Mark was still on good terms with Duke, called him up at home to see if he could turn him on to some kind of gig in L.A.

Duke could. His old service buddy Rex had a liquor store too, in Hollywood, was always griping that he couldn't get good help. Duke called L.A, then called Mark back.

Green light. Or a green light for an interview, at least. If Mark moved to L.A., Rex wanted to talk to him.

Mark mulled over the idea all night. He made three phone calls to SoCal, connected on the third with Crystal, his old L.A. girlfriend's kid sister. Second green light: if Mark could chip in some bread for the rent, he could crash in their living room in Silver Lake. He could come anytime. He'd have a roof over his head.

By morning, Mark knew he was going.

Fortunately, both his roomies were at home, nodding sleepily over breakfast cereal on the plywood 4-x-8 on cinder blocks they used as a dining table. Mark made his pitch. January was coming up, he wasn't going to stiff them but didn't want to be on the hook for a whole month of rent if he was planning to leave ASAP. How about if he paid one week, and then let them keep most of his stuff? All his albums, his Fillmore West posters, his underground comics. For sure they could sell the albums for good bread.

They exchanged looks, shrugged, said yes. Mark felt excited. Wheels were turning. It was happening.

Next: how was he going to get down to L.A.?

He considered a bus trip, but quickly ruled it out: too much money. The Santa stint had paid well, but he didn't know when Rex would pay him, or even if Rex would hire him, and he'd need bread to put a roof over his head. And how many times had he hitchhiked to and from L.A.? At least a half-dozen.

But never with the big beard.

Which he absolutely, positively did not want to shave off, but no question: the beard had shot his hitchhiking to hell, totally. Thumbing rides around town was one thing, but hundreds of miles downstate, no way. Drivers now seemed to size him up as

Sam the Serial Killer whenever he had his thumb out. The trip might take twice as long.

Or, worse: he could be stranded. That happened. If a driver was nice enough to pull over, you didn't want to be a dick and push hard to be dropped off at a decent freeway exit, where there was traffic and space for drivers to pull over to give you a lift. But if you *didn't* push, you could get dropped off in the middle of nowhere.

Mark's longest wait for a ride had been five hours, but that had been in his clean-shaven days. He'd talked to other hitch-hikers, knew he'd been lucky. One guy had been stuck for a full day, more than twenty-four hours, marooned with almost no traffic at a north Fresno on-ramp to the 99. (And had sweat bullets throughout, as Bakersfield and the whole redneck Route 99 corridor were unfriendly turf for hitchhikers.) Another guy had been stuck for *three* days near Barstow, had finally bartered work as a truck stop lumper to get as far south as San Berdoo.

But he wouldn't risk getting stuck if he could find a chick to go with him.

Mark grinned as he fleshed out the idea. Even without the beard, he'd never bagged rides as quickly alone as he had when traveling with a woman. (Two or three guys hitchhiking together = forget it.) It was a good deal for her, too. A chick solo could get rides faster, but solo female hitchhikers dealt with major hassles. He'd met women who'd had to jump out of moving cars to get away from perverts. A female/male duo was the ideal combination.

He could put up an ad.

Where?

Mark called the *Thrifty Gazette* to check rates, but hung up on a recording that said they'd be closed until January 6.

So he could do it the hard way.

Mark had planned to celebrate New Years' Day by dropping acid with his roomies and taking in a marathon *Planet of the Apes* triple feature at the Roxie. Instead he spent the whole day hustling from restaurants to corner stores to gas stations to every other store that was open on New Years', tacking or pasting up his hand-lettered flyers on everything that looked like a bulletin board:

FEMALE HITCHHIKING PARTNER WANTED

EXPERIENCED HITCHHIKER LOOKING FOR
FEMALE TRAVEL PARTNER
FOR ONE WAY TRIP TO LOS ANGELES.
DEPARTURE ASAP.

Mark put his home phone number, but didn't trust his roomies to take a message, and also wanted to size up the woman who answered the ad. So he added:

IF INTERESTED:
COME TO DUERNER'S
(CORNER WAGNER/SEELY)
ON SAT. 10:00 A.M. TO TALK DETAILS.

He almost skipped Knockers. He *wanted* to skip it, didn't want to run into anyone he knew at the mall. But there was a big community billboard near the East Tit entrance, and he figured that lots of likely-age-range-for-hitchhiking young people would be at the mall, returning their relatives' bad ideas for Christmas gifts. So the next day Mark rode the 830 yet again, and decided while there to put up a flyer on the smaller West Tit bulletin board, too. You never knew.

CHAPTER TWENTY-FIVE

Mark had occasionally bought coffee at Duerner's when he volunteered at the hotline. It imitated the look and feel of a corporate coffee shop in a big city financial district, bustled with white-collar workers on weekdays and was quiet on weekends. Mark wouldn't have trouble on a Saturday spotting a woman who'd come about the ad.

He was in rocky shape. His upcoming departure had made his roomies sentimental; they'd wanted to party, and he'd guzzled beer and passed the bong with them until 5:00 a.m. Mark had finally hit the sack, but then a neighbor's horn had got stuck, and the noise set off a chorus of barking dogs.

Result: zero shut-eye. None. He'd showered, combed and scrubbed himself to make a decent impression on any woman who showed up, knew he could talk, but not much else.

9:58 a.m. He was on time. Mark entered.

As he'd expected, Duerner's was almost empty. There was an old geezer fussing over a newspaper crossword puzzle, and then a black chick hunched over a table in the corner.

Mark glanced at them woozily, went to the counter to order. It was only as he turned with his coffee to choose a table that he looked at the black woman again.

And recognized her.

She wore jeans and a green sweater. He'd never expected to see a harpy out of the maroon-and-yellow corporate colors.

Ms. Runsen.

Ms. Runsen glanced at him for a micro-second, then with unconcealed disgust lowered her eyes to her coffee and didn't look at him again. Mark felt a quick panic, then indignation. Why should he freak out seeing a harpy now? He wasn't gigging at the mall anymore. She was another local, period. He'd had the bad luck to pick a meeting place where a harpy bought coffee. That was all. Maybe she liked looking out the window, writing tattle notes for the cops on pedestrians who looked like they might want to get stoned someday.

Well, he had to look out the window, too. Mark threw back his shoulders, and with an attitude of outraged dignity passed Ms. Runsen without looking at her and turned a chair at a nearby table to face the door. He'd see his future hitchhiking partner when she entered, greet her, talk to her as if Ms. Runsen weren't there. And if Ms. Runsen overheard, well, she'd learn that he wasn't just a townie. Mark was going places.

10:05, said his trusty wind-up wristwatch.

A middle-aged woman tied her dog at a parking meter, entered Duerner's. Mark looked at her expectantly, wondered about traveling with someone old enough to be his mom. But the woman paid no attention to him, went to the counter.

10:10, said his wristwatch.

When it said 10:15, he heard a sudden, unfriendly, one-syllable exclamation from his right side.

"*You*!!"

Mark turned in time to see Ms. Runsen get up. She stood over him, looked at him contemptuously, angrily. She looked ready to whack him with a chair.

"*You* put up the flyer!" she said. "*You*!"

Mark leaned back, tried to blink the fuzz out of his brain as he stared up at her. Things weren't computing.

"Yeah, that was me. I put up the flyer," he said slowly. "On the bulletin boards, which are there so people can put flyers on them." He nodded at his cup. "I also bought coffee here, because I'm in a coffee shop. So what?"

Ms. Runsen turned away, shook her head disbelievingly as she stared out the window, as if she could hardly believe her bad luck. She shot him another disgusted look, then stamped out of Duerner's, shutting the door behind her hard enough to draw a glance from the cashier.

Mark blinked, briefly considered and dismissed the possibility that he'd just had a hallucination, told himself to never do another all-nighter.

He still hadn't digested Ms. Runsen's departure — or her presence, for that matter — when she returned. She yanked out the chair opposite his, dropped onto it, looked at him furiously.

"Okay," she said. "Tell me about it."

"Tell you about what?"

"The hitchhiking trip. Go ahead. I'm here. Explain."

Mark curled an amused lip.

"Why should I? You're not going anywhere with me."

Ms. Runsen looked around the coffee shop. "Do you see anyone else here? Did anyone else answer your flyer? Go ahead. Tell me about it."

Mark took a long time to answer, struggled to prod the fatigue-crusted gears in his brain to turn, function.

Ms. Runsen was worked up over something. She was off-duty, yes, had shed her dippy yellow and maroon harpy outfit, could be expected to loosen up a little. Even four star generals likely took off their neckties and dress Oxfords before bed. But there was more than that, a lot more, and he didn't think it had to do with him. She looked harried, on edge. Maybe he wasn't the only one who'd done an all-nighter.

Mark noticed that she had sunglasses crooked into the top of her green pullover. Sunglasses, on a gray, overcast morning.

Ms. Runsen rolled impatient eyes, waiting for him to answer. Mark managed an unfriendly smile.

"I don't know exactly how to lay this on you, Ms. *Runsen*," said Mark, with sarcastic emphasis on her last name, "but you're not exactly my favorite human being in this state. Okay? I mean, if the Secret Service came in here and told me that Tricky Dick Nixon wanted to go hitchhiking with me, I think I'd rather ..."

"Do you have to like someone to have her as a hitchhiking partner?" Ms. Runsen shot back. "Is that a requirement?"

The fatigue-gummed mental gears shuddered, stalled, turned slowly. Mark blinked repeatedly, looked at the sober, agitated black woman waiting for his reply.

No, he admitted to himself, they didn't have to like each other to hitchhike together. And she was right: no one else had answered the flyer.

Mark looked at her differently, appraisingly. Hitchhiking with a black chick would be tougher. He'd never done it before. A black woman traveling with a white man: they might run into racists. Violent perverts were a hitchhiker's biggest danger, way ahead of drunks who wanted someone to yak to while weaving across lanes. An interracial couple might attract more of them.

Absolutely no travel on Route 99. Fresno, Bakersfield, that whole shitkicker redneck corridor. Could he even imagine, even imagine trying to thumb a ride out of Bakersfield with a black chick?! Brrr.

But she was his age, looked good otherwise.

Slowly, matter-of-factly, amazed at himself, amazed that he was seriously considering travel with Ms. Runsen, Mark explained. They might get lucky and make the trip in a single day, he said, but his guess was two days, and it could take longer. It depended on luck, and depended on where they got dropped off by Ride #1 to stick out their thumbs for Ride #2.

Eating and sleeping were pick-up, decided on the fly. He'd slept in a cow pasture, in roadside ivy plants, on the asphalt under a truck in a car dealership, had bought food at service stations if a driver stopped for gas, or at any restaurant or market if dropped off in town. It was up to her what to bring along — money for food, for sure, a sleeping bag and a backpack, if she had them — but the more baggage they had, the more they'd discourage potential rides.

He wondered if he should mention the knife, decided against it. He'd bought a boot knife after a gay Marine had made a hard pass north of Camp Pendleton, but had never had to take it out of his ankle holster, dearly hoped he never would and liked to pretend it wasn't there. Instead he told her that hitchhiking could be risky, that he'd dealt with problem rides, that they might have to deal with one, too.

"How many times have you done the trip?" Ms. Runsen asked.

Mark shrugged. "At least six times, to and from. I'd have to count."

"When can we leave?"

When can *we* leave, she'd said. Like it was settled.

Mark squirmed, imagined himself standing with Ms. Runsen at a Route 99 on-ramp in Bakersfield, watching a redneck's pick-up truck hurtling toward them with a shotgun barrel pointed out the window, like the last scene in *Easy Rider*.

"I don't know," he said.

"Don't know about what?"

"Well, you're black."

"I am?! No!" Ms. Runsen mocked a gasp, without humor, glowered at him. "Are you a racist, Mark?"

Mark curled his lip. "No, but other people are, and some of them have driver's licenses." Mark remembered a long-ago driver who had bragged about harassing anyone of color seen after dark in an Alabama 'sundown town.' "I've met them."

"Do you want to go or don't you?"

Mark hesitated, openly assessing the tense, unsmiling woman who glared at him across the table, so different from the aloof harpy who had hounded him on the Santa throne only weeks before. What was the *deal* with this chick, anyway? What kind of weird Jekyll and Hyde life was she leading?

"Okay," Mark said.

"Then when can we leave?"

Mark shrugged. "For me, it's flexible," he said. "I'm ready to go anytime."

"Can we leave this afternoon?"

CHAPTER TWENTY-SIX

This afternoon.

And now it was almost 11:00 a.m.. Mark checked his watch and quickened his pace toward home, Duerner's now blocks behind him. They'd made a deal. At 4:00 p.m. they'd meet west of auto row on the old Peters Creek highway, stick out their thumbs. Peters Creek had space for drivers to pull over, led straight to on-ramps to Route 101, southbound and northbound. If there were other hitchhikers they could walk a block to put a buffer between them, so drivers wouldn't think they had to give rides to everyone bunched in a group.

The planning was all up to him. She'd said she was new in town, didn't know the area, had only started at Knockers a few months before he'd signed on as Santa. And he was the veteran hitchhiker.

So why had he said yes to a late afternoon start for a trip to L.A.? That was horrible, ridiculous. They'd have only one hour of daylight left, were guaranteed to have to spend an extra night sleeping in the open. But 'today' was what she'd wanted, and he'd felt too groggy and shell-shocked to argue.

Mark had already told his plans to his mom, but at home called her work number to leave a message: he was leaving early, would call after he hit L.A. Then he went to his nearly-cleaned-out bedroom and started stuffing clothes into his backpack. It was already close to noon. He didn't have much time. Goddamn Ms. Runsen. He was so groggy; he was going to forget to bring something. He thought of a nap, but knew that if he shut his eyes for a moment he'd be out cold for hours.

Goddamn her. It was like they were still at the mall, like he was still being bossed around by a harpy. A 4:00 p.m. start for a trip to L.A.

· · ·

His roomies were sacked out on the living room couch, still recovering from the binge the night before. Mark asked if they had any uppers.

"No, man, sorry ... hey, are you going today? *Today*?!"

Mark said he was. The roomies exchanged looks. One went into his bedroom, returned with his stash box, proudly showed the interior. Mark saw three skewers of fiber-tied thai stick.

"We've got to give you a good send-off," the roomie said.

Say no, Mark told himself. No way. Smoking super-strong Thai stick marijuana now, *now*, as wiped out as he was, with the meet at Peters Creek Highway only hours away? Crazy.

But wasn't Ms. Runsen the *reason* he thought he should say no? He'd hitchhiked stoned before. Plenty of times.

Was he scared of what she'd say?

Mark ground his teeth, suddenly angry, remembered how he'd felt while watching Ms. Goody Two Shoes trot up to the Santa throne every three hours to do the big bloodhound sniff sniff of his beard. With her harpy skirt and blouse pressed and her hair just so, and a sparkle in her shiny black dress pumps. He'd thought of her as an apparition, an acid flashback: the token TV African-American sprung into wrathful three dimensional life from a detergent or ass wipe commercial, out to punish him for leaving ring around the collar, not getting his shirts their whitest white.

Well, they weren't at the mall anymore. If she liked sniffing his breath, today he'd give her something to sniff for real, and Mark grinned defiantly, nodded at his roomies, and pulled up a chair.

• • •

At 4:00 p.m., toting backpack and sleeping bag, Mark walked stiffly past the auto dealers on Peters Creek highway to meet his hitchhiking partner. The gray sidewalk seemed to ripple and wave under his feet, like a Möbius strip, undulating alongside the rumbling, honking herd of early rush hour traffic. In the distance he glimpsed Ms. Runsen, but didn't gesture or increase his pace. He stared at his feet, concentrated on planting one shoe after another on the untrustworthy sidewalk. If he didn't, he might keel over.

He was as blitzed as he'd ever been in public. The thai sticks had been spiked with something. Maybe PCP; he wasn't sure — was too wasted to be sure of anything — but the combination of exhaustion with whatever it was he'd smoked had left him barely able to navigate under his own power. His red, bloodshot eyes were wide open. He was sure that if he shut them for even a moment, he'd fall onto the fake grass fronting the car dealers.

A hundred yards to go. Ms. Runsen saw him, turned. She'd bound her hair up in some kind of yellow shawl.

Mark realized that he'd forgotten to bring a sign.

Long-distance hitchhiking 101: a sign, written with a thick marker on cardboard, that you held up so drivers could see your destination.

He had a marker, stuffed in his backpack.

Could he tell her to wait while he hunted up some cardboard?

No; he was much, much too polluted. No sign. Just stand behind her with his thumb out and stay on his feet and stay conscious.

Twenty yards to go. Ms. Runsen was wearing the sunglasses. Mark squinted at the yellow shawl, wondered if he were hallucinating.

It wasn't a shawl: it was a blonde wig. A blonde *wig*! She looked like a hooker.

"I'm here," Mark said.

Ms. Runsen looked him up and down, saw how stoned he was. She turned her head silently, grimaced at the oncoming traffic. Utterly revolted.

"Put your thumb out," Mark said, "and try to meet the drivers' eyes. And smile."

He dumped his backpack and sleeping bag beside her gear on the sidewalk and then stood behind her, with his arm out and thumb up. Ready or not, he was the leader. She'd never hitchhiked before.

Fifteen minutes passed. Then twenty, then thirty. Mark shook his head to try to stay awake, glanced bewilderedly down at the yellow tufts of the blonde wig, felt as if he were sleepwalking, dreaming. A long time to have to wait while hitchhiking with a woman, maybe he'd been wrong about Peters Creek or maybe about hitchhiking with a black chick, who knew?, but it was getting darker, a few drivers had their headlights on, and they'd have to find a streetlight to stand under if they didn't get a ride fast. He was so so so wiped out, it was like the red and gray dusk colors and the rumbling roaring whining traffic were a stereograph photo scene that he was seeing under water, if he could just stay on his feet and maintain ...

A driver pulled over, a rusty old pick-up painted with dayglow hippy flowers and a blocky camper shell bolted on the truck bed.

Mark stepped up, almost toppled into the fender. The driver leaned over a big suitcase on the passenger seat to roll down the passenger window.

A guy their age, a NorCal hippy commune type, with a round face and a no-mustache Amish beard.

"Where you headed?" Mark asked, and looked dizzily at the driver's face through the underwater-distorted stereograph, and then as he listened to the driver's answer thought that the God that Rhaytana didn't believe in had just reached down personally from above to protect them both, because what he heard the driver say was:

Past Inglewood, near Newport. Which was *past* the L.A. airport on Route 405. Inglewood and Newport Beach, they'd just nailed the whole trip to L.A. with the first ride.

"You know where that is?" the driver asked.

"Definitely. We're going all the way."

"You can ride in the back," said the driver, and then said he had to make two quick errand stops before he hit the freeway. "But I'll get you there."

Mark grabbed his gear, told Ms. Runsen to get her stuff, almost stumbled into the truck again as he went to the rear. He got the camper shell door open, slung in their backpacks and sleeping bags, crawled in after her.

The camper shell roof was low, with a thin mattress on the bed, some tools, narrow slit side windows that he couldn't see out of. They had just enough room to sit or lie down.

The pick-up pulled away from the curb. Mark braced his hand on the wheel well as the driver pulled off the Peters Creek main drag and started to go round and round on side streets for whatever stops the driver had to make.

Ms. Runsen was sitting on the other side of the pick-up bed, the yellow wig brushing the camper shell top. She looked at him with unconcealed disgust, as if she'd had to share a ride with

Charles Manson or the Zodiac Killer. Mark realized he must stink of weed.

"We're set," Mark said. "He's going all the way to L.A. We scored."

Ms. Runsen didn't answer. "I'm going to sack out," Mark said, and turned on his side facing the wheel well, and was fast asleep less than a minute later.

CHAPTER TWENTY-SEVEN

Mark dreamed that he was taking a driving test at the DMV. In the dream he was back in his junky gray VW squareback, with the DMV examiner sitting beside him, the same middle-aged bald guy who had tested him in real life when he was sixteen.

He was talking to the DMV examiner in the dream, talking and smiling, and the DMV examiner was talking to him, and smiling too, and then Mark put the squareback in reverse and started driving backwards. Not just to park or back up a few feet, but to take the test that way, twisted in his seat and staring past the headrest out the rear window. And the DMV examiner was smiling and saying something like 'attaboy,' as if Mark had hit on a special way to pass the test that no one else had thought of.

•   •   •

Mark woke up.

Ms. Runsen was shaking his ankle. Hard.

"Get out!" she said. "Out!"

Mark blinked. It was night. Their gear wasn't in the truck anymore.

"Get out!!"

Mark crawled out of the camper shell, stood.

They were parked on a gravel pull-out overlooking the ocean, next to the highway. A two-lane highway, not four lanes. With no traffic. Amish Beard must have decided to take Route 1 to L.A.

The pick-up was pointing the wrong way.

Amish Beard looked upset.

"What's happening?" Mark mumbled.

"I told you Ingle*nook*," Amish Beard said.

"Where are we?!?!" Ms. Runsen stood in front of Mark, glowered at him furiously. The blonde wig and sunglasses had disappeared.

Mark blinked, shook his head, stared vaguely at their gear on the gravel next to the truck. Without looking at Amish Beard, he muttered:

"You said Inglewood, man. Past Inglewood to Newport Beach."

"No!"

Amish Beard shook his head adamantly. He was shorter than Mark, looked like he was afraid that Mark might hit him.

"I told you Ingle*nook*," Amish Beard insisted. "Past Ingle-*nook* to Newport. Not Newport Beach. And I asked you if you knew where that is, and you said yes, and that you were going all the way."

Mark groaned, shut his eyes, slouched against the pick-up. It was sinking in. Amish Beard looked at Ms. Runsen defensively.

"Look, this isn't my hassle. He screwed up, not me."

"Are we close to Fort Bragg?" Mark asked quietly. He might have been asking a cop if anything could be salvaged from a house after a fire.

"No, man, we passed Fort Bragg fifteen minutes ago. We're past Ingle*nook*, almost to Newport."

Amish Beard told Ms. Runsen that he was sorry, but that he'd told Mark Inglenook, and that this wasn't his hassle.

And goodbye.

He climbed into the truck, drove off.

• • •

"Where ARE we?!?!" shouted Ms. Runsen.

She planted her feet in front of him, her fists balled at her sides, wild-eyed.

Mark groaned, covered his face with his hands.

"I said where the FUCK are we?!" She stamped her foot. "What have you gotten us into?!"

Mark dragged his fingers off of his cheeks, made himself look at his shaking-with-rage traveling companion, as the fire victim might stare at the smoldering ashes of a destroyed living room.

"Well, let's see." Mark looked up, as if calculating. "He said we passed Fort Bragg about fifteen minutes ago. So I'd reckon that puts us about ... oh ... only about a hundred and fifty miles and maybe three hours in the wrong direction."

"WHAT?!?!"

Mark didn't answer. He hoisted his gear to his shoulder, ambled resignedly across the turn-out, then down a short path to the edge of a cliff overlooking the ocean. Behind him he heard the drone of an approaching car, going the wrong way, followed by the crunch of Ms. Runsen's footsteps. Mark looked down at a narrow strip of sand and rocks far below, and, beyond it, the mighty, moonlit Pacific, sprawling as far as the eye could see, vanishing on the horizon beneath a canopy of glittering stars.

A choice place to be stranded, at least. And he'd more or less sobered up, too. He'd be able to pay attention when Ms. Runsen chewed him out.

"Hey! HEY! I'm talking to you!" She dumped her bags beside him, looked at him murderously. "WHERE ARE WE?!"

Mark nodded at the water. "I think that big thing is the Pacific Ocean."

"What are we GOING TO DO?!?!"

"I think I'm going to look at the big thing for awhile."

Ms. Runsen continued to glower at him, then seemed to realize she wasn't getting anywhere, and stopped. A minute of silence passed. She stood beside him, arms folded disgustedly across her sweater.

"The expert hitchhiker," said Ms. Runsen sarcastically. She lowered her voice to mimic his. "'Oh, don't worry. I've done this lots of times. I know what I'm doing.'"

Mark stared resolutely at the ocean. "Look. I thought he told me Inglewood. Okay? And Newport Beach. I mean, those are real places that people *drive* to, okay? That's where somebody picking up a hitchhiker would be going. Who ever heard of Ingle*nook*?"

"But that's not why you screwed up," said Ms. Runsen icily. "And you know it. It's because you were *stoned*."

Mark made himself look at her. Ms. Runsen was smiling coldly, contemptuously.

"You *stunk* of marijuana. The smell in that little camper thing was so bad I thought I was going to *vomit*."

"Okay ..."

"You just couldn't do without your little druggie high before the trip, could you? Nothing could be worse than being sober for a day when you had a chance to be high. Where are you going to take us to next by accident, Mark? Vancouver? Alaska?"

"Okay, look." Mark felt happier if he continued to speak to the Pacific. "It was my fault. You're right. I admit it. I messed up. Now, if you don't have food, if you thought we'd have a chance to buy something, I've got some grub in my backpack. You can have it. If one of us is going to be hungry, it ought to be me."

"That's not what I want."

Something in her voice told Mark to look at her. Ms. Runsen didn't seem so angry now. Which worried him more. She stared at him with set, defiant jaw. Determined.

"Then what do you want?"

"You know perfectly well what I want."

For a full ten seconds they stared at each other without speaking.

Ms. Runsen held out her hand.

"Your marijuana."

"What?"

"Your *stash*. The rest of your marijuana." Ms. Runsen stepped closer, her expression ferocious. "Don't try to tell me you don't have it. Do. Not. Dare."

Mark grimaced, decided that it was better to look at the ocean after all.

"You might have to think and see the world with your sober brain all day. Wouldn't that be horrible?"

"Look," said Mark, to the ocean, "you're mad. Okay? I understand. This is my fault. But that ..." He made himself glance at her. "That's really extreme, okay? That's not necessary."

"Oh?"

"You're going to be with me from here on in. I'm not going to get high in front of you. So anything I do is going to be limited. You're talking about a complete waste of primo ... a complete waste for nothing." Mark tried to look solicitous. "If you're thirsty, I've got a canteen. You can have it. If your sleeping bag isn't comfortable, we can swap. I know I messed up ..."

"Because of the marijuana," interrupted Ms. Runsen frostily, boring in. "If you want to know the correct, decent way to make up for what you did, I just told you what it is. Your marijuana is the problem, so, I want the marijuana. And any other drugs you have. Period."

Five seconds of silence, then ten, then fifteen.

Mark looked at her.

Ms. Runsen was still holding out her hand.

A vivid memory returned, still only weeks old, of looking at Ms. Runsen's pressed blouse as she hovered over him, watching her nostrils flare as she sniffed his beard. Mark cast about wildly for a decent reason to refuse.

But: one hundred fifty miles and three hours in the wrong direction. He felt sunk.

"Fuckin' harpy," muttered Mark under his breath. He thrust his hand into his jeans, pulled out the baggie of pot, handed it to her.

"Is that all of it? Do you have any other drugs?"

"Yes, that's all. No, I don't." Mark looked at her defiantly. "I'm not going to give you my pipe. Okay? All it's got is ashes in it. I couldn't get high if I *ate* the thing."

Ms. Runsen dropped to one knee, rummaged in her backpack, came up with a rubber band and a cliffside rock. She strapped the baggie to the rock, held it up.

"You know what I'm going to do with this?" she asked.

"Yes, Ms. Runsen," Mark shot back, in sarcastic sing-song. "I know what you're going to do with it."

"You do it."

She handed the rock to him.

"What?"

"You do it. To show yourself that you *can* do it. Go ahead."

Mark held the rock, allowed himself a last, miserable look at the green marijuana buds through the clear plastic. Then, resigned, committed, he reared back and hurled the pot-baggie-weighted-with-rock as far as he could into the ocean.

All his weed. Gone.

"Thank you," said Ms. Runsen primly.

"You're not welcome."

They looked out at the ocean without speaking. Mark tilted his head to take in the starry vault, remembered leafing through one of his roomie's coffee table books about constellations. He'd been high, didn't remember any of the names.

No toke til they hit L.A. Jesus.

"It's not as cold as I thought it would be," said Ms. Runsen. She sounded like she was making nice after getting her way.

"It doesn't usually get that bad next to the ocean."

"What do we do now, Mr. Expert Hitchhiker? Go back to the highway and put out our thumbs?"

Mark shook his head. "Naw. Not at night. No way." He reached for his gear. "I saw some open field on the other side of the highway. We can sleep there. In the morning ... there'll be traffic, we can see who we're going to ride with. Maybe I can hunt up some cardboard to make a sign."

Ms. Runsen hoisted her pack and sleeping bag, followed him up the path to the turn-out. A car approached, headed south, twin light rays spearing through the night. Ms. Runsen looked at him questioningly.

"Not at night."

They crossed Route 1, pushed bramble and pampas grass aside to clamber up the embankment on the other side. At the top was a short, reasonably flat stretch of grass, out of sight of the highway.

"This'll do," said Mark, and dropped his backpack.

Ms. Runsen hesitated. She looked at the grass, then at Mark.

"There's not a Hilton here, Ms. Runsen."

"Are you going to behave yourself?"

"Behave myself how?"

"You know what I mean."

She held her head up, regarded him stubbornly, defiantly. Mark rolled his eyes, offered a bemused expression to the stars, as if to share a joke with an imaginary onlooker.

"I don't know how to tell you this, Ms. Runsen, but you're not exactly choice sexual fantasy material for me. Okay? Having you sniff my beard never turned me on much."

Ms. Runsen pursed her lips, looked offended. Mark didn't care. Nearly a half-ounce of quality weed, chucked in the drink.

"In fact, Ms. Runsen ..." He knelt by his back pack, pulled open the straps, "... if it came to that, if I really couldn't wait to fulfill my masculine needs, I think I'd rather go off hunting in the fields here for a nice cooperative heifer than bother you any. I think we're still in cattle country, even up this far north."

"What a perfectly crude thing to say."

Mark shrugged, wrestled his sleeping bag out of his back-pack. "I guess I'm a perfectly crude guy." He gestured expansively at the surroundings. "You're free to bed down anywhere you like. Go wander off and hide from me, if you want. But if you get in trouble, I might not hear you."

Mark unrolled his foam pad and positioned the sleeping bag on top of it. He heard Ms. Runsen grumble, then saw her backpack drop on the ground next to him. The grassy area was flat, but not big. The only reasonable choice was to put her sleeping bag beside his.

Mark pulled off his shoes, slid clothed into his sleeping bag. He watched with mild interest as Ms. Runsen wound a stocking wrap around her hair, then raised her arms to don a puffy shower cap. Her sweater bottom hiked up; Mark gaped at a thick bandage at her waist.

"Jesus, what happened to your ribs?!"

Ms. Runsen glanced at him unpleasantly.

"Something that I'd want to put a bandage on."

"Top secret, huh?"

"If you want to call it that."

"Like why you were wearing that yellow wig."

Ms. Runsen was silent for nearly a minute. She pulled off her shoes, followed Mark's lead in sliding clothed into her bag. She looked defensive.

"I thought it would help us get a ride."

Mark snorted. "Oh, suuuure. With the sunglasses."

Ms. Runsen didn't answer. Mark turned on his side, facing her, propped his weight on his elbow.

"You've got something going on, Ms. Runsen. Maybe I was too out-of-it this morning to pay attention, but I'm not now. Since when do straight arrow, goody two shoes types like you ditch their jobs to hitch to L.A. with a weedie like me? With five hours lead time and a blonde hooker wig? Unh unh. I don't think so."

Ms. Runsen frowned, said nothing. Mark thought she looked embarrassed. She pulled her backpack closer, used it as a pillow, lay looking up at the stars.

"You don't want to tell me anything, that's fine. We're teamed for L.A. Done deal. But between the two of us, Ms. Runsen, maybe *I'm* the one who's got more reason to worry about my hitchhiking partner attacking *me* in the middle of the night."

Chapter Twenty-Seven

Ms. Runsen turned her head on the backpack, looked at him mildly.

"Don't you think it's a little rude to keep calling me by my last name?"

Mark snorted. "Well, that's something else you never told me. Your first name. What else am I supposed to call you?"

"Odetta," Ms. Runsen said quietly. "Two Ts. Odetta. Good night."

She turned on her side away from him. Mark looked at the back of her head in the shower cap, then wriggled under his sleeping bag, shut his eyes.

Odetta. That was a weird name, wasn't it? No, wait; wasn't there a black folk singer named 'Odetta?' Odetta Holmes. Maybe she'd been named after the singer.

But, no: likely no one had heard of 'Odetta Holmes' then. So she'd gotten the weird name for some other reason.

At least he was finding out something about her. A Christian cross necklace had come out of her sweater while she'd been fussing with her hair. Maybe he'd ask her to wear it in the open when they hitched. It might help them get rides.

Mark felt consciousness fading, the phantasms of sleep begin to drift before his mind's eye. He thought drowsily of trying to clamber down the cliff to retrieve his pot after she fell asleep, calculated the odds of grave injury or death at better than fifty percent, decided against it. (Plus it was soaked in salt water. Which might add a weird kick to the high. Who knew?) His last waking thought was that he felt uneasy about some part of what she'd just said. Bothered, but he didn't know why. He felt like he was missing something.

CHAPTER TWENTY-EIGHT

The next morning Mark awakened in a purplish predawn to the sight of a jagged cardboard rectangle lying next to his sleeping bag. He blinked, looked up. Ms. Runsen — Odetta — was standing above him, winding a flower print cloth around her hair. Mark thought she looked like an African singer he'd seen on the Ed Sullivan show.

"You said you wanted to make a sign." She nodded at the cardboard.

While he lettered L-O-S A-N-G-E-L-E-S on the rectangle, Mark talked about what he was expecting in the day ahead.

Hitchhiking, he said, was like shooting pool; you wanted to make the shot, but also wanted to give yourself a good "leave" for the shot you'd take next. In hitchhiking, the leave could be much more important, but there wasn't much you could do about it without giving a driver the third degree before you got in.

If you were dropped off in a spot with good leave — with plenty of traffic, good visibility and room for drivers to pull over — you could be better off than you were before. But being dropped in a bad spot could be worse than any sand trap in golf, and hitchhikers couldn't take a penalty to be magically transported to a good spot instead. You might be stuck for hours, or have to walk for hours to get to a better place.

Hitchhikers sometimes left graffiti on road signs. If the graffiti was bad enough — the equivalent of, 'I've been stuck in this hole for six hours,' written by different hitchhikers on different days — they might be better off quitting before they started and hiking to a different on-ramp.

They'd want to be polite and friendly to drivers who picked them up, partly because it was only decent and partly because a driver who liked them would be likelier to drop them off with a good leave. But before they climbed aboard in the first place:

"... let me talk to the driver first," said Mark, and waited to see Odetta's nod before continuing. "There are people you don't want to get in the car with. You've got to rely a lot on instinct."

•   •   •

Their first ride was from someone Mark never would have expected to stop: a Scandinavian-looking gray hair in a navy blazer and a nearly new Eldorado. The dude had to be at least sixty years old, Mark guessed. The oldster pulled onto the turn-out, gave them a doorman-at-the-Sheraton treatment while loading their gear into his trunk, and politely blocked Mark off while opening the front door for Odetta.

Carl was his name. He seemed disappointed to learn that they weren't a couple.

"I was one of the Freedom Riders," Carl said proudly. He talked about joining the civil rights protests of the early 1960s: sit-ins at segregated lunch counters in North and South Carolina; mob attacks against integrated bus rides in Alabama.

"I sat one chair away from Martin Luther King Jr. at a rally," he said. He tapped his sideburn. "I was close enough to see the nick on his cheek where he'd shaved. Right here. A half-inch nick." He nodded at Mark in the back seat. "As close to him as you are to me right now. Martin Luther King, Jr."

Carl dropped them off north of Fort Bragg, shook both their hands, and insisted that they accept a bag of trail mix as a parting gift.

"Don't expect many rides like that," Mark told Odetta.

Their next ride was from a fat, frizzy-haired, raspy-voiced New Yorker who said she'd barter a ride for help reading a map. "I'm farsighted," she said. Mark sat next to her, studied the map, guided her to the desired exit. The woman promptly pulled over in a bad place, said "Out! Out! I don't have all day!" and sped off as soon as they had their gear on the sidewalk.

"I told you that first guy wasn't typical," Mark said.

Their third ride was from a hippified commercial step van, a spiritual cousin of Amish Beard's pick-up, bound for a commune near Albion. Mark had felt unsurprised to spot a few other likely commune-dwellers alongside Route 1, all young, all long-haired: a couple trekking north in his-and-hers tie-dyed shirts, stooped under backpacks at least twice the size of Mark's; a shirtless no-older-than-fourteen year old with waist-length blond dread-locks, gamely pushing a wheelbarrow stacked high with lumber. And others.

Mark ceded the step van wheel well seat to an obviously ill-at-ease Odetta, offered a sociable nod to the van's other rider, an intense-looking, Viking-maned youth who asked if he'd met them at Table Mountain.

"What's Table Mountain?" Mark asked.

"A commune," the rider answered, and added that new communes were still sprouting up on the Northern California coast. "People want to get back to the land."

He showed Mark a page from the *Whole Earth Catalog* about geodesic domes, said that he wanted to help build them at their commune. "Like at Drop City," he said.

•   •   •

The driver pulled off the highway near Albion, let them off next to a combination grocery store and gas station. Mark checked his wristwatch.

"We're making pretty good time. If you want to buy some food, we're not going to do any better than this place."

Odetta shrugged. A laconic clerk with a beer belly sagging through a Woodstock t-shirt sold them food and drinks to accompany the trail mix. Mark spotted a weathered bench facing the highway, placed the open trail mix bag in the middle. They sat on opposite sides, taking turns to dip fingers into the bag between them for nuts and raisins, gazing across Route 1 at the shimmering blue Pacific as they drank and chewed.

A great place to toke up, Mark thought, and unhappily imagined a lucky halibut getting a big flatfish high from his tied-to-the-rock weed.

"Do you care which way we head south?" Mark asked.

Odetta looked at him questioningly. Mark explained: the junction of Route 1 and Route 128 was only a few miles south. 128 would take them back to 101 and a straight southbound shot to S.F., but there were far more places on 101 to get stuck with a bad leave. Route 1 was slower, but mellower and way prettier, and mostly free of hitchhiking sand traps.

"You're the expert," said Odetta. "I've never done this before."

In that case, Mark said, he'd play it by ear, make the call when they got their next ride. Then:

"Who snitched me off?"

Odetta kept chewing, looked at him with raised eyebrows.

"At the mall." Mark pursed his fingers as if holding a joint, brought them to his lips. "About the weed. You can tell me now. Who?"

Odetta swallowed, frowned at the highway for a few seconds before answering, then seemed to shrug.

"One of the mothers knew I worked as a mall ambassador and told me that Santa smelled like marijuana."

"A mall ambassador." Mark snorted. "Ambassador! What's that?"

"A harpy."

"Who was it?" Mark tried to remember the mothers who had looked at him suspiciously. "A redheaded chick, with her hair in a bun? Was it her?"

Odetta chewed her sandwich before answering. "So you can look her up and get revenge when you go back north? Is that why you want to know?"

Mark rolled his eyes. Odetta looked at him defiantly.

"Because if you're looking for the person to avenge yourself against, you're sitting next to her right now."

"Oh, Christ. Would you give me a break ..."

"I meant what I told you, Mark. If I'd gotten close enough on my own to smell you, I would have ..."

"Are you through eating?" Mark interrupted hotly.

Odetta held up her half-eaten sandwich. "Does it look like I'm through?"

But Odetta took another bite, chewed, stopped talking. Mark felt disgusted.

"I wasn't going to get revenge against anyone. Okay? I happened to be curious." He gestured imploringly. "I mean, big fucking wow. Frankly. Santa's a stoner. Big deal. So what? I had one kid, exactly one kid say that Santa smelled funny. For that you stop the whole line, rat me off to Bill, make a whole federal case out of it ... Did you ever think about those kids who didn't get a chance to talk to Santa after you shut down the line? Ms. Runsen?"

"I'm through," said Odetta abruptly, and stood.

"You've still got part of your sandwich left."

"I'd rather save it or throw it away than listen to anymore from you."

She started to walk back to the highway, then stopped abruptly and faced him. She again looked defiant, but now also slightly uncomfortable.

"I have something I want to say to you."

Mark waited.

"Last night I used an obscenity with you when we got out of the pick-up. I am *not* apologizing to you personally, but I want to say aloud that I do not want to be a person who uses such language and that I'm not going to do it again."

She turned and continued toward the highway.

"Oh my fucking *God*! My *God*." Mark roared. "What kind of a nutcase Bible thumper am I traveling with?!"

Odetta didn't answer, and they took up their positions roadside in silence. Odetta stood in front, held up the "Los Angeles" sign with a friendly smile whenever a vehicle approached, didn't smile or speak to Mark otherwise. Mark stood behind her, stole occasional thoughtful glances at his hitchhiking partner.

She had something going on, all right. Mark remembered the shades and the blonde wig, the obvious lie she'd told about why wearing a blonde hooker wig would help them get rides. The way she'd looked when she'd stomped back into the café, asked if he could leave the same day. She was toughing something out, whatever it was, keeping her jaw set, being Miss Cool and Composed, like she'd been at the mall, but Mark wasn't blind; every once in awhile he'd spot a crack in the front she was putting up, and see she was holding back something. Something painful.

Mark felt a faint, fleeting pang of sympathy, quickly suppressed it. She was still a giant pain, she'd cost him a half-ounce of pot that some stupid fish was grooving on and that he'd missed all morning. Her issues were her issues. He'd put up with her a day or two more, depending on their luck, then: adios and good riddance, Ms. Odetta Runsen. So harpies could have problems, too.

CHAPTER TWENTY-NINE

Their next ride was from a Cloverdale therapist driving home from a monthly family reunion in Little River. By then Mark had decided that he would have preferred staying with Route 1 on the coast, but a Route 128 ride to Cloverdale was too good to pass up. Cloverdale didn't just connect with Route 101; the 101 lanes ran on Cloverdale's main drag, through the center of town. Perfect hitchhiking.

The therapist's name was Walt. He was fortyish, tall and burly, sported a dense beard that could have graced the backside of a well-fed black bear. Mark had pegged him as a sawmill worker when they'd climbed in, but soon had noted that their driver spoke in an unusually gentle, sympathetic way, and hadn't been surprised when Walt said that he counseled families.

Mark decided to ask about the step van rider's comment about north coast communes. Walt smiled wistfully, resignedly. The question had struck a chord.

"There *are* a lot of communes. Most of them don't last, but then others start up." Walt smiled wryly. "The young want to flee the evils of the modern world. Go back to the land, as that fellow told you."

Odetta was in the back seat, gazing up at the huge redwood trees that towered to either side of the road, that cast the winding two lane highway in dappled shadow, dwarfed it, made it feel like an alley cut through the woods. Route 128 ran through the Navarro redwoods park. Walt piloted the car easily around the curves and bends that he traveled every month, looked like he was trying to decide what to say.

"The trouble is," he said, "that to live on the land, you have to know about homesteading, and be ready for the work involved. A lot of the kids who come up here grew up in the suburbs. They don't understand that these beautiful forests don't have electrical outlets, or plumbing, or gas lines." He sighed. "So they wind up getting money from Mom and Dad, or going on welfare. And eventually, leaving."

He looked at Mark confidingly. "The modern world *is* evil. Uncle Sam sent my nephew to Vietnam. No one has to convince me. But ..." He held up his right arm, tapped his shirt sleeve. "I don't know how to sew, but the modern world lets me buy this comfortable shirt to stay warm. It would take me a couple of days to hike from Little River to Cloverdale, but I can go there in an hour and a half on a modern road I wouldn't know how to build in a vehicle I don't know how to make. The kids who come up here find out the hard way how much we take for granted."

He drove for the next minute in silence, seemed to be reflecting unhappily about whatever Mark's question had reminded him of. Then, sadly, with resignation:

"I've had families consult with me because their children ran off to the communes. Maybe I ought to be grateful for the business."

.   .   .

Walt dropped them off downtown, between a gas station and a drive-in restaurant. Mark wrinkled his nose at a stench of gasoline mixed with grill-fried hamburger, surveyed the traffic-choked lanes of Route 101 running on Cloverdale Boulevard. A lumber town. He held out an arm to warn Odetta as a flat bed truck rumbled in front of them, a Peterbilt strapped high with half-ton logs.

"Let's find a better place to stand," Mark said. "We're going to want to be fussy here. Okay? Not take just any ride. If we hold out, we might get a lift all the way to L.A."

He explained his opinion as they walked, tilting his head toward her and raising his voice to be heard over the traffic. The best hitchhiking spot he knew of in California was south of San Jose near Morgan Hill, where a stretch of the 101 turned onto a slow, pedestrians-permitted road with room for a driver to pull over. Hitchhikers Shangri-la. A Los Angeles-bound traveler lucky enough to hang out a thumb in that spot would be nuts to take a ride to, say, Bakersfield, or even Lancaster. You'd hold out, be picky, even super picky, wait for a lift all the way to L.A. Because with a leave that good, you'd get one.

"This place isn't going to be that good, but it looks close. Anybody doing a big West Coast tour could pass through here. So if I turn down a couple of rides, don't be surprised."

• • •

But it didn't work out that way.

They reached a good place to stand, an unmarked pull-out on the far side of a traffic light. This time Mark held the "Los Angeles" sign, surveyed traffic as Odetta stood next to him with arm extended and upright thumb.

Maybe if their million dollar ride had come within a minute, he wouldn't have had time to notice that Cloverdale felt more rural and redneck than he remembered. But the ride didn't come, and he soon decided that they should have stayed on the coast. He'd forgotten Odetta's color, that he was a white man hitchhiking with a black woman.

They were being stared at. Not by every driver, not even by twenty-nine out of thirty. Most drivers glanced at or looked past them with the empty, expressionless, disinterested faces that Mark knew from every hitchhiking trip he'd ever taken; the faces of drivers who wouldn't stop, the faces that told him to lower his thumb and wait for the next car.

But every once in awhile they were being sized up with a frank hostility that Mark hadn't seen since his last regretted blunder onto redneck Route 99. Maybe it was chance; maybe they'd caught the town on a bad day. Cloverdale looked like it would be a nice burg if it didn't have a giant freeway jammed through the middle of it like a turd on a salad. But it didn't feel nice now.

"This might not be such a good place to be fussy," Mark said.

"Why not?"

Mark didn't answer. Two white teenagers in a fat-tired pick-up were checking them out. From the northbound lanes, so they wouldn't be in sight for long. But still. The driver was blond, crew cut, glared at them with open incredulity, contemptuous and amused, as if they had been carrying a communist recruitment banner. Mark watched the driver's lips move as he spoke to his companion, thought he made out a racial epithet.

The pick-up's traffic light changed; the teenagers drove off. Mark glanced at Odetta; she hadn't noticed. Mark squirmed, glanced at the sky, recognized his own anxiety, and wished for the umpteenth time that morning that he still had his stash. If that million dollar ride would just come soon. They had the whole of southbound 101 rolling past them, car after car, with room to pull over, a clear view of their 'Los Angeles' sign. They'd be in motion and on the way to friendlier turf, with Cloverdale only a memory.

But then he heard, from behind, loud and unmistakable: "Nigger pussy!"

"Don't look," Mark said quickly.

Odetta didn't look. But she'd obviously heard. He risked a quick sideways glance. She looked surprised. Hurt. Worried.

Mark lowered the "Los Angeles" sign, held out his arm and thumb.

"The first ride that comes, we'll take it," Mark said.

.   .   .

A half hour later, Mark stood looking at an unsmiling Odetta as she sat on her backpack at a scenic, desolate 101 on-ramp north of Healdsburg. A portly young lumber salesman had dropped them off there ten minutes earlier.

Dropped them off with an apology. "This probably isn't a great place to get rides," he'd said, with prescience.

They'd been passed since then by all of three vehicles. Mark had glanced at the on-ramp road sign, then had looked away before Odetta could see him studying it. It was covered with angry graffiti left by other hitchhikers.

"I'm sorry that happened," said Mark self-consciously.

"Sorry that what happened?"

"What that guy yelled at you at the last stop."

Odetta shrugged, gazed off stonily at the untrafficked traffic lanes extending to either side of them. She'd still looked worried when they'd climbed into the car with the lumber salesman, but since then had recovered. Or was stuffing however she felt about being yelled at, as she'd been stuffing everything else since she'd met Mark at Duerner's.

"I mean, that you'd have to listen to that kind of racist crap in 1975. Anyway, I'm sorry."

Odetta grimaced, looked away, said nothing. Well, fuck me, thought Mark; that was what he got for trying to be nice. He wandered back to the road sign, this time didn't conceal his interest in the graffiti.

It was horrible. He'd give it another twenty minutes, tops, then eyeball his map and see how far they'd have to walk to the next on-ramp. A major setback.

"We can't try going up on the freeway?"

Mark shook his head. "Extremely illegal. One way trip to jail. And dangerous."

"Are we still north of where we started yesterday?"

Mark groaned. "Yes, we're still a few miles north of where we started yesterday," he said, in a sing-song voice. "And I still don't have the weed that someone made me chuck in the ocean."

•   •   •

But it was the next ride that got under Odetta's skin. He was reminded of the time at the mall, when he'd given up trying to get her goat and then had gotten it without wanting to, with an innocent joke.

The newish Buick pulled over just as Mark was about to suggest the long hike south to the next on-ramp. Scoring a ride so soon at such a zero on-ramp was fantastic luck, like nailing a flush golf shot into the hole from a bad lie in a sand trap. Mark and Odetta climbed into the back, behind a middle class-looking black couple and a grade-school aged son. They looked too straight to pick up hitchhikers. Mark guessed that they'd pulled over for Odetta.

Or that the driver had pulled over for Odetta, as the lift obviously hadn't been his wife's idea. She ignored them conspicuously, as if her civic-minded husband had spotted two sacks of garbage next to the road and decided to cart them to the nearest dump.

The driver told them he was going to Santa Rosa, then returned to what seemed to be day-long argument with his wife about her weight. Mark learned from the back-and-forth that they were taking a winter wine country tour during hubby's vacation.

"A vacation is for our personal *pleasure*," the wife said. Mark guessed she was about thirty pounds overweight. "Who diets on a vacation? Restaurants are a vacation *highlight*. I enjoy eating."

"You certainly do."

"What's that supposed to mean?"

And so forth. The wife occasionally interrupted the quarrel to tell their son to sit still. But the boy was an extrovert, wanted to look over the seat to socialize with the unexpected newcomers in the back seat.

"I know my times tables," he said proudly.

"*All* of them?" Mark asked, and eased back into his Santa role, quizzing the boy lightly as the Buick motored south on the freeway. He felt relaxed, grateful for the rescue from the no-man's-land on-ramp and the change-of-pace ride in a clean, nearly new car.

But Odetta hardly spoke. She pursed her lips into a tight grimace as she watched the boy's banter with Mark, then turned to look out the window on her side. As if she didn't want her face to be seen.

•   •   •

"College Avenue would have been better," mused Mark, twenty minutes later. He glanced inattentively at Odetta walking behind him, felt absorbed in thought. "This might be okay, though." He squinted at the western horizon, tried to gauge how many daylight hours they had left. "We're not going to bag a ride to L.A. from here, but we might make it to Frisco."

They were walking south on Santa Rosa Avenue, single file, far south of Santa Rosa's city center, through a flat, underdeveloped industrial district of gas stations, warehouses, vacant lots. Mark had hitchhiked there once before, remembered good visibility and too little traffic. The freeway on-ramp was about a third of a mile ahead, marked by a small thicket of trees.

"Maybe I could have leaned on him harder to drop us off on College," Mark said. "See, that's the problem with hitchhiking. That dude saved our fanny getting us out of that hole. And then to twist his arm to drive out of his way ... who wants to be a creep, to someone who did you a favor?

"How do you think he would have taken it?"

He turned to look at Odetta then, shifting his backpack on his shoulders, twisting his head as he clumped through roadside gravel and weeds. She didn't answer. She was staring morosely at the ground ahead of her, hands hooked through her pack's shoulder straps.

"What's wrong?"

"Nothing's wrong," said Odetta.

"You could have fooled me."

He studied her a moment longer, then turned his eyes back to the road. Not his problem. Ships passing in the night. He couldn't figure her out, but there were a lot of things in life he couldn't figure out, and in another day or two she'd be something he hadn't figured out that he'd never see again.

Boy, did he wish he still had his stash. That antsy, fidgety feeling, like his skin didn't fit.

The trees marking the freeway on-ramp were only a few yards ahead. Mark stopped, tried to picture a driver's view of the nearby roadside, to choose an ideal place to stand.

"Maybe if we go back about ten feet ..." he muttered, and then turned to his travel companion.

Odetta was crying.

Helplessly, with lowered eyes, shuddering lips. The tears shone on her cheeks.

"What is it?" Mark felt bewildered.

Odetta didn't answer.

"We can't hitch if you're crying."

Odetta said nothing. Mark pulled off his backpack, dumped it on the gravel next to a chain link fence fronting a mobile home dealer.

"You better sit down."

"I ... I'm okay," Odetta stammered.

"I don't think so. Take off your pack, put it on top of mine. Have a seat. We'll take a break."

Odetta hesitated a moment longer, then complied. She sat on the backpacks as if she were sitting on a stool, not looking at Mark, her chest heaving jerkily under her sweater. Mark squinted at Santa Rosa Avenue, watched the occasional car motor south toward the on-ramp, wondered which one might have given them a lift to Frisco.

Well, that was what he got, wasn't it? He'd been too out-of-it at Duerner's and at Peters Creek to pay attention to the warning signs — the sunglasses, the blonde wig, the willingness of a straight arrow to hitchhike — and now he was paying the price. She might pull a full-on wingding, wind up in a mental hospital. They might never make it out of Santa Rosa.

A driver slowed near the curb, looked at Mark and his crying companion with a questioning, solicitous expression. Trying to help. Mark shook his head, smiled; the driver sped off. For sure the dude would have given them a ride. Maybe a big ride, to Frisco, beyond. For sure ...

Odetta had stopped crying. She sat with her hands on her knees, staring fixedly at a spot on the sidewalk, her chest rising and falling steadily. Mark studied her, and as he remembered the big bandage around her waist felt his impression change. Maybe she really was the sober goody-goody who'd picked on him at Knockers, but also a goody-goody who was going through something super, super heavy that he didn't know about. That would bust up absolutely anyone.

"I'm okay now," Odetta said. She wiped her eyes.

"Take your time." Mark stretched, held his arms over his head, looked at the traffic. "Go ahead and cry. I was getting stiff, carrying that pack all day."

Mark glimpsed the bandage again as Odetta pulled a cloth out of her jeans to wipe her eyes. She put her hands on her knees again, stared fixedly ahead, concentrated on her breathing.

"Look, what's the deal with you, anyway?" Mark asked. "How come you're doing a trip like this? What happened?"

"*I'm not going to talk about my private life with you!!*" she said hotly.

She had almost shouted at him. With a sudden furious, defiant stare, jaw set and trembling. It was as if he'd asked her to confide in the lowest criminal: a rapist, a pedophile. Was that what she thought of him?

Mark stepped back, startled, hurt. As if she'd slapped him.

"Oh. Okay. Screw Mark, right?" His voice hardened. "Are you done with your little boo-hoo-hoo, then, Ms. Runsen? Can we go?"

Odetta nodded, stood.

CHAPTER THIRTY

Mark turned down two offers before their ride turned up. The first was from a pair of hardhats in a jumbo-tired double-cab pick-up that looked like it should have been hauling in ammo and AR-15s at a gun show. Mark didn't like the up-and-down way they eyeballed Odetta, said they'd hold out for a longer ride. The second was from a harried, bookish, long-lost-sister-of-Woody-Allen-type who said she was supposed to pick up hymn books from a church near Two Rock. She didn't know where the church was, and Mark didn't know where Two Rock was, either.

Their big one-way ticket south turned out to be in a clapped-out Rambler piloted by a white, bald, bearded oldster with a sea-shell necklace draped over a dashiki. He could take them all the way to the Haight in San Francisco, he said, but wanted to travel there via a scenic route: east to McNears Beach, at least, and then maybe with another detour to Tiburon, if the light held.

"This is memory lane for me, man," he said. "I haven't been this far south in at least five years."

The front seat was stacked high with New Age books (crystal healing, tantra, pyramid power), so they piled into the back with their bags. The Rambler was a beater. It shuddered and wheezed its way to fifty miles per hour, and in the slow lane on the 101 went no faster, while every third driver passing in the middle lane threw them the evil eye for driving so slowly.

Baldie was a true blue hippy. All the way south past Petaluma and Novato he talked up the Summer of Love glory days, Love-Ins and Be-Ins, Janis and Jimi and the time he'd scored LSD personally from the one and only Owsley at one of the first acid tests. Odetta stiffened as soon as he said 'LSD,' but Mark always wanted to humor a driver, and ignored her. He chatted with Baldie about trips past, told the story of his roomie's nightmare trip on a 300 mic blotter at Altamont, when mid-peak he'd seen Meredith Hunter knifed by the Hells Angel. "Major BUMMER!" cried Baldie, and Mark glimpsed Odetta's head shake and eye roll.

North of San Rafael Baldie turned off the freeway to start the scenic route. The Rambler lurched and coughed drunkenly through a ritzy suburb, and then the 'suburb' part thinned out to valley oak and almond-tan hills as the Rambler fought its way up a long, gentle grade.

Ten minutes later they were bumping along in the Marin County middle of nowhere. Practically backwoods of Saskatchewan nowhere. A couple of football fields worth of soupy green tidal marsh stretched off to the east, with the shore of San Pablo Bay beyond it, and woodsy hills flanking the road ahead. They'd passed a jogger five minutes earlier, and a bicyclist a minute before that, and nobody since.

Baldie had flicked on his headlights. He might have still seen to drive without them, but not for much longer. The light was fading fast, had weakened to soft shades of purple and pink. Mark figured that Baldie would skip the detour to Tiburon, as it would be full night long before they got there.

"About where are we?" Mark asked.

"On the road to McNears Beach!" said Baldie happily. "We used to trip out here. And the next best thing ..."

Baldie pulled out a fat joint, lit it, passed it back to Mark while he held in the smoke.

Mark came close. Oh, God, did he ever want that weed! He could practically taste the spit-damp joint between his lips, feel the marijuana smoke coursing through his bronchial tubes to deliver R-E-L-I-E-F. He even started to reach for it.

But then he thought of Odetta.

The sticking-it-to-her part didn't bother him. He would have been happy to stick it to her. It was knowing that she *expected* him to take the joint, like what a cynical vice cop would expect of a peeper left alone in a women's dormitory. He couldn't give her the satisfaction.

So he said:

"Sorry, man. I'd love to. But she's trying to quit. If I toke up with you, she's going to go on another binge." He looked at her innocently. "Odetta, how many days have you been sober?"

That was all the cue she needed. Odetta spoke up.

"Could you please stop the car and let us out?"

Mark stared. Baldie tilted his head at her.

"I do not feel comfortable being in a vehicle with a driver who is smoking marijuana," Odetta said icily.

Baldie didn't like that. Mark saw his jaw tighten.

"Now, hold on ..." Mark started, but that was as far as he got. He was shocked, gaped at Odetta, flapped his jaw like a hooked trout.

Baldie swerved to the right and braked.

"Out!" he said.

•   •   •

A half-minute later, Mark stood next to his gear and his travel partner, watching the Rambler's tail lights fading in the distance.

Mark turned to her, his face stiff with shock, anger.

"Are. you. out. of. your. fucking. *MIND*?!?!"

Odetta stood straight and met his stare haughtily, self-righteously. Mark felt like he was hallucinating. He imagined a basketball player returning to the bench after going 0 for 3 on a game-deciding three-shot foul, chewing out his coach for not having asked the referee to change to a less worn-out ball.

"What are you ... he was going to take us to ... do you know where we *are*?!" he sputtered.

"He was smoking marijuana."

"And? So? What are we supposed to do now?"

"We can hitchhike a ride with a sober driver."

"Who is *where*, exactly? A sober driver who is where?!" Mark waved his arms, gestured at the marsh and dark hills. "Do you see anyone around, Ms. Runsen? Anyone at all?" He cupped his hands around his mouth. "Hel-loo, Mr. Sober Driver! Please take us to San Francisco!"

And Mark saw that this had registered. At least a little. Finally. As if she were a straight A star student whose chemistry experiment had just flopped at the science fair. Odetta frowned, the self-righteous expression blanching at the edges.

Mark snorted disgustedly, hoisted his backpack and started to trek south on the middle-of-nowhere road. A few seconds later he heard her footsteps behind him.

"We're hitchhiking. Okay? Ms. Runsen? We're not getting rides from paid chauffeurs." Mark kept walking, figured he could tell her the facts of hitchhiking life without looking back. Looking at her would only make me mad. "We don't get everything our way. Now, if he'd been weaving, if he'd been about to get us in a wreck, that would have been different. But not the second he lights up a doobie. Okay? Not if he's our only ticket back to civilization."

"What are we going to do now?"

"Well, we can try to get a ride. Even at night. That shows how desperate I am." Mark looked off toward San Pablo Bay. "Tell you what I'll do. Tomorrow under 'Los Angeles' on our sign I'll write: 'Rides Accepted Exclusively from Sober, Employed, God-Fearing Christians.' How's that? Ms. Runsen?"

"Are you calling me by my last name because you're mad at me?"

That did it. Mark turned to confront her. She stopped, stood with her thumbs hooked under the straps of the backpack that looked too large for her, seemed to be waiting for him to tell her off. The light was almost gone. Everything was hazy, dim, dreamlike, a medley of violets and blues in the deepening night. He couldn't see her face clearly, even from a few feet away. Her expression seemed different than any he'd seen her with before: resigned, calm. Sad.

"Well, how am I *supposed* to act with you, *Ms. Runsen*? If I'm a despicable, selfish little boy, if I'm not even good enough to try to be nice to you when you start crying? Maybe I don't *like* you enough to call you by your first name. *Ms. Runsen*."

Mark turned on his heel and returned to the angry march along the road. Pointlessly, he knew; they were too far away from civilization to get anywhere on foot, but at least when he walked he didn't have to look at her. Mark heard the crunch of her footsteps, brooded over the nearly-night landscape before him, black-shadowed hills and woods almost merging in color with the winding road.

"Mark, may I ask you a personal question?"

Mark snorted. "You can try."

"How old were you the first time you rolled a joint?"

"What?"

"How old were you?"

"The first time I *rolled* one?" Mark frowned; what kind of a question was that? "Well, the first time would be the first time I smoked one. I was fourteen."

"Then I've got you beat," Odetta said quietly. "I was eight."

That got to him.

Mark stopped, turned to face her. She was looking at him with a regretful little smile, as if she'd decided to confess a family secret that she'd known would shock him.

"What?!?!"

"It was my little chore when I stayed with my father," said Odetta, matter-of-factly. "I'd empty the bag on the table ..." She moved her hands, as if she were separating marijuana into piles on a newspaper. "... put all the seeds and twigs on one side, and all the marijuana on the other. My father was proud of me. He liked my joints better than the ones he made with a rolling machine."

And kept looking at him with the half-smile, resigned and a little sad. Mark goggled at her for another few seconds, then turned and started walking again. Mostly so she wouldn't be looking at him, so he could think his thoughts in private.

Rolling joints when she was eight years old. That was for the record books, all right; even if his ditzy mom had been a stone pothead, she never would have given him that kind of chore in grade school. But why had she wanted to tell him now?

Mark heard her footsteps behind him, the steady sound of her foot soles on the gravel.

"Of course, my father's main thing was alcohol," Odetta continued. "But he liked marijuana almost as much. That's why I got so angry when you made your little joke about my daddy being a dealer. That was a little too close to home.

"So I do know marijuana, Mark. Better than I wish I did. But I don't know hitchhiking. So if you think I really should have put up with that man in spite of what he was smoking, then I'm sorry."

So that was why she'd told him. To lead up to an apology.

Mark didn't answer right away. The marsh paralleled the road on the bay side, but he could see that ahead the asphalt rose between two low hills crowned with trees. He'd already guessed that they'd be spending the night there.

"That's okay," he said, finally. "I got us in a hole yesterday, and today it was your turn. So we're even."

•　　•　　•

In the next hour they offered their thumbs and happy-face smiles to exactly three drivers. When the third car passed, Mark decided that they'd been masochists long enough for one evening.

"We might as well hang it up. This ain't happening."

"What do we do?"

He nodded at the hills flanking the road ahead of them. "Basically the same thing we did yesterday. Camp out. We'll do better tomorrow when they can see us."

She let him lead the way, as if knowing about hitchhiking would mean he'd know where to camp, too. He turned off the road to clamber up a short hill on the inland side, heard Odetta snapping branches behind him as he picked his way between oak and shrubs in search of a clearing. He had to push deeper through the bush than the night before, but eventually found an area that was broad and flat enough for two sleeping bags. This time Odetta spread out her sleeping bag next to his without comment.

Mark wandered into the brush to take a leak. When he returned, Odetta was winding a stocking wrap around her hair, as she had the night before. Mark slid into his bag and glanced at her as she tugged her hair into the shower cap, then crawled into the bag next to his.

But it was early, thanks to being stranded, and he figured that she wasn't sleepy yet either, and she was the one who'd brought up her father's pot habit. So he asked:

"Did you ever smoke with him?"

"I'm sorry?"

"Weed. When you were eight."

He turned toward her in the bag with his weight propped up on one elbow. She didn't answer right away. She lay on her back with her hands folded behind her head as she had the night before, looking up at the stars.

"I'm afraid so," she said, finally. "Twice. Unfortunately. Then my mother found out. She isn't the world's bravest woman, but that time she put her foot down."

"Did you like it?"

She screwed up her mouth, like she was trying to decide. "I did, but I didn't. I knew Daddy was getting me to do something bad." She looked at him. "Even an eight year old has a sense of what children should be doing."

And then, after a pause, she asked, quietly:

"You know you have a problem, don't you, Mark?"

"A problem with what?"

"You know what I mean."

"Oh, Jeez ..."

He flopped on his back and shook his head at the sky. Fed up.

"That again. Mother of God. Look, could you give it a rest? I'm clean now. Didn't I turn down that guy in the car? What else do you want?"

Odetta didn't answer. Mark kept staring disgustedly at the stars, like one of them had to be the home of a hitchhiking god that would appreciate what a royal pain she was. She gets them stranded in the middle of nowhere, and now she was going to be his psychoanalyst. 'You know you have a problem, don't you, Mark?' Like the trip his high school counselor had laid on him when he'd pulled three Fs in his sophomore year. With that 'I care about you so deeply' manner.

But he also knew that he was irritated partly because she'd asked him about something he felt touchy about, touchy and defensive, and as he looked up at the endless astral panoply of glittering white stars Mark thought again of how he'd flipped slack-jawed and dull-eyed through his roomie's book about constellations. That he'd been too stoned to understand or remember, and that was why he couldn't recognize any of what was shimmering above now.

"Okay, you've got me," he said, and turned his head to look at her. "You want me to admit it, I'll admit it. I have a problem. I smoke too much weed. How's that? But if I were you, Ms. Runsen, if I were trying to skip town by tagging along by thumb with a stoner in a blonde hooker wig and shades, I don't think I'd be too quick to harp on people about *their* problems. Okay? Because between the two of us, I'd say the one who looks to have a bigger problem isn't yours truly."

Odetta didn't say anything. Mark fussed with his backpack to make a better pillow and looked up at the stars again. Touché. Served her right. So she wouldn't try that high school counselor holier-than-thou trip anytime again soon, but then as he was congratulating himself and eyeballing the stars he remembered how she'd looked earlier that day in Santa Rosa while trying not to cry, and the feeling that he'd had then: that maybe she hadn't done anything wrong, and was a victim, even if she wouldn't tell him why.

So on impulse Mark turned toward her, and:

"Okay, I'm sorry I said that. I apologize. Odetta."

No answer.

"Odetta?"

"What?"

"Did you hear me? I said I was sorry."

"You have the right to say what you think," she said. Evenly, as if she were reciting a verse from a children's poem.

"I mean, you don't want to talk about it. Fine. You don't need me getting on your case about it. I don't know what it is, but I can tell you've got major stuff going on."

Which she didn't answer, and in the silence he felt awkward and weird, so added: "Look, can you at least tell me where you're going in L.A.? That makes a difference for hitchhiking."

"I'm going to Lynwood to stay with some relatives," Odetta said quietly.

They talked off and on for another half-hour. It was early. She wasn't tired either. After awhile she decided that she hadn't done up her hair properly, and he asked why she had to truss it up. "So it won't get messed up," she said, and he asked why she couldn't just wear an afro, and she asked if he thought Knockers would have hired her if she'd had hair like Angela Davis. "No," Mark said, and then said that she didn't sound particularly black, either, and that he didn't think it was right that black Americans just because they were black would try to have hair like whites or sound like whites, either.

And then he didn't know if she was going to hit him or start laughing, but finally she said in an exaggerated patient way that if she didn't sound negro-ey enough for him it was because while she was growing up her mother had worked for a dozen years as a domestic for a family from Berlin and she'd grown up playing with their kids ("Who *didn't* smoke marijuana," she added.) and even celebrating holidays with them. But by then finally Mark felt drowsy and said fine, fine, have it your way, and they stopped talking.

But before he fell asleep he had the same feeling he'd had the night before, that he'd forgotten something, overlooked something, that she'd just told him something important and that he'd missed what it was.

CHAPTER THIRTY-ONE

11/5

Paul,

You have shocked me. Really and truly, without exaggeration: shocked me. If only you could have been a voyeuristic fly on the wall at the supermarket magazine stand this morning, when fleeting impulse spurred your continent-wandering friend to pluck a copy of *White Rhino* from the rack and take a peek inside.

Fix my flat if that magazine didn't include me! Where did you dig up that old photo they used, Paul? It must have been shot for a tour ID badge, but I've forgotten particulars. I can't imagine what passing market patrons might have thought of me at that moment of discovery: an anonymous, nondescript, indifferently-dressed fellow shopper at the magazine rack; a middle-aged man, alone, unfamiliar (as I am only passing through town), eyes wide and mouth agape as with dumbfounded mien he inspects the open *White Rhino* grasped between trembling fingers.

"*Letters from Rhaytana*." Simple. To the point. Did you suggest the series title? "*Rhaytana on the Road*" would have been alliterative.

It's not as if you didn't warn me. My error was in not taking the request seriously. 'So Paul wants to share my letters with a 'zine,' thought I. 'What difference would it make? Who reads a 'zine?' What I neglected

to consider is that 'zines grow into magazines. *White Rhino* now has a national cir-
culation, and *Letters from Rhaytana* is along
for the ride.

For better or worse, however, knowledge
of this unexpected celebrity burdens me with
a sense of responsibility. My life can be
an open book (I suppose), but am I to write
as uninhibitedly as I did before, without
knowledge that my words may be read by per-
haps-impressionable minds?

I have misgivings about my career, Paul.
The rock-and-roll titans whose tours I managed too frequently appear in my rear-view
mirror as pied pipers, leading their credulous young fans to ruin, particularly in
their use of drugs. Consider the scorecard
at the mortuary: Jimi Hendrix, Janis Joplin,
Jim Morrison, all dead of overdoses. And how
many others went privately and gradually to
seed, landed in hospitals, jail cells, psych
wards, largely thanks to their drug consumption? They didn't bill themselves as role
models, but a fifteen year old's favorite
singer or guitarist will inevitably serve as
such ... and as role models were akin to the
sleaziest used car salesmen on the sleaziest lot in the country, con artists who turn
back odometers, disconnect warning lights,
pour sealant into radiators and sawdust in
transmissions. They burned their followers,
led them grossly astray. One rarely imagines
a Jimi, Jim or Janis in a cheap polyester
suit under an E-ZEE-credit-Used-Cars sign,
leering at potential victims, but that's how
I sometimes picture them today.

I so often managed tours for musicians with fans in their teens and early twenties. *White Rhino* is obviously geared for that age bracket. These young people might not have asked to be born (and may angrily brandish that point in disputes with beleaguered parents), but born they certainly have been, and they will fare far, far better in their unasked-for lives if they develop personal habits proven to be compatible with often-difficult earthling living.

Self-discipline. To not eat the sundae if forty pounds overweight, to not sleep in til 10:00 if your job starts at 8:00, to be disciplined enough simply to take your own good advice for yourself. Self-control. You can't steal it because you want it or kill him because you don't like him.

And perhaps especially, sobriety. I need my clear-thinking, unsullied-by-intoxicants brain to navigate life, to show me what forks in the road to take, what to believe. Should I assume that future world-famous athletes / musicians / movie stars like me needn't bother with dull vocational planning, or take up kick boxing for my health, or ride pillion with the drunk motorcyclist because I think he's got a cool bike? And for purely aesthetic reasons: if we are our planet's most intelligent beings, isn't it rather tasteless to corrupt the nucleus of that intelligence with drugs or booze?

I now venture uncomfortably close to an admission that pains me.

I may be more agnostic than atheist, but also am no fan of the world's religions, as you know. Creationism, the Scopes Monkey Trial, youth brainwashed and terrified by scientifically baseless doctrine, disgraceful bloody wars waged with teenage cannon fodder to see whose concocted comic book deity is holier than the other. But with all that said, I believe that the world's religions make at least some attempt to shield their young from the age-old vices aggressively celebrated in pop music culture, in the pages of magazines like *White Rhino*. I can think offhand of three acquaintances who have sworn that they wouldn't have survived American ghetto childhoods without their churches.

(And in so writing certainly seal the coffin on future serialization. Feel absolutely free to send this missive to *White Rhino*! I spotted ads for rolling papers, hookahs, hydroponics and jeweled roach clips while thumbing that copy in the supermarket. If they publish this, or even mention me again, I'll eat my Basque beret.)

CHAPTER THIRTY-TWO

The next morning they got lucky. Hitchhiking could be like shooting pool, as he'd told Odetta, but it could be like roulette, too, or craps ... or trying to pick the quickest check-out line to stand in, for that matter, or nearly any other human activity that could go well or badly when having a good or bad day.

At first light they packed up their gear and hoisted their backpacks, picked and stumbled their way through bush and bramble downhill to the road. At dawn it looked even more deserted than it had the night before, but just as Mark was steeling himself for a two hour wait and missing his morning bowl a beige Citroën DS shaped like a giant joint appeared at the bend, and son of a gun if that very first vehicle of the day didn't give them a lift.

And their luck held. Like being on a roll in a casino. In all of ten minutes at a lousy on-ramp they bagged a ride onto the southbound 101, and the driver turned out to be a hitchhiking old hand, made a just-for-them detour to drop them off at an on-ramp by a funky old tavern a mile north of the Sausalito exit, with room for drivers to pull over and time for drivers to size them up before they did.

"Let's hold out here for something good," Mark said.

"Something good" didn't pull up for over an hour. Mark turned down rides to North Beach and Daly City, suppressed nerves. He felt like he was staying in a big stake poker hand with only four cards of a flush.

But the fifth card of the flush pulled up just as he was ready to fold: a bulbous, white, round-fendered old Volvo with a ski rack clamped on the roof.

"How far're you going?" Mark asked ...

... and grabbed his bag with a thumbs up nod at Odetta as soon as he heard the answer: San Luis Obispo. Two hundred fifty miles south, far clear of the city and the San Mateo/Santa Clara peninsula suburb clutter where he'd been hung up hitchhiking at least four times. Their big ride.

•   •   •

"I'm Wyatt," the driver said, and offered a handshake after they'd piled in. Odetta said she wanted to nap, had climbed in the back.

Mark thought he looked like a 'Wyatt,' was half-tempted to check under the seat for spurs and a lasso. Wyatt was broad shouldered, pushing forty, looked like a long-haired, hippified outlaw who could have drawn down on Marshall Matt Dillon in a *Gunsmoke* re-run. But first impressions deceived: Wyatt had worked as a roadie, had even known Rhaytana.

"Not as a friend," Wyatt stressed. "He was a higher-up, way up the totem pole from me. I might see him rapping with my stage manager, but that was about all." Wyatt glanced at him. "I was strictly grunt labor. I dipped my toe in the music business, had the experience, but that was all."

For the past seven years, Wyatt added, he'd worked as a corporate auditor.

Mark thought he might as well ask for leads, as a back-up. They were south of the city by then, nearing the airport; Mark had swung his head to look over the napping Odetta's head at the 'South San Francisco' letters on Sign Hill.

Surprisingly, Wyatt had some:

"You could look up Zeke Wilson and Cal McGrath. They were tight with Rhaytana. I've got no idea where they are, even if they're still in California, but you could check the book." Wyatt furrowed his brow, thought. "Plus there was a motel that a lot of music guys stayed at. The Dixon ... Dixie ... Dix something or other. Near the 405, around Culver City. Rhaytana didn't, he had his own place, but if he's just in town for this charity, who knows?"

Mark fished out a pen, scribbled the names on the back of a receipt. He felt stoked. Which was nuts, the leads were seven years old, but the fact that he'd gotten them at all, that on the way to L.A. he'd already met a former music biz pro who'd worked with Rhaytana. It was a like a sign.

Wyatt downshifted to pass a truck. Mark snuck a look at his profile. Wyatt looked like someone who had just politely answered questions about an unwelcome, disowned relative.

"Did you dislike him?"

"Who? Rhaytana?" Wyatt shrugged. "I couldn't like or dislike him. I never knew him. It's just ..." He looked uncomfortable. "That stuff he wrote about Jimi and Janis. And Lizard King. Writing that he pictured them as sleazy used car salesmen, in polyester suits ... that's pretty cold." Wyatt shook his head reproachfully. "I mean, they were our whole era. When we get old, when we look back at our time on earth, Jimi, Janis, Jim, that's who we'll remember."

Wyatt looked at Mark, to see if Mark understood.

"Maybe they were bad examples," Wyatt said, "but they were *our* bad examples."

•   •   •

A couple of hours later they approached the first off-ramps for Salinas, a sleepy agricultural city inland from California's Central Coast. Wyatt said he had to make a quick stop there to check on a friend's mother.

"To make sure she's okay, taking her meds," he explained. "We might as well stop for lunch. I used to live here."

Wyatt drove them to a cheery, sun-bleached cafe under two woolly palm trees. Odetta peppered him with polite questions about his auditor job. Her turn to humor the driver, Mark thought, and concentrated on his hamburger.

But while he was mopping up ketchup with his fries, Mark happened to mention how his beard had killed his luck as a hitchhiker.

Wyatt leaned back, offered a broad smile. Mark sensed that he'd brought up something their driver had an opinion about.

"Man, I'll be straight with you," Wyatt said. "I almost didn't stop to pick you up." He nodded at Mark's whiskers. "From behind the wheel, that looks pretty intimidating. You could go on stage with ZZ Top."

Mark squirmed. Odetta looked amused. Wyatt checked his wristwatch, pushed back his chair.

"It's going to take me about forty minutes to check on Moms," he said. "You guys can hang out here, if you want, but I'll make you an offer."

And then he made his pitch: that he knew a barber only a block away, and would comp Mark to a shave, if he wanted one.

"My treat," he said. "I'm white collar corporate now. I can afford it." He held up conciliatory hands. "But only if you feel like it, man. It's your life, your hair, your business."

And Mark heard himself said yes.

Six months to grow the beard this long. He'd thought he wouldn't trade his beard for a kilo of Hawaiian pot. But the 'yes' was out of his mouth before he had time to think, and then he was standing, ignoring a surprised Odetta as he took the bill from Wyatt and listened to Wyatt's directions on how to find the barber.

He knew that she was the reason. To show her. She could think he was a potaholic sleaze like her dad, that for whatever her personal reasons were she'd had to team with a ridiculous-looking stoner bumpkin with a beard half as big as his chest, and she could wash her hands and disinfect her clothes once they parted company in L.A. Fine; she could think that, but he'd show her that under that beard he at least had looks going for him. Even if not much else.

• • •

Mark found the barber dozing in the shop's single barber chair, under a poster showing men's hair styles from the fifties. He was completely bald, grossly overweight, introduced himself as Slim, and said he cut hair out of envy.

"Like a eunuch who crews for porn flicks," said Slim, and tapped his bald noggin.

A half-hour later, Mark rose from the barber chair and inspected his clean-shaven reflection for the first time in two years. Slim stood beside him, offered a light wolf whistle.

"Jesus Pesus," Slim said, "Would you look at what I've unleashed on the world!"

He turned toward a closed door at the back of the shop.

"Mabel. I said MABEL! Get your ass out here and see what the stud farm brought to Salinas."

The door opened, emitting Mabel, Slim's rival for corpulence, sporting a foot tall, safety orange beehive that looked as if it had been set with a tack welder. Mabel looked Mark up and down, let her tongue loll out, thrust her pelvis suggestively at Slim's hips.

"Ten percent off if you screw my wife," said Slim.

•   •   •

Back in the ranks of the Romeos, thought Mark, resignedly, and ignored two tittering teenage girls as he walked back to the cafe. Decision made; he couldn't glue the hair back.

Odetta was standing in front of the cafe. Mark kept his eye on her face as he walked up, felt gratified to get the reaction he'd hoped for. She was obviously startled, flustered, tried and failed to conceal her surprise. He'd gotten one in under her guard.

"How do I look?" said Mark.

"Fine," said Odetta, quietly. She averted her eyes. "Very different."

"Fine?! Is that all?"

She recovered, managed a chuckle. "Aren't *we* conceited?!"

Wyatt returned five minutes later, looked at Mark more seriously as they climbed back into the Volvo.

"You were *hiding* behind that beard," he said, matter-of-factly.

CHAPTER THIRTY-THREE

But in San Luis Obispo they caught a bad ride.

Wyatt dropped them off downtown. Odetta and Mark said their thank-yous, hiked back to the freeway. The on-ramp was only so-so, but San Luis Obispo was a friendly, mellow little town. Mark figured they'd bag their next lift within a half-hour. A good thing, too, because it was getting late. They only had an hour of daylight left.

But no one stopped. Thirty minutes passed, then forty, fifty. Mark winced as they were approached by the first cars with lit headlights. They weren't close to a streetlight; in full dark, drivers would see them clearly for only a moment in the sweep of their headlights. Which would be the absolute pits for their prospects.

So maybe that was why he accepted the ride in that boxy, puke pink Valiant. Even though he'd had a bad vibe as soon as it pulled over.

• • •

The driver leaned across the seat to push open the passenger door. Mark saw him in the dome light: white, thin, mid-thirties, with big ears, a narrow jaw, and hair that had receded evenly from his forehead, like a blanket rolled up to expose part of an egg.

The rear seat was piled high with boxes, but there was room for three on the Valiant's split front bench seat.

"Where you headed?" Mark asked.

The driver grinned, waved an impatient hand. "Santa Barbara." His voice was nasal, gritty. "Go ahead and put your stuff on the boxes."

Mark opened the back door, grabbed Odetta's backpack by the strap. He was stacking it on top of the boxes when he saw that Odetta already had opened the door, was sliding in next to the driver. His stomach tightened. He should have said something. He didn't want her sitting next to this guy.

Too late now. Mark grabbed his backpack and slung it in along with their 'Los Angeles' sign, and as he slid onto the bench seat next to Odetta turned his head for another look at the back seat as he was closing his door. To make sure that the backpacks wouldn't fall off and crumple the sides of the driver's boxes and maybe make the guy mad.

That was when he saw the porn magazine. As the driver was putting the Valiant in gear, accelerating toward the on-ramp. Maybe Mark had knocked it loose when he'd stacked the backpacks.

SUCK was the title, huge white letters on blood red, and then beneath it taking almost the whole front cover was the photo. Which of course was of a guy getting a blow job, what else would it be with that title?, but even though it was very weird to carry that kind of magazine in an open box, even in 1975, what made Mark's skin crawl was the way the guy was getting it. With his fingers shown digging hard into the woman's temple in the photo and her mouth jammed full and a whole vibe of her being *forced* into it. Like showing the woman being forced to do it against her will was the whole point of the shot.

"So how far are you two coming from?" the driver asked. He checked his mirror, joined traffic on the southbound 101.

"North of San Francisco," Mark said. "Thanks for the lift."

"Long trip," the driver mused.

He stayed in the slow lane. Mark saw him checking out Odetta, looking at her body, too directly, too obviously. Odetta didn't seem to notice. She was staring straight ahead, silently. The bench seat was barely wide enough for the three of them. Her leg was almost touching the driver's; maybe she felt uncomfortable to be so close to a stranger. Or maybe by then she'd picked up a bad vibe about him, too.

But he drove well enough. Mark looked through the windshield, at the ever-shifting sea of red tail lights in the deepening night, the shadowed silhouettes of trees and buildings next to the 101. A couple of minutes passed.

Maybe it was a false alarm. So the guy liked to jack off with a porn rag. What did he care?

"Are you two going to a commune?" the driver asked.

Odetta shook her head. "We have separate destinations."

"I thought all you hippies lived in communes." He leered, as if he expected one of them to deliver a punch line.

"We're not exactly hippies," Mark said.

"I'd like to check out one of those communes," the driver said.

"I'd be curious, too," said Mark.

The driver's lip curled in a leer. "I heard about one, all they do all day is screw. That's it. They fuck all day like rabbits."

No, Mark thought, maybe not a false alarm after all.

Mark flicked the side of his left foot twice quickly against Odetta's ankle, as much warning as he could give her, twisted on his end of the bench seat so he could better face the driver.

The driver was chuckling, grinning, knowingly, cynically. His profile came in and out of view, intermittently lit by the passing beams of headlights in the northbound lanes. Grinning like he was on to something, like he knew the score about how hippies really spent their time.

"What I heard is, some of the chickies there fuck ten times a day," the driver said. "With all the dudes in the commune. You know. Free love. Sometimes the commune pimps them out to buy drugs."

"I wouldn't know about that," Mark said.

Odetta stared straight ahead, eyes wide, eyes fixed on the freeway. Paralyzed. Maybe because Mark had warned her with his foot. Or maybe because this sick white man already was so far out of the orbit of anything she'd encountered that she didn't know how to communicate with him as a human. As if she'd encountered a rabid animal.

So it would be up to him, Mark thought.

Unhappily, resignedly, Mark let his right hand slide down past the door map pocket, checked for the presence of the knife's shallow metallic bulge on the outside of his right ankle under his pants leg. It was there.

A precaution, after the near wrestling match with the horny Marine. He'd never thought he'd even think of taking it out of its holster.

"They've got little teenies in the communes, too." the driver said. He laughed. "If a hippie chick is old enough to be on the rag, then she's old enough to fuck. Right? One of the older studs busts her cherry, then she can fuck like a pro, earn her keep."

The driver grinned, ran a quick tongue around his mouth, as if pleasurably smacking his lips on the image he'd offered. Mark scanned the freeway shoulder for possible escape routes. His heart was pounding.

There weren't any good escapes. This part of the 101 cut through open country: hills, trees, grass, no buildings. He couldn't invent an excuse to get the guy to stop the car, and if the guy did — pulled over by the freeway, let them open the door, get their backpacks out — they'd be fleeing into the woods. If Sicko had a gun tucked away and felt like following them for some target practice ...

But they were coming up on Pismo Beach. Mark racked memory for past hitchhiking trips on the 101, the route south of San Luis Obispo. Pismo, the beach; they had to be close. They'd crest a hill and then on the west there they'd be.

"How'd you two hook up?" the driver asked.

"We didn't," Mark said. "We teamed up to hitchhike together. That's it."

The driver leered. "Just someone to fuck on the road, huh?"

"It's not like that, man," Mark said. "Please don't talk that way."

He dropped his right hand past the map pocket again, pulled up his pants leg and pulled the knife out of its ankle holster, reminding himself as he did — begging, pleading with himself — to be careful, c-a-r-e-f-u-l, in spite of his fear, because if he dropped it and it slid under the seat of an unfamiliar car at speed on the freeway he might as well have never had it.

Could this diseased bastard have a knife of his own on his side of the car? Or a gun? Mark looked at the driver's hands, intermittently cast in wan yellow by streaking headlight beams, the bony fingers tapping lightly on the top of the plastic steering wheel. If he did have a knife or a gun, how fast could he get it out?

Maybe it still wouldn't come to that. Maybe this guy was nothing but sick, angry mouth, and he'd fill the car with his diseased rap about sex communes and teenie whores and freak Odetta out, but still let them out at Pismo if Mark said they wanted to get out early. Maybe, but it didn't look like it, not the way this guy was ramping up his sick spiel from 0 to 100 only minutes after they'd gotten in the Valiant, and Mark tightened his grip on the knife handle and looked at the driver without expression, and waited.

Ahead through the windshield Mark glimpsed the black shadows of low hills. They were coming up on a rise; the freeway was curving up and east. Pismo, the beach. He was sure.

The driver snorted, as if Mark had taken him as a sucker.

"Oh, come on! Not fucking a *black* chick?! The way spades fuck? Who're you kidding?"

Mark's voice hardened. "Man, this ride's over. Pull over and let us out of the car. You've got us wrong."

Odetta was shaking. Stiff, petrified, eyes wide, glued to the road.

The driver chortled, more loudly, ignored him, made no move to pull over. "I don't think so. I'll bet your nigger girlfriend loves to fuck. Don't you, sugar?"

And then Mark noticed the driver's right hand.

He'd slid it off the steering wheel. Maybe when Mark had been looking ahead at the rise in the freeway.

The driver had his right hand on Odetta's thigh. High up on her thigh, with the fingers pushing between them. Squeezing. Steering with his left hand on top of the wheel.

"Oh, man, you don't want *her!*" Mark said.

He moved quickly, banged his head on the dome light as he scrambled sideways across Odetta, holding the knife tight. The driver swore; the Valiant swerved. Mark jammed himself onto the seat between Odetta and the driver, twisted sideways to face him.

"She's got the clap, man! You fuck her, you're going to get scabs all over your dick. You can do me instead."

"Get away from me!" the driver yelled.

"But you're so handsome."

"Fucking faggot!"

The driver dropped his left hand toward the door side pocket, started to grope for something on his side of the car.

Mark swung up the knife, pushed the tip hard against the side of the driver's neck.

"BOTH HANDS ON THE WHEEL!" Mark shouted.

As loudly as he could, his mouth inches from the driver's ear, twisting the knife tip onto the neck stubble so the driver would know what it was and clapping his left hand hard on the back of the driver's neck. An indignant chorus of horns sounded behind them as the Valiant swerved briefly across lanes.

The driver gasped. His eyes bugged open as he felt the knife blade. He pulled up his left hand quickly, both hands now trembling atop the steering wheel.

"Keep them both on the wheel," said Mark. Harshly, but not shouting. "If I don't see your hands you're going to get stuck."

"Motherfucking FAGGOT!" shouted the driver. But kept his hands on sight on the wheel.

"I'll tell you where to pull over," Mark said.

They'd passed the crest. Mark kept his eyes on the driver's hands and terrified face, flicked his gaze west. He'd been right; the beach. The land west of the freeway sloped down to the ocean. He glimpsed scattered house lights below.

"Pull over when I tell you to," he told the driver. "Like you've got a flat tire. I don't want to stick you."

Seconds passed. Five, ten, twenty; agonizing, miserable, excruciating. Mark kept the knife hard on the driver's neck, stared at the driver's hands and the freeway ahead, watched for a stretch of the shoulder that would be wide enough for the car.

"Right here," Mark said. "Nice and slow. Both hands on the wheel."

The driver pulled over. Obediently, fingers clenched tight on the wheel, face contorted with fear.

"Turn off the ignition. With your right hand."

The driver turned it off.

They were next to trees and a couple of yards of scrubby freeway landscaping, sloping to a short, wobbly chain link fence they could roll over, and then a road. They could get out of Sicko's sight, if he had a gun and wanted revenge.

But, it was still safer to humor him.

"No hard feelings, man," said Mark, with the blade still pressing onto his neck. "It didn't work out for you, it didn't work out for us." And then: "Odetta, get our bags out."

Odetta did, quickly. Her arm bumped Mark's neck as she grabbed the second backpack.

Mark kept his eyes on the driver's hands as he slid across the bench seat to the open door, and put feet to the soft shoulder pavement.

Then, to Odetta:

"Get your pack! Go!"

He grabbed his pack, skidded down the slope, rolled over the fence, turned to help Odetta. But as soon as he turned he saw they were in the clear. The Valiant's turn signal was blinking; Sicko wasn't interested in sticking around. Mark watched it accelerate to merge into southbound traffic.

They were safe.

CHAPTER THIRTY-FOUR

"A real Mr. Right, wasn't he?" Mark stooped, slid the knife back into the ankle holster.

The Valiant was gone. Mark stared for a moment longer at the freeway lanes where it had disappeared, his heartbeat pounding in his temples. He hadn't gotten the license plate numbers.

"We've gotta get that dude on the *Dating Game* ... hey!"

Odetta had hoisted her back pack, was marching determinedly south on the dark road paralleling the freeway.

"Where're you going?!"

Odetta didn't answer. Mark grabbed his gear and trotted to catch up to her.

"Where're you going?," he asked again, when he was beside her.

"Back to the freeway."

Then Mark saw how agitated she was. Her face was rigid, mask-like. As if she had been shocked out of range of rational thought, had become a mad automaton, a broken wind-up robot. She glanced at him, wide-eyed, kept hiking.

"What?!?!"

"We need to get another ride."

"No, no. Come on ..."

He trotted to step in front of her. She tried to walk around him. He stepped sideways, blocking her path.

"Not after that, Odetta. Come on."

She stared at him fixedly for a moment longer, then lowered her eyes and nodded jerkily at the pavement. Meekly, as if mortified to acknowledge her own upset.

Mark looked around. A block away a neon sign flickered weakly in front of a yellow-lit store front; a customer came out with a bag, climbed into a car at the curb. Mark saw the lights of other businesses farther away, but nothing else close by. So they weren't in downtown Pismo, if they were close to Pismo at all.

To the west a narrow street slanted gently into what looked from a distance at night like a dark void: the ocean. Mark gestured, hitched his back pack.

"We can find a place to sit down there."

He started walking, checked to be sure that Odetta was following him as he tramped down the quiet street, past snug, compact beach homes, some already dark in the early winter evening. A mustachioed senior raised a highball glass in salute from a lawn chair as they passed his front yard; no one else was in sight.

He could still hear and feel his pulse throb. It had all happened so fast. He'd tensed up when he'd seen what a problem the driver would be, but after that he'd been too busy thinking survival to feel frightened. And now all the panic and fear that he'd dammed up was flooding through him. He felt dazed, like someone had clubbed him from behind and he was trying to blink colored lights away from his eyes.

They reached the ocean. At the foot of the street was a pocket park crowning the bluff, with weathered benches facing the surf. In the distance Mark saw the stick-like silhouettes of beachgoers wandering the shore, but they were far away. They were alone.

They sat on one of the benches. Mark gripped his knees and struggled to control his breathing, made himself count backwards 10 - 9 - 8 - 7 as he stared at the midnight blue ocean shimmering to the horizon under moon and stars, and the pale, silvery whitewater crests of the surf breaking beneath them.

"Well, I'm sorry," he said finally. "I've been hitchhiking a long time, but that's the worst guy I've been in a car with."

Odetta didn't say anything.

She was a mess. Trembling, panting through her nose, staring at nothing. Shell-shocked. Mark winced, tried to imagine how it would feel for the straight-laced black woman who'd worn her yellow and maroon uniform at the mall to be groped by that bastard and spoken to in that horrible, diseased, racist way, on top of the mysterious whatever else she was going through.

"Do you want my jacket?" Mark asked.

She shook her head quickly. Boy, she looked bad.

"Okay, why don't we say that's it for hitchhiking," Mark said. "We'll find some place to camp out here and then tomorrow, there's got to be some kind of bus to L.A. We made it to SoCal. L.A.'s not that far away. How's that sound?"

Odetta didn't speak.

"Look, could you please be human? Yell. Scream. Cry. Throw something. That guy was awful. You don't have to be so tough."

Odetta shuddered, covered her face with her hands. Her shoulders trembled.

It took her another quarter hour to settle down. Or to settle down more. She slid her hands from her face, sat staring at the ocean with her elbows on her knees, breathing more steadily.

And then Mark remembered the store he'd seen on the commercial street, with the flickering sign.

"Look, why don't I get us some eats?" he said. "You ate like a bird with Wyatt. Something to drink. A treat. Like compensation for what we went through. Will you be okay by yourself here?"

Odetta nodded. She'd like some aspirin, too, please, if the store had any.

"You're sure you'll be okay here?"

She nodded. Mark hiked back up the narrow street, offered a quick wave and smile to the mustachioed senior. A retired who-knew-what, Mark thought: civil engineer, postal inspector, bus driver, even a cop; how many thousands of L.A. worker bees could there be, who dreamed of hanging up their 9 to 5 duds in a cushy spot like this on the central state coast?

The flickering neon sign, Mark saw, was for a brand of beer. He entered, was offered a laconic nod from the cash register by a pot-bellied clerk. Mark plucked sandwiches and sodas from a cooler, found the aspirin between the toothpaste and shaving cream. It was only as he stepped up to pay that he noticed the neat row of pints and fifths behind the cashier's head.

So Mark bought a pint of eighty proof whiskey, and a roll of paper cups for them to drink it from.

Because Odetta wouldn't complain. *Couldn't* complain now, not after what they'd just been through. His nerves were shot, and hers had to be worse. He'd have a cup and she'd have a cup and they'd drink it while they ate and r-e-l-a-x, mellow out like normal human beings.

And if she wouldn't drink any, she couldn't complain if he did. Liquor wasn't his thing, but he was wrapping up his second day stone cold totally sober, and the weirded-out feeling had grated and gnawed and scraped at him all day. And now Prince Charming in the Valiant. He had a right to take something to settle down.

Mark hiked quickly back to the pocket park, feeling the neck of the pint through the paper as he cradled the bag under his arm. Odetta was as he'd left her. Mark sat on the bench beside her, felt guiltily aware that he was holding the bag so that she couldn't glimpse the pint through the paper. He handed her the aspirin, then placed the sodas and sandwiches on the bench between them.

Then the roll of cups. Which weren't needed with the canned sodas. Odetta stared at the roll, looked at him quizzically. Mark sat with the bag on his knee, his hand covering the bag opening.

"And I bought one more thing, Odetta, so we can relax. Okay? So we can sleep."

Mark took out the whiskey.

He thought later that he might as well have taken out a gun, or an autographed photo of the Valiant driver. Odetta reared back, lips curled, looked at the bottle indignantly.

"I don't want that!!"

"You don't have to be like that," Mark said patiently. He unscrewed the cap. "It's like a medicine. Like in the Alps, with those rescue dogs ..."

"Mark, how can you do this to me?!"

She was shaking, wide-eyed, almost hysterical. Mark screwed the cap resignedly back on the bottle.

"Look, Odetta ..."

"After what I told you about my father? Do you hate me that much? I do not want to get *drunk* with you, Mark."

Mark put the whiskey back in the bag.

"You can't stand to be sober for two full days. That's what this is about, isn't it?"

She stared at him, trembling, wide-eyed. Her lips twitched.

Mark met her eyes with a grimace, felt a mixture of shame and indignation. What was *wrong* with having a legal drink of alcohol if they weren't driving anywhere? After what they'd been through?

But he knew as he looked at her that he wouldn't have the drink, and that in his angriest and ugliest thoughts about the beard-sniffing harpy at the mall he'd never imagined or wanted to see Ms. Runsen as broken and hysterical as she was now. It was as if the sight of the bottle had ripped the scab off of a wound, and now she might crack up completely.

"All right, Odetta," said Mark. "We won't have a drink. I shouldn't have bought the whiskey."

Mark stood, started toward a trash can by the sidewalk. Then he thought of something, turned to stand in front of her.

"I'm going to go ahead and chuck this, but I want something in return."

Odetta looked at him. She sat with her arms folded across her stomach, her hands clasping her elbows. Calming down.

"I want to know why you're doing this trip with me."

Odetta immediately averted her eyes. Mark stepped closer.

"*I* need this," he said, and tapped the bottle through the bag. "To settle down. But I'm not going to drink it, because I don't like seeing you this upset. I don't hate you, Odetta. Believe it or not, but I don't.

"But if I chuck this legal whiskey that I paid for, then I want to know what the score is with you and this trip. Okay? You didn't wear that blonde hooker wig because you thought it would help get rides. If I chuck this, will you tell me what's going on?"

Odetta grimaced, looked toward the ocean. Seconds passed. She raised her head, met his eyes.

"All right, Mark. I'll tell you."

In full martyr mode, Mark moved to the edge of the bluff, made sure that Odetta was watching as he uncapped the bottle and poured the whiskey onto the rocks. He walked to the sidewalk to drop the bottle and bag into the trash, then returned to sit beside her on the bench.

"Shoot," he said.

Odetta leaned forward, sat with her arms crossed across her stomach and her hands clasping her elbows, rocked lightly and stared at the grass as she sadly and calmly told Mark the story of the violent husband she'd left in Northern California, of his threats to use contacts in the police department to detain her if she tried to take a bus or leave town another way. Of how he'd finally gone too far, and how she'd seen Mark's flier on the mall bulletin board only hours after her husband had put the steaming clothes iron on her bare ribs.

Her husband Phillip.

Mark immediately recognized the story: about Phillip, Vietnam, the punji sticks, the below-the-knee amputation. As soon as he recognized it he felt disconnected from the physical world, as if he were floating in a non-dimensional ether before the sitting couple in the pocket park while simultaneously listening to the woman's steady, pained, matter-of-fact voice and watching the young, now clean-shaven, former mall Santa Claus sitting beside her and listening.

It then did not immediately register that the story she was telling was truthful. She did not look at him as she spoke, and so did not see signs of his surging, indignant fury: that someone would conspire to play some hideous trick on him, that the mall had known all along why he wanted to work there, that his hitch-hiking companion was akin to a paid actress in a methodical, detailed, unspeakably cruel sham.

But such a sham wasn't possible. It wasn't a trick. It couldn't be. Not possibly.

Mark reeled, thought that he might faint, dug his fingers into the bench's wood slats to maintain balance. For that moment, at least, he believed in God, utterly, profoundly, absolutely. After all his effort, after he'd practically given up, abandoned almost all hope of meeting her: God or fate or ESP or outrageous coincidence had delivered her to sit beside him now. Mark had finally met his Greta.

PART IV

CHAPTER THIRTY-FIVE

The next morning they wound up hitchhiking again after all. Odetta insisted that she'd recovered from the bad ride, and Mark admitted that it would be easier to try their luck at the on-ramp than figure out transit options. He still had only a general idea of where they were.

The on-ramp wasn't particularly good, but their luck was: they caught a ride within fifteen minutes, and the ride would take them all the way to L.A. The driver asked Mark when they climbed in if he were an actor or male model, but otherwise was content to chat mostly with Odetta, who sat in front.

Mark slouched in the back, pretended to doze while silently studying her profile: contemplating it intently, tirelessly, for the hours of the drive, in fascination: the smooth sepia skin of her cheeks, jawline, temple; her lower ears visible beneath the flower-print head wrap, her lips and teeth moving in animated chat with the driver; cheerfully, as she had recovered from the trauma of the night before. The true owner of the sometimes barely-audible voice that had shared its secrets with him, that he had waited for every night at the hotline. A young black woman, not German. His Greta in disguise.

What had she confessed in that one phone call? That she didn't think about Parker more than eight hours a day.

· · ·

The night before he had almost told her his role with the hotline. Almost, but he hadn't. By morning he had known that he would never tell, never; that torture couldn't have dragged the secret out of him, that it would go with him to his grave.

How could he tell her that he of all people had been the man she had imagined as — what had she said? — a psychiatrist, a priest, a fiftyish professor with graying temples in a Victorian armchair in a lounging robe? How cruel it would have been to her and to himself to force her to see that her savior all the long had only been loser stoner amounted-to-nothing Mark, in his Santa suit and weed-stinking beard. It would have been almost like taunting a pig-tailed four year old at the mall, with her Christmas list and fantasies of Santa and his elves; jeering at her, mocking her, hurting her to pointlessly and unnecessarily expose a harmless illusion.

As long as she believed that Parker was real then at least that part of Parker that genuinely existed in Mark would remain valid, alive. In his sorry life he'd managed to do this one good, important thing that absolutely no one could take away from him, and as they cruised south in light Route 101 traffic past Santa Barbara, Ventura, Camarillo Mark continued to discreetly study Odetta, and smiled sentimentally with his secret knowledge, and felt warmed by it. For his sake at least as much as hers: he'd never tell.

. . .

The driver dropped them off at Sunset and Western, on the outskirts of Hollywood. Odetta thanked him for the ride as Mark pulled their packs out of the back, squinted in the mid-day sun at the traffic-choked lanes and curbside, single-file troop line of skinny-trunk fan palms that towered over Sunset to east and west. Back in L.A.

They were next to the parking lot of a fast food restaurant. Mark fished out his dog-eared fold-out city map, opened it on the waist-high barrier separating the lot from the sidewalk. Odetta stood next to him, held her side of the map open.

"There's Lynwood." Mark tapped crisp-printed black letters on a spot on the map. "Southeast. Do you need any help figuring out the route?"

Odetta shook her head. "I'll be fine. I can take the bus on Western. Then south I think she told me there's another bus on Imperial." Odetta smiled. "I wouldn't want to, but from here I could walk."

She chuckled at the idea, smiling in the expectation that he would see the humor; a pleasant-faced young black woman in her rumpled on-the-road clothes, backdropped by the Los Angeles asphalt and traffic and high-above green crowns of the palm trees.

His Greta. He'd never see her again. When she turned to take the bus on Western she'd disappear from his life forever, would become part of his unrecoverable past, like Toby. If only he had some way of asking questions without making her suspicious. Why hadn't she gone to Saint Catherine's? She'd always struck him as a woman of her word, on the phone and now in person. Why hadn't she kept her promise?

Would she be all right in Lynwood? On the bus going there? He felt so protective of her now, absurdly so. She wasn't the one with the drug problem.

Mark folded the map, handed it to her.

"Why don't you take this? I've got another one."

"I won't need it, Mark. It's your map."

"Can you please take it as a gift?"

She looked at him for a long, quizzical moment, then accepted the map, slid it into her pocket, looked at him with the same expression of gentle humor.

"Mark, you have been acting so strange all day."

"I guess I have."

"Where are you going to go to get some pot?"

"Excuse me?"

Odetta smiled. "Now that you won't have me around anymore to *harp* on you, to be a *harpy*, you can get *stoned* again." She bugged out her eyes and drew air through pursed lips, then laughed at her imitation of a marijuana smoker. Trying to make a joke. "What a relief, not to have me picking on you."

Mark blinked, stared. He felt hurt.

"Well, no," he said hesitantly. He averted his eyes, shifted his weight self-consciously on the balls of his feet. When he spoke again he realized that he was saying something important, that the words he now uttered without any contemplation or inner debate represented a firm decision.

"No, as a matter of fact, that's not what I'm going to do at all." He raised his head, met her eyes. "This has kind of ... shown me a new way. Almost three days sober. I've made it this far, I'm going to ... stick it out. Try staying straight. Maybe not forever, but for now. That's what I'm going to do."

And then added, a moment later:

"I wish you hadn't said that to me."

This obviously startled her, even more than he had startled himself in saying it. She looked at him in bewildered surprise for almost ten seconds, seemed torn between a reflexive desire to apologize and knowledge that his history made an apology inappropriate. Mark squirmed, almost shyly, shuffled his feet. Greta.

"Well, I think this is it," she said at last. She smiled affably. "You got us here, Mark. Thank you. We had quite an adventure. I even got to see Fort Bragg. I don't think I'm ever going to hitchhike again, but now I know what it's like."

She raised her arm, shook his hand.

"Look," said Mark, "What do you think if we arrange to meet back here on the weekend? To be safe?"

She listened without expression as he explained his reasoning, both to her and to himself, as he again spoke words that he had never planned to say, hadn't imagined even minutes before. Odetta hadn't seen her Lynwood relatives for years, Mark pointed out, didn't know what would be waiting there for her. His situation was similar.

"You and me, we know each other now," Mark said. "We're not exactly ... the most similar people, but I think you trust me now, and I trust you, too."

And then suggested that they meet there at noon on the coming Saturday. To see if one of them needed help with something.

"I'll be sober," Mark said.

Odetta thought for a moment, then shrugged, nodded. He was right, she said; she did trust him now. And it sounded like a good idea.

So, she said: noon on Saturday.

CHAPTER THIRTY-SIX

Nine hours later Mark sat in the back yard of a dilapidated house in the hills south of the Silver Lake reservoir. He was sopping wet, stripped to his jockey shorts, dripped water onto the weeds under a rusty-framed lawn chair. His wet clothes hung from a clothesline. Maybe they'd be dry by tomorrow morning. Or damp enough to wear, at least. He'd improvised shower and laundry with the back yard garden hose.

Crystal had been a no show. She'd moved out, had split for Maui with her boyfriend. The gum-chewing redhead who had opened the door hadn't known anything about an arrangement to let Mark shack up there for a couple of days. No, he couldn't come in to use the bathroom to wash up — did she know him? — but for a buck he could spend the night in the backyard, as long as he got along with her dog Karma. "He's introverted," said the redhead. As for the bathroom, why didn't he try the coffee shop on Sunset near Vendrome? She knew lots of people who'd taken a dump there.

Karma was a bear-sized German shepherd mix who now eyed Mark suspiciously from the other side of the yard. He had barked indignantly when Mark had opened the gate, but seemed to have resigned himself since to the interloper's presence, and now growled only occasionally. His main concern now seemed to be that Mark might try to invade his dog house.

Well, it beat sleeping in the ivy plants next to the freeway, didn't it? He wouldn't have to worry about the CHP rousting him in the middle of the night. And there was a level patch of grass for his sleeping bag.

Mark straightened his fingers into a karate knife hand, used the side of his hand to squeegee off water from chest and legs. He'd be dry enough soon to get into his sleeping bag. Tomorrow he'd find something better. The redhead's roommate Avo had visited the back yard long enough to offer Mark a lead on a place in East Hollywood. The landlords were right-wing whackos, Avo said, but if he'd pay in cash they'd probably let him move in with no notice. If that didn't work out, there was Griffith Park. He'd get by. And the liquor store lead had worked out, at least. Mark had called from a gas station phone booth. The owner Rex had said that the gig was still open, had given Mark an address south of the Hollywood Cemetery. They'd meet there tomorrow at 10:00. Work. Income, money. He'd get by.

Mark squeegeed off more water. He was dry enough for the bag now, but didn't feel sleepy yet. He slouched on the lawn chair, gazed past rooftops and night-silhouetted trees at what he could glimpse of the vast, glittering city below. Back in L.A. Streets in Silver Lake and Echo Park could feel like hilly oases, but the smog still made the city lights reflect a hellish red on the night horizon, and he could hear the distant thunder of traffic below.

L.A. could be cruel. He thought of the sleazy XXX sex stores in Hollywood, the sad platoons of hookers who walked Sunset Boulevard east of the strip. The corporate moguls or movie execs who lived in the Hollywood Hills or Bel Air or Beverly Glen could pick up the little run-away druggie whores and use them like tissue paper. All very free, liberated, open, heartless.

He wondered how Odetta was doing. He'd opened his second map to look up Lynwood, had seen that it was near Watts, Compton. Black neighborhoods, he guessed; for Mark unknown, foreign, forbidding places that he only would have visited with an escort, like Beirut, Angola. He remembered watching TV footage of the 1965 riots in Watts: snipers, national guardsmen, buildings and cars aflame. Was that what those neighborhoods were like now?

No; that couldn't be; Odetta wouldn't move to a place like that. Mark tried to picture a working class black neighbor-hood, drew on his memories of TV documentaries about Martin Luther King Jr., black America. There'd be rows of neat, modest homes, and her family's home at least would have good paint and the lawn mowed and the walkway trimmed, as Mark pictured them all as conservative, sober, church-going types like Odetta. Except for her dad. Would they be having a special dinner for her? Would she tell them she'd hitchhiked?

If only he could have still been at the hotline. Mark smiled dreamily as the fantasy bloomed, took shape within. She could excuse herself from the dining table, take the phone into the bedroom, call. He would be Parker again, would hear Greta's eager, breathless account of how she had finally, finally decided to leave Phillip, escape from town, hitchhike downstate with the sleazy pothead Santa from the mall, join relatives in Los Angeles. Greta wouldn't hide her vulnerabilities in a talk with Parker. She would be human, female, vulnerable and frightened, unsure, brave. Everything that Odetta refused to be with Mark. He could be her protector again.

No, he'd never tell her about the hotline. Never. *He* knew what he'd been to her. That was enough. No one could take that away from him, and Mark smiled, felt a wistful, sentimental affection as he contemplated the decision, and was surprised to realize that he looked forward to their reunion on Saturday at least as much as he did to meeting Rhaytana.

CHAPTER THIRTY-SEVEN

"The chinks I don't worry about much," said Rex the next morning. "But you get jigs or spics in the store, you keep an eye on them.

"The minorities think they own this country."

He leaned on his cane next to the beer cooler and looked at Mark broodily. About fifty-five, Mark guessed, a walking, talking advertising campaign against everything sold in his liquor store, with a chain smoker's hoarse, emphysemic wheeze and a Mr. Potato Head nose blistered red with the spider veins of a hardcore alcoholic.

Mark didn't answer. He felt depressed. His wallet wasn't thick with twenties. It was either take this gig or start sleeping outdoors, or maybe turn his first trick with the male hustlers on Santa Monica Boulevard.

Rex explained terms. He didn't have the up-and-at-'em he used to, what with his arteries and bronchitis. The store was a one man operation, but if he could pay Mark to take over the register, he could stay home, recuperate. Paid in cash, strictly off the books, no paperwork. Mark would be an independent contractor.

Mark said yes. He figured he had to. The place was a total downer, a drab, gray cave on a shabby stretch of Melrose, with sun-faded liquor decals in the storefront and a broken neon sign. Rex wobbled unsteadily on his cane from the cooler to the cash register. He stunk of whiskey.

"If you steal," he said, "I'll kill you."

• • •

Avo's room-to-rent lead turned out to be some dead architect's bad idea of an English Tudor, a squat, homely single family home hunkered between modern, boxy multi-story apartment buildings in East Hollywood. Mark opened a wrought iron gate hung with campaign placards for Ronald Reagan and Bob Dornan, stepped up a driveway flanked by American flags.

"Old lady Mrs. Dobson lives there with her weird-o son Melvin," Avo had said. "They're totally right-wing, but for the room they rent all they care about getting paid under the table in cash. They'd rent to Karl Marx if he showed them the lettuce."

Mrs. Dobson answered Mark's knock: gray-haired, spectacled, dressed like Dorothy's rural Kansas Aunt Em in *Wizard of Oz*, with a conspicuous mustache. Mark spotted framed portraits of Barry Goldwater and Joe McCarthy on the living room walls behind her. All the living room furniture was covered with shiny transparent plastic, and the carpet was crisscrossed with wide lanes of vinyl carpet protector.

Mark stood at the door smiling with his wallet in his hand, slightly open, so Mrs. Dobson could see the bills.

"I'm a friend of Avo's. He said you might have a room to rent here."

She did. Mrs. Dobson directed him to a plastic-covered easy chair, interviewed him with a clipboard on her knee from a plastic-covered sofa. Most questions were standard fare — full name, date of birth, previous address — until:

"Are you a socialist?"

Mark blinked, shook his head.

"Are you or have you ever been a member of the Communist Party?"

A pudgy forty-something in a lime green leisure suit had appeared in the hall doorway, regarded Mark blankly through square black glasses under a slippery-looking Elvis hair-do. Melvin.

"He spends most of the day writing right-wing letters to the editor," Avo had said. "That, and masturbating. The dude must flog off five times a day. You can hear his elbow thumping against the wall. It's gross."

Mrs. Dobson showed him the room: small, unfurnished, with a slit ceiling window, a droning mini-fridge and a closet-sized bathroom with the sink and mirror mounted in the shower stall. But it beat negotiating space with Karma in the backyard; Mark paid cash up front for a week.

•   •   •

The first interfaith concert was booked for a high school auditorium in the San Fernando Valley. Mark had to take three buses and wait forty minutes between the second and third, slumped on a bus bench fronting a strip mall, forcing an occasional good-humored smile when a teenager regarded him with amused pity from a passing muscle car. He'd have to save for wheels, if he stayed in Los Angeles. It was like the SoCal big shots had set things up so you couldn't live there without a car.

He reached the high school by late afternoon, felt his pulse quicken as he crossed the parking lot and saw roadies wheeling black flight cases into what had to be the auditorium's stage door. He was about to meet Rhaytana. Really, truly, finally. Three hours before the gig, with the crew rushing around and the bands doing their sound checks: how could Rhaytana *not* be in the auditorium? He'd be busy as all hell, sure, but if Mark said he'd come all the way from NorCal to get *Letters* autographed, how could the Rhaytana he felt he'd gotten to know through his words ever be heartless enough to refuse to sign? And to talk with him for a few seconds, and arrange to meet later? When Mark was standing in front of him, when Rhaytana could see that he wasn't some con artist.

Mark walked through the stage door, behind a roadie lugging an amplifier. The auditorium was chaotic, with crew members scurrying to and fro like Disney dwarves on, around and in front of the stage, arranging cables, fussing with lights, speakers.

Mark started to follow the roadie, then noticed that he was being watched by a gangly twenty-something perched on a tall stool by the door.

"What's up?" He was tall, hook-nosed, spoke with a British accent.

"Is Daniel Velasco around?" Mark tried to look as if he were running an errand. "The production manager?"

The Brit curled an ironic lip. "Otherwise known as the great Rhaytana."

He grinned, hopped off the stool with a cheerful, knowing expression, as if Mark had posed a riddle to which he already knew the answer. Mark felt something deflate in his torso, almost like air hissing out of a leak.

At the gig he was supposed to be Daniel Velasco. Production manager, part of the crew. Period. If the Brit was calling him Rhaytana ...

"You're the second fanboy today." The Brit chuckled. "If we get anymore, I'm going to have to put up a sign."

"Well, where is he, then?"

The meek, humiliated question seemed to have come from someone else. His stomach was cramping.

The Brit threw up his hands.

"Absolutely anywhere in the world but here, mate. He quit the tour."

Mark groaned, covered his face with his hands.

"Take it easy now," the Brit said. He sounded as if he thought Mark would start screaming.

Mark slid his hands from his cheeks, made a miserable gesture to show that he was okay.

Unreal. Unreal. The flier had said that Rhaytana would be the production manager for eight consecutive Los Angeles concerts. How could he have missed on that? Did something in the universe have it in for him? Had the flier from Fielder about the interfaith concerts been like a squishy rubber mouse toy that someone would tie to a string to tease a cat, that the cat would pounce for and always miss without knowing why, because making the cat miss and look stupid was the reason the human string puller had bought the mouse in the first place?

In a gentle voice, the Brit explained:

Rhaytana *had* been booked as the production manager. The promoter's big mistake had been listing him by his real name in the flier.

"There's some dude with a Rhaytana 'zine, he got the word out," the Brit said. "At the office they got calls every day. Multiple calls. And visits.

"He must have realized what he'd be in here if he showed up. Whatever this guy wants, it's not publicity. He bailed. Passed the torch to one of his old buddies in the biz."

Mark figured that he might as well show the Brit the flier that Fielder had sent, with the oval and exclamation points around Rhaytana's name. He told how he'd pulled up stakes, hitched to L.A.

The Brit winced. A sympathetic type.

"I just might have something for you. I think he's still in L.A." The Brit surveyed the auditorium floor, raised his hand to offer a loud finger whistle to a passing roadie.

"Jimmy! Come over here for a sec."

Jimmy waddled over, a fat, frog-faced redhead in a Bob Marley t-shirt.

"Didn't you say that Rhaytana chap is still in Los Angeles?"

Jimmy nodded. It was second hand information, but Jimmy thought it was good. Rhaytana was supposed to have told his friend Leonard that he'd be sticking around for awhile. He'd spent most of his adult life in Los Angeles, had Southern California fences and bridges to mend.

"And how can this gentleman get ahold of Leonard?" asked the Brit.

Jimmy looked at him skeptically. The Brit scoffed.

"Now, now. We don't know Rhaytana or Leonard from Adam, do we? No one asked us to keep a secret." He tilted his head toward Mark. "Does this man look like a terrorist?"

Jimmy came back five minutes later with a phone number written on note paper.

"You didn't get that from us," said the Brit.

•   •   •

At a quarter to twelve on Saturday, Mark sat waiting for Odetta on the Sunset and Western parking lot barrier where he'd shown her the map. It was sunny, clear, an only-in-L.A. late morning in January. A small breeze wafted the fronds of the high-overhead palms. Mark watched passersby, contemplated an elderly has-been actress type in a slit skirt as she hobbled along the sidewalk on carmine red evening heels.

He'd wait hours for Odetta, if he had to, but had decided she wouldn't come. Why should she? She hadn't described her Lynwood relatives, but Mark assumed that they were a real family, unlike his ditzy mom; stable, sane, grown-up. She'd escaped Phillip. What use did she have now for someone like him?

So: he'd wait, and she wouldn't come, and then Mark figured he'd go look for some weed.

He'd almost tried to cop the night before, when he'd stepped off the third bus coming back from the Valley and spotted a couple of dudes toking up behind a gas station. Mark had started walking toward them, figured he could buy a bud if they didn't want to share. Only remembering Odetta had made him stop.

But if she didn't show up today: not anymore. He could take the bus west to the Strip, around Gazzarri's, the Whisky: for sure he'd be able to score dope there. Tomorrow would make one solid week with no cannabis in his body, but this clean and sober shit was getting him nowhere.

He was worse off than he'd been in Norcal. The liquor store gig was the pukes. Rex was a chip-on-his-shoulder racist, it was like he could compensate for being a lame old dough boy who'd nearly chain-smoked his way into an oxygen tank by talking smack about how he'd shoot any Watts so-and-so who tried to steal from him.

The Dobson dump was a joke. The sink was built into the *shower*. He had to step into the *shower* to wash his hands, and then when he'd try to sleep he'd get to hear the thump-thump-thump of Melvin's elbow hitting the wall. The only positive was that he had a space of his own to write a few more entries of The Trials of Parker in his diary. Parker in L.A. Although so far he hadn't written anything.

So why couldn't he go back to hitting the pipe to take the edge off, and not be so bothered by all this crap? He wasn't some go-getter Mr. Career type. He didn't have any idea what that was. He could chill, get high, take his medicine, be There when he had to be and only part-way There the rest of the time. Like before.

At 11:50, the northbound Western Avenue bus pulled up at the stop catty-corner from Mark's seat on the parking lot barrier.

Mark sat up, watched. That was probably the bus she'd take coming from Lynwood.

The bus pulled away from the curb, showing the riders who'd stepped off.

Mark blinked. Odetta.

She wasn't wearing the flower-print head wrap. That was the first thing Mark noticed, although it shouldn't have been.

Chapter Thirty-Seven

He saw what he should have noticed first when she stepped to the crosswalk.

She was carrying her backpack and sleeping bag.

·   ·   ·

"They don't have any room for me," Odetta said.

She sat next to him on the waist-high wall, squinting in the sunlight, occasionally raising her voice to be heard over accelerating traffic when the intersection's lights turned green.

"My uncle has, in the same house, a little two bedroom..." Odetta held up her hand, counted off fingers. " ... my great-uncle and great-aunt, who are waiting for spots in assisted living. My second cousin Wilbur from Oklahoma, who is looking for work here, like me, *and* Wilbur's wife, *and* Wilbur's three children, counting the baby.

"Then I called."

Odetta smiled wryly, resignedly.

"I can keep staying there. They won't kick me out. But it's a madhouse. I've slept in a different spot on the floor every night, and every night someone has fallen over me.

"So I told them this morning, 'Maybe Mark has found something.' If not, back to Lynwood. You might be sleeping in Griffith Park, for all I know."

Mark described his life at the Dobson house. Odetta made a face.

"Do they have another room for rent?"

Mark shook his head. "Do you want to give it a try? We can go ask. If they get more money, they might not care if we double up."

"Well ..."

Odetta fell silent, looked off at the horizon with a helpless, accepting expression. Trying to think of alternatives, and not seeing any.

"I guess, Mark. It will be like when we were hitchhiking."

Mark stood, reached for her backpack, tried not to show how happy he felt. But Odetta still looked uncomfortable while they walked east on Sunset, and so Mark added that he hadn't touched pot since she'd made him chuck his stash north of Fort Bragg, and promised to stay straight while she was with him at the Dobson's. And realized in an ambivalent, well-what-do-you-know way that he had again made an unplanned-for commitment as he spoke the words, and that he'd wind up clocking more than a week sober after all.

CHAPTER THIRTY-EIGHT

They became roommates.

Melvin asked Odetta if she knew Huey Newton or belonged to the Black Panthers. Mrs. Dobson grumbled about seeing a marriage certificate, but by then Mark knew that all they really cared about was under-the-table cash, and sealed the deal by saying they could pay a seventy-five percent increase for two people on the original rent.

"Besides, it's not what you think," he added. "We basically hate each other." Odetta nodded.

They settled into a routine that was in some ways a continuation of their hitchhiking life on the road, except that the routine was now confined to a single room indoors, and included the tiny bathroom and droning mini-fridge. Mark bought used sheets at a thrift store, strung them up as a barrier to divide the room. Odetta said it was at least better than having her Lynwood relatives fall over her at four in the morning. Mark took the side of the room that shared a wall with Melvin's bedroom, tried to explain the thump-thump-thump of Melvin's elbow as a plumbing problem.

At night, they usually talked before sleep, as they had talked before sleep while hitchhiking, Odetta from her sleeping bag on her side of the sheets and Mark from the bag on his side. Mark would lie in the dark and look at the small gap between the sheets and floor as she spoke, illogically, as if the gap were a speaker. They might exchange only a few words, but often talked much longer than they had on the road, sometimes for more than an hour.

• • •

Mournfully, stubbornly, obsessively, apologetically, Odetta talked about the life that Vietnam had stolen from her: a content marriage with a husband who she adamantly insisted had been loving, kind, faithful, hard-working and a good provider before the war; their realistic plans to settle down, open a mortgage on a nice home; and, perhaps more importantly, their determination to build a church-going Christian family in that home, when

Odetta sired that good husband's children. It was as if she could only heal the wounds of her own childhood by becoming the parent her dysfunctional, masochistic mother hadn't been.

"I even used to think," Odetta said, "that if I had a baby and cared for it well, my mother's spirit could come into the baby and be healed, too. Like I could be a good mother in the present and heal the past at the same time."

Mark finally saw Phillip's photo, congratulated himself for concealing interest, replying with only a casual 'Sure, I'd be curious' when Odetta offered to show it to him. The black man staring out at him from the rectangle of treated paper — contritely, Mark thought — was indeed homely, as Odetta had described him, or average-looking at best, with too-large ears and a face nearly as round as a pie pan.

Mark listened, surprised Odetta with his attentiveness, marvelled privately at the difference between hearing her clear, human voice from a few feet away and his past effort to decipher every crackling, barely-audible syllable at the hotline. He felt as he lay listening in the dark that the gap between the floor and the hanging sheet was like the answer pane in the Magic 8 ball crystal-gazer game, or an arcade fortune-telling machine, that if he asked questions and was patient the quiet, mournful, confiding voice that seemed to issue from the gap eventually would resolve the mysteries about Greta that had troubled him on the phone. He still wanted to know why she hadn't gone to Saint Catherine's, but ordered himself to wait. He couldn't ask specifically without revealing his secret: who he had been to her all the long, before he himself had known that he was that person.

• • •

One night she talked about her calls to the hotline.

They had been talking for about twenty minutes. Mark had asked if she'd ever spoken to her mother about the problems with Phillip. No, Odetta said, never with her mother, Mark would understand why if he met her, and then added casually that she used to call a hotline.

"A hotline?" Mark said, as carelessly as he could, and when she didn't answer right away the moment felt almost surreal in its misery, he couldn't remember ever so badly wanting anyone to tell him anything and yet couldn't say a word more without showing his hand.

At last she continued on her own.

Yes, she said, a hotline; a suicide hotline, but people could call for other things. The line quality had been horrible, sometimes she could barely hear, but had still called dozens of times. She'd spoken to only one volunteer, she said, had only felt comfortable with that one.

And then:

"I swear, Mark, some day I'm going to go back north and find that man to thank him. Even if I have to put an ad in the newspaper. I don't know if he was a professor or a retired therapist or what. I don't know what I would have done without him."

And on his side of the sheet Mark goggled in open-mouthed wonder at the Magic 8 ball answer pane gap between sheet and floor in amused ecstasy, vindication. He could have been Clark Kent, listening to Lois Lane's account of how she'd been rescued from peril by the Man of Steel. No, he'd never tell. Never.

•   •   •

It took her only a few days to book her first job interview at a Los Angeles mall. Mark was surprised; he had thought she had burned bridges at Knockers by leaving town so quickly. But he learned that this wasn't entirely so. Odetta had sensed impending danger before the final crisis with Phillip, had arranged a private, frank conversation with higher-ups to explain her situation. The bridge was singed, but not burned. And Mark deduced that her references otherwise were excellent.

Further, huge, megalopolitan Los Angeles had more opportunities. The first interview was followed days later by a second, and then a third. Odetta reported breathlessly one night that she might even get hired with a promotion, a big one. But, there was a catch: the mall manager wanted her to know about visual merchandising, and said that he expected a new hire to help him research security cameras. Banks had them now, Odetta explained. Big malls wanted them, too.

Odetta rolled up her sleeves. She returned every night to sleep, but seemed to spend the rest of her life aboard Los Angeles RTD buses: on the eastbound line to downtown, where she could read about 'visual merchandising' at the Central Library, or visiting other malls. Once Mark had to console her after she dealt with naked racism at a bank; the assistant branch manager had thought that any black person interested in the security cameras had to be a criminal.

·   ·   ·

Wyatt's 'Dixon' or 'Dixie' turned out to be an insiders' nickname for a north-of-the-Hollywood-Bowl motel that indeed had been booked frequently by music tour crews through the late sixties. The clerk on duty recognized the name when Mark visited, but could offer no other help. Management had changed; the new owners wanted business conventioneers, not roadies.

Wyatt's two other Rhaytana leads flamed out, too. "Cal McGrath" was nowhere to be found, might as well have never existed. "Zeke Wilson" was now a middle-aged music executive who owned a condo near Marina del Rey, but the nasal-voiced woman who answered his phone said he wouldn't return from the East Coast until spring.

That left Leonard, the lead from the interfaith concert.

And the Leonard lead turned out to be live.

It took five ring-ring-ring-no-answer phone calls, but the number that roadie Jimmy had scribbled on the piece of paper was finally picked up by a laconic, gruff-sounding male who answered to Leonard. Yes, he knew Daniel Velasco, although he thought it was a stretch to call 'Danny' a 'friend.'

"More like an acquaintance," Leonard said. "I haven't seen him for a week."

Mark tightened his grip on the receiver, braced his hand on the grimy glass wall of the phone booth to steady himself.

"You saw him a week ago?"

"That's what I just said." Leonard sounded suspicious. "Hey, who is this?"

In occasionally quavering voice, Mark explained why he had come to Los Angeles, his dashed hopes at the interfaith concert, his hopes of speaking to Rhaytana face to face.

"How'd you get my number?" Leonard asked.

"Well, they … I'm not supposed to tell."

Leonard snorted. "You won't tell me how you heard about me, and I'm supposed to help you meet Danny."

Mark pled, lobbied, miserably, twisting his fingers on the receiver, aware that this was his first real chance of meeting Rhaytana and that he was probably blowing it.

Leonard was firm.

"If I were his friend, what kind of pal would I be if gave the information you want to a complete stranger? I don't know you from Adam."

Mark started to answer, but Leonard cut him off.

"Write me a letter telling me why you want to see him. With *your* contact information. So he can get ahold of *you*. Not the other way around."

Leonard gave him the address of a Studio City post office box.

•   •   •

Mark wrote a seven page letter, asked Odetta to read it on Sunday morning while he was brushing his teeth in the shower sink. He'd told her about Rhaytana by then.

"What do you think?" He took a big swig of water, then held back the hanging sheet so he could look at her side of the room while he swished the water to rinse out the toothpaste. She was dressed, sitting on the floor cross-legged with the letter open on her lap.

"I don't know, Mark." She looked at him with a sympathetic wince. "It's pretty long. Do you think he'll read it?"

Mark said he hoped so, asked her again to thank her uncle for letting Mark use the Lynwood address, and then as he leaned against the wall on his side of the sheet to pull on his socks Mark asked what church she was planning to check out. She'd said she wanted to visit a new church every weekend until she found a good match.

"I think it's called Renewal Beacon," Odetta said, but then added that she didn't think she'd go, she didn't have a good feeling about it, and asked what Mark was planning to do. And Mark said he thought he'd hike up to the Ferndell nature trail and then the Griffith Observatory. "I'd like to do that sometime," Odetta said, and Mark looked at the gap under the sheet as he knelt to tie his shoes and said, "Why don't you come with me?"

.   .   .

They hiked north on Western to the Los Feliz turn, took the stairs and path into Ferndell. Odetta was impressed, marveled at how green and secluded and cool the little trail felt, like an oasis. They paused on a footbridge to watch the stream bubble past, and Odetta caressed the green fronds of the dense ferns that flanked the winding trail path in the deep, cool shade of the sycamore, redwood, ash trees, and said that some day when she was a mother if she were still in California she'd take her child here. Then a quarter or a third of a mile north the tree cover ended abruptly as they turned onto the spartan fire road that wound up the hillside, and then they spoke mostly in short, breath-conserving sentences as they concentrated on the uphill climb.

At the Observatory they looked at the pendulum and the telescopes and then wandered out to the art deco-ish arches covering the promenade walkway, a narrow balcony that encircled the south-facing main observatory dome like the rim of a cup and offered spectacular views of the vast, flat, sprawling city below. They stood side by side looking out at the city with their elbows resting on the broad stone wall, and Odetta said:

"Phillip hung up on me."

Mark looked at her. Her expression was matter-of-fact, as if she'd told him what bus she planned to take to a job interview.

"Hung up on you when?"

"Last night."

Mark shook his head, made a disgusted sound.

"He's my husband," Odetta said quietly. "We're still married. I wanted him to know that I'm still alive."

"Through no fault of his," Mark snorted, and then intermittently off-and-on for the next ninety minutes as they went back inside and looked at the pendulum and telescopes and other exhibits and then returned to the fire road for the long down-hill clump-clump-clump back to Hollywood offered each other variations-on-a-theme of arguments already expressed in a half-dozen conversations past, like actors improvising dialogue in an already-familiar play. What else does he have to do to you?, asked Mark. What part of torturing you with a hot iron did you not understand? And Odetta: could Mark at least understand that he had been different before the war? Was it such a sin to still care about the husband she had loved and to be hurt to see him falling steadily apart, even if she couldn't go back to him, to see him losing his mind because of a war that he'd entered as a draftee, a slave?

"Slaves like our ancestors, Mark. Not your ancestors. Like ours."

And then, emphatically.

"I was going to bear Phillip's children. He wanted me to. The father of my *children*."

They were back in cool, shady Ferndell, had paused to sit on a bench by the trail. She was upset. He spoke to her much more directly now than he ever had on the hotline, she wasn't a crackling, barely-audible voice that he could alienate, lose forever, but he still wondered now if he'd picked a bad moment to be so straight-forward. She looked close to tears.

Mark decided not to answer, picked up a twig under the bench, flicked it idly at the trail. They fell silent.

A young mother appeared at a curve in the narrow trail, approaching them. She was Latina, perhaps twenty-five, smiling, gently clasped the small, pudgy hands of two toddlers. Mark guessed that it was to restrain them, as they were both old enough to walk, but the children looked content, tranquilly fascinated by the ferns and trees and greenery that was likely new to them.

A good mother, Mark decided. He'd seen all types from the Santa throne, thought he could judge. The kids were lucky.

"That's going to be me some day," said Odetta.

•   •   •

On Western south of Franklin was a health food store, and Mark saw as they were walking past that it adjoined or included a restaurant: small, arty, hippyish, and out of place, Mark thought, as it was precariously close to a nearby sex club and adult bookstore.

Odetta paused so that Mark could read the offerings and prices chalk-written on a small easel blackboard next to the entrance. He gestured to the entry for banana nut bread.

"We can afford that, anyway," he said.

They entered, amidst a faint aroma of sandalwood oil, crossed a woolly hemp rug to a rickety wooden table under a photo of a bearded Indian guru. The restaurant was crowded. Students, artists, latter-day hippies; white, black, Latino, Asian, a crowd he might have expected to see in Laurel or Topanga Canyon. For once, Mark realized, they weren't being stared at. He'd become accustomed to furtive stares when outdoors with Odetta.

They ordered the banana nut bread from a Mama Cass of a waitress, grimaced at the price of smoothies and decided to settle for water. Odetta asked if he thought he was breathing better now that he wasn't smoking pot and Mark shrugged, he guessed so, and Odetta said he was doing way better than her father would have, her dad wouldn't have lasted two days sober, and Mark said he wished she wouldn't compare him to her dad. All right, I'm sorry, said Odetta, and then while they were talking about why exactly she was so keen on finding another church a skinny forty something in a rumpled cook's apron appeared at the kitchen door holding a big transparent bag of seed rolls, and in a friendly voice cried:

"Listen up, people!"

Loudly enough to get the room's attention. The cook was smiling.

"This morning we have a bargain basement *giveaway!*" He held up the rolls, said that they were still tasty, tasty, yum, yum, yum!!, but they were too old to sell, so he'd decided to have a department store giveaway, like at Sears or Montgomery Ward.

"These wonderful rolls are yours," he said, "if you've come today for a special occasion! Not just because you're hung over on Sunday and are too lazy to cook. Who's here for a special occasion?"

Chapter Thirty-Eight

Without thinking, Mark was the first to raise his hand.

"Oh, joy!" said the cook, with a hand clap. "Tell us, young man! What's your special occasion?"

Everyone in the restaurant was quiet, looking at them. Odetta seemed frozen.

Mark sat up, cleared his throat.

"Well, the two of us met up north about a month ago, at work, and we pretty much hated each other. I mean, major arch enemies."

Mark smiled self-consciously as the cook made a face and the diners offered a playing-along groan.

"But then, it turned out, we had to travel together," Mark continued. "I mean, had to. Necessity. And we got to know each other better, and today ..." He glanced at Odetta. "Today is the first time we've done something purely social together. Other times, it was for something one or both of us had to do, but today it was a hundred percent just to hang out and be friends."

"That's special enough for me!" cried the cook, and led the diners in a short wave of applause before crossing the room and depositing the bag on their table.

"We're set for eats," said Mark to Odetta, after the cook had disappeared in the kitchen and the other diners had returned to their conversations.

Odetta smiled faintly, looked at the table. Her cheeks looked darker. Mark wondered briefly if it was the restaurant light, and then realized that she was blushing. Blushing a lot, he guessed, for it to show, as she wasn't light-skinned.

"Sorry if I put you on the spot."

She shook her head ever so slightly to show she hadn't minded.

"You're not so bad," she said softly.

And at last sat up and raised her head to meet his eyes. With a simple, frank candor, slightly sad, nothing else, an open, guileless vulnerability she would show to a friend who knew all about her.

Mark blinked, startled. It was as if until that moment her face had been in camouflage, visible and yet simultaneously hidden, shrouded, as if by a magical veil from a child's fairy tale that allowed the sight of some features, but not all. At last the veil had fallen away, and for the first time he saw her clearly. Even when he had most loathed her at the mall he had reluctantly acknowledged that she was 'not unattractive,' but now this grudging admission seemed so grossly inadequate and understated as to be simply untrue.

Odetta was beautiful.

CHAPTER THIRTY-NINE

A week later Odetta was hired by a glitzy new mall near the 405 freeway. She was an assistant manager now, not only supervised mall staff as she had at Knockers but would work with the individual mall stores on "visual merchandising." The top manager Rory was obsessed with this, said that any store with an unattractive window display was hurting both itself and the mall as a whole.

It wasn't a dream job. Rory was moody, difficult. Odetta knew that the job had been available because he'd fired two predecessors. Worse: the mall was more than fifteen miles south of East Hollywood, almost as far as the junction with Route 110. Bus transit was at least an hour and a half each way.

Odetta was resigned, stoic. The Vietnam war had stolen the life she'd built with Phillip; now there was nothing to do but buckle down and start from scratch. Rory lent her glossy trade publications; Odetta studied them during the bus rides, cradled them open in the crook of her arm if a bus was full and she had to stand. If she had to work late, she occasionally slept on the floor in a mall storage room.

"You can at least let me take care of the laundry," said Mark, as Odetta wouldn't let him wait on Western to walk her home if she had to catch a late bus. Odetta relented; Mark learned how to wash bras in the sink.

•　　•　　•

Rex still came to the liquor store almost every day, cheerfully volunteered that he had nothing better to do. He greeted old customers from a tall stool behind the counter, talked and chain-smoked while Mark stood at the cash register or stocked the shelves and coolers. He was always at least tipsy, and sometimes drunk enough to slur words or lurch into the counter when he slid off of the stool. His lungs were shot; he couldn't carry a six pack between the cooler and the counter without panting, wheezing.

Mark wished he'd stay home with the TV. He knew that he wouldn't have been bothered by Rex if he'd still been getting high every day, that he would have grouped his racist old boss among the other only vaguely and dreamily perceived irritants in a stoner's life, realities necessarily tolerated between joints, bowls. But he was sober now, clear-headed. It was tough to listen to Rex's racist jokes, or hear him tell for the fifth time the story of his supposed show-down with the taco or spade who'd tried to shoplift or pass a bad check. Even if Odetta told him to take it in stride, that at least Rex could be generous. Rory wasn't.

This was the kind of gig he could expect without a high school diploma. He hadn't thought twice about dropping out at seventeen. More time to get high, to screw, to make money; a slave no longer. But now ... the trouble with being straight and clear-headed so long was that it had restored his sense of the fourth dimension. He could see where he stood now in relation to time, the life arc, his past and future. He wasn't going anywhere.

. . .

One afternoon Mark spotted a 'Get your GED' flier on the bulletin board at the laundromat. The flier showed a rainbow coalition of beaming young graduates in cap and gown, listed courses and test dates at the L.A. City College. L.A.C.C., on Vermont, north of Melrose. He could walk there.

He thought about the flier while he was folding the laundry, and realized that he was still thinking about it when he returned to the room and divvied up their duds. When he finished he decided to go out for a walk. Odetta wouldn't be back for awhile.

Mark hit Fountain Avenue and headed east, told himself that it was about time he checked out the views from the hill at Barnsdall Park, but when he reached Edgemont where he would have turned north to get to the park he instead found himself still walking east to Vermont, so that soon without a conscious decision or even conscious thought there he was: turning off Vermont and stepping onto the L.A.C.C. campus.

A sleepy-eyed, gum-chewing Latina clerk in an administration office provided a GED overview. There were five test areas: Writing, Reading, Math, Social Studies and Natural Sciences.

The tests would take ten hours over several days, and to pass he'd need at least a thirty-five score on every test, or an average score of forty-five on all tests combined.

Yes, he could sign up there, she said, and showed him a list of test dates.

Mark picked a date a month away.

"Are you sure?" the clerk asked. "If you don't pass, you'll have to take courses or wait six months to take it again."

Mark was sure.

He left, walked back out to Vermont among students strolling the campus with books and binders under their arms. He felt simultaneously exultant and foolhardy, as if he'd just signed on to a bout with Muhammad Ali. He hadn't cracked a textbook in six years.

CHAPTER FORTY

One regular customer at the liquor store was Fernando, a mechanic who often picked up soda and snacks for his crew at a nearby garage. Mark liked talking to him when Rex wasn't around. Fernando was his age, said he was a 'chilango' who'd grown up with 'a socket wrench in my hand' at his dad's Mexico City gas station.

Mark told Fernando that he'd signed up for a GED test.

Fernando leaned across the counter and looked behind the register.

"So where's your prep book?"

"You think I'll need one?" asked Mark, and Fernando nodded emphatically. The GED wasn't a slam dunk. Their tranny guy at the garage had flunked.

So after work Mark entered a bookstore for the first time since he'd read up on hydroponic dope growing. They had three books on GED prep. Thick books. Mark picked up one, scanned the questions, thought he would be physically sick, but again it was as if a part of him knew that he would only follow through if he engaged in a kind of internal conspiracy, if he snuck behind his own back, so even as he told himself that it was hopeless he still took the book to the cash register.

And hours later he decided — as he sat on his side of the hanging sheet with the book open on his lap — that maybe it wasn't so hopeless after all. He was thinking night and day better now that he wasn't hitting the pipe. He remembered what he read, picked up on the core point of a paragraph without staring at it in a 'du-uhhhhh' stupor with his mouth open. He had a chance. Maybe what he was sending in the GED ring against Muhammad Ali wasn't a loadie lard bucket pulled off the bar stool but someone who could really fight.

He studied. At first he tucked the prep book under the counter when Rex was in the liquor store, but then read it openly even as Rex smoked and drank and did his racist rap on the stool behind him. He decided he ought to hit the library for extra help on math and science, and when he saw that the bespectacled young librarian was attracted to him repressed guilt feelings and turned up the charm so he could get a library card with only one of the Dobson's utility bills as proof of residence, and checked out two high school textbooks.

Odetta became used to coming home from the mall to find him sitting with an open book on his lap. She complimented him. Encouraged him. Which he'd expected her to do. It didn't matter so much to him.

What did matter was that he noticed a difference in how she acted around him. How she spoke to him, how she looked at him. Not a big difference, but enough of one. Although it was again as if he journeyed through his days with different levels of thought, of self, of awareness, so that he might think he was doing something for one reason when the real reason was something else. He hadn't yet consciously wondered why Odetta's opinion of him was important, or why he wasn't growing back the big camouflage beard now that they were living together.

• • •

Mark called Leonard about his Rhaytana letter the night before the first GED test. Odetta's uncle had never received any kind of response in Lynwood. Mark figured that a good word from Leonard could buoy his mood. "Danny said he'll get back to you," Leonard might say. Then Mark would be psyched, encouraged, would go into the GED test with a full head of steam.

But the idea backfired. Leonard interrupted him brusquely mid-sentence.

"Your letter arrived," Leonard said. "That's all I've got to say to you, Mark. You could call me until I see a lawyer about a restraining order, and the answer would be the same. 'Your letter arrived.' Nothing else."

Then, "Don't call me again," and the line went dead.

Odetta promised to treat him to lunch in Long Beach whether or not he passed. She had a car now, a rusty F-85 that Fernando had tipped off Mark about. Two fenders were dented and the trunk didn't open, but the drivetrain and chassis were solid. Rory had congratulated her and immediately boosted her work load, but at least she wasn't spending hours on the bus every day.

. . .

Mark took the GED tests in a windowless room with fake wood paneling and a droning ventilator, with three other test takers for the Reading, Math and Social Studies tests on the first day and four others for the Writing and Natural Sciences test the next. The first day he sat next to a middle-aged longshoreman who told the room that he had a malignant tumor and didn't want to die without a high school diploma. The second day his desk was behind a fat woman with a Doris Day pouf who obsessively picked her nose with a red lacquered fingernail.

The reading test wasn't bad, but the first two math questions were quadratic equations. The very first two. Mark felt panicky, but shut his eyes, talked himself back to earth. He needed a thirty-five. That was all. He didn't have to get every question right. Sometimes on multiple choice he'd score with a lucky guess. And he was here. He could try.

The next week when he returned for his scores the elated, triumphant Mark who left the test center had already decided that thirty-seven was his new lucky number. Maybe he'd tattoo it on his chest. Thirty-seven was his math score, the lowest of his five scores in the five subject areas. Two points over the minimum. He'd passed the GED.

. . .

A few days later Rex fired him.

Mark had thought that he'd look for a better job now that he had his GED, and quit once he had one. But he didn't last that long. Or maybe he didn't last that long precisely because he knew he'd passed and had better prospects and didn't have to keep listening to Rex's us-against-them racist BS.

So one afternoon when they were alone in the store and Rex asked with a wheeze if he'd heard what happened to the coons in the coal mine, Mark shut his eyes and pressed his fingers onto the counter and said:

"No, and I really don't want to hear that joke, Rex. I truly don't," and turned to face him.

The argument lasted about five minutes. Mark felt as if their roles had been reversed, as if he were a parent reasoning with a kid. Why do all blacks have to be the same, Rex, do you really think that all the black doctors and lawyers are plotting ways to clean out your cash register? He told Rex about Odetta, tried to explain how much it hurt to hear the ugly jokes when he saw her every day. Even if she'd told him not to pay any attention.

But by then he saw that Rex was getting too upset. Rex slid off the stool, leaned hard on the cane. He was panting. His cheeks were red, sweaty. He looked like he was going to work himself into a heart attack.

"Get your day's pay out of the register and get out of my store."

•   •   •

Odetta helped him get a job as a security guard at a different mall on the Westside. A mall cop. Or a mall cop provisional hire; the mall said he'd have to complete two half-day classes on his own time to get a guard card. But they put him on the payroll, gave him a uniform, and Mark got used to hacking the long westbound grind every morning aboard the Santa Monica bus.

Mostly he walked around. The instructor in the first half-day class told them how far up the creek they'd be if they made a bad citizen's arrest, and how much farther up it they'd be if they made it without a guard card. Plus the mall didn't want them to detain anyone. 'Be there, let people see the uniform, and call the real police if anything serious happens.'

It wasn't bad. It was a step up from the liquor store; he couldn't have gotten the gig without the GED, and a drug test that he wouldn't have gone anywhere near up north. The only hours he didn't like were weekday afternoons, when teenagers swarmed in after school and he was supposed to 'show a presence' around stores with shoplifting problems.

"Oh, isn't he *ravishing!*" one girl squealed at him the first day, and that set the pattern. Once a giggling trio followed him around the mall. He didn't have to wear a security guard Pershing cap, but decided it made him uglier, and wore it in the afternoons. It helped.

• • •

Occasionally on his block Mark exchanged greetings with a seriously pregnant twenty something who lived in the next door apartment building. Mark thought of her as 'Janis;' she looked like a freckled blonde Janis Joplin. Janis usually wore maternity tank tops, which showed off a biker tattoo on her shoulder, but once had waddled out in an enormous man's Appalachia Trail t-shirt that had flapped around her knees like a dress.

"Is that where you're from?" Mark had asked, and she'd laughed and replied "Kind of," and added that her state was West Virginia. Since then they'd gone back to simple 'hellos.' Janis seemed pleasant.

Then one day after work, as he was hiking north from the bus stop on Santa Monica, Mark spotted an ambulance with flashing rooftop lights double parked on his block near Janis' building. His first, selfish thought was that old Mrs. Dobson had pulled a cardiac and that Odetta and he would have to move out.

But the EMTs weren't inside the Dobson's. Mark walked closer, saw the backs of two blue uniform shirts side by side on the sidewalk. They were kneeling in front of a stretcher, heads down, busy with their patient. Mark heard moans, then to the right of one blue uniform saw a woman's pudgy white leg splayed and raised with her knee toward her shoulder, a sheet draped over her crotch. He glimpsed Janis' face, now contorted with some-thing more than pain. Anger.

The EMTs were talking to her. The moans grew louder, much louder.

"The fucking nurse told me I could go home!!"

Then Mark knew what he was about to witness.

The block had been quiet, but now neighbors were drifting out to see what was going on. A skateboard-clutching teenager and a matronly black woman stepped up behind Mark. A car slowed; the driver leaned out the window, stared, open-mouthed. Across the street a cluster had formed. The crowd behind Mark grew larger.

By now Janis' moans had become bellows. Unrestrained, blood-curdling, furious. Obscene: "FUUUUUUUCK, OH FUUUUUUUCK, FUUUUUUUCCCKK!" Mark cringed, felt a vague shock. Did she howl only for the sheer pain, or for the pain coupled with her anger at the nurse who apparently had thought she didn't yet need the hospital, or, likeliest, for everything in her unknown-to-Mark life, for whatever maze of past decisions and circumstances had put her alone on her back on a Hollywood sidewalk, giving birth without painkillers? What was it?, but then even as he was wondering one EMT moved to one side, said something about 'the cord,' and the other EMT leaned in closer with one gloved hand above the other, holding something, something hidden by the draped sheet, and in a rocking motion Mark saw the EMT's arms move.

And then there was the baby.

Mark only saw it for a second, before the EMTs' huddling shoulders blocked his view. As if he were supposed to see it, he would think later, as if fate had conspired to put him on a certain bus coming back from the mall, and not another, had conspired to induce Janis' crisis when he would be witness. To see the tiny, sticky, helpless, eyes closed baby, with dangling umbilical cord, wizened little face flecked with white crust.

Janis' bellows had turned into a low, desolate moan. The EMTs were busy, shoulders and arms moving.

The baby cried.

"It's a boy," one EMT said.

The kid with the skateboard started clapping. A wave of applause broke out, then a shy cheer. The group across the street joined in. Mark joined in. An EMT briefly raised a gloved hand without turning his back, flashed a victory sign.

The birth of a mammal, all right, like in the Rhaytana letter: raw, unlovely, with seeping fluids, kin to the birth of a calf, a puppy. The letter had been true enough. Nature camouflaged, deceived; a dude who drooled over a centerfold never thought that the whole evolutionary purpose of his drooling was to yield the scene now before him on the sidewalk.

But if that was all there was to it, why did he feel so moved by what he'd just seen? His eyes were wet. He was trembling.

CHAPTER FORTY-ONE

A few months later they had enough saved to rent an apartment. An apartment together; neither suggested not continuing as roommates. They were used to each other, got along, would have had to stay months longer at the Dobson's if they couldn't have pooled funds to pay move-in costs.

They wound up staying in the same neighborhood, rented a sunny second story two bedroom in a stately, cream-colored stucco that Mark associated with Old Hollywood. The landlady was a retired actress, stooped and cheery, who startled them by showing off an early thirties publicity shot of her younger self in garters and hiked-to-the-hips skirt. "Those legs got me work!" she said proudly. "Then the goddamn Hays Code kicked in, and I was out on the street." She said they'd be doing her a favor by hauling up some old furniture gathering dust in the basement.

They split space in the refrigerator and bathroom medicine cabinet, saw each other occasionally in the morning and almost always in the evening. Odetta had finally found a church she 'kind of' liked on Slauson east of La Brea, nine miles south. "A black church," she said, apologetically. Mark went once. Everyone was nice, but he was the only white in the building. One little boy turned in his pew and stared at him with open mouth and wide eyes, as if he were Bigfoot or the Loch Ness Monster.

．　　．　　．

When did he recognize that he had fallen in love?

Or if 'in love' didn't feel true enough, accurate enough, complete enough, if the phrase's commercial overuse had stripped it of real meaning, then when had his attachment to Odetta swelled to an intensity far greater than any he had felt in the past for any other woman?

One morning when their work schedules coincided she padded sleepily to the kitchen table in slippers and bathrobe. The kitchen window faced south; already at daybreak the light streamed in, illuminating the tableware and weathered table top. Odetta half-smiled in drowsy greeting, paused at the stove to fill a plate with the eggs and hash browns that it had been Mark's turn to prepare, sat across from him.

He had forgotten to return the basket of toast to the middle of the table. That was all. She looked bemusedly at the basket sitting next to his plate and through a light yawn said:

"I don't deserve any toast this morning?"

And that was really all, all that the utterly ordinary and commonplace moment included, consisted of, but it was as he passed the basket that he realized with a start that even after months of having lived like sardines at the Dobson's he was still mildly thrilled to be in the same room with her, and never wanted to live apart from her again. To look at her, hear her, even in a few fleeting moments of close proximity to smell her.

When had it begun? The night somewhere near Pismo Beach, when he had learned that she was Greta? Had his profound astonishment and protective affection triggered a switch or ripped off an emotional safety barrier to let love or tender feeling enter, penetrate, propagate, like a microbiological culture introduced by a scientist's swab in a petri dish? Was that why he had never grown back the beard, in an unknowing effort to be attractive to her? Or if not near Pismo, then surely when they had won the seed rolls in the restaurant. When she had blushed, when he had recognized her beauty, felt startled by it.

He felt that he had been caught absolutely unaware, like a boxer felled unconscious while glancing out of the ring. In his late teens he had trysted once with a black woman in his hitchhiking-to-L.A. days, but he had been stoned, now recalled the contact only vaguely, through a fog. He had otherwise never thought of a black woman as a partner, not sexually and certainly not romantically. For that matter, he remembered no romantic depiction of a black woman in any movie or television show. His high school had included perhaps a dozen blacks; his junior high and elementary school, none. How had this happened to him?

Had a part of him resisted admission — or perhaps even in his wordless unconscious mind waged hysterical, terrified, selfish and self-preserving war against admission — because of what a relationship with Odetta would entail? She wanted to be a mother. She stocked no birth control pills on her side of the medicine cabinet, likely would have considered a lobotomy before an abortion. Was a now twenty-three year old mall cop with a new GED so unusual if a panic-stricken part of him desperately did *not* want to so smitten with a woman so unwaveringly committed to motherhood? Particularly if the mall cop possessed unusual good looks, when not camouflaged by the sternum-length Klondike beard, was regularly flirted with, given the eye, knew that he could have his pick. Why couldn't he have fallen for a woman who just wanted to date and screw?

●　　●　　●

He finally told her how he felt the next Saturday afternoon. Or part of how he felt.

They had decided to visit Santa Monica. Odetta had never been to the pier, but a strong wind came up almost as soon as they walked under the big blue and white arch, and Odetta said apologetically that she hadn't brought enough protection for her hair. So instead they explored the narrow Palisades park that hugged the bluffs overlooking the ocean, and Odetta soon said that she'd found another favorite place in Los Angeles. It reminded her of a painting, she said, an impressionist painting she'd once seen in an art magazine of women with bustles and men with top hats on the banks of a river in Paris. Except that the Palisades were even nicer.

They walked north, between squat, extravagant palms and towering eucalyptuses and figs with sprawling boughs, past little lawns upon which sat or slouched or slept hippies, teenagers, homeless, retirees, faces in a crowd; a leathery-cheeked Mexican Charles Bronson frowning at a chess board; an unsmiling middle-aged actress type with an unsuccessful face lift and an aura of depression. Then they felt like sitting, and found a bench next to spiky green aloe plants in a succulents garden at the bluff edge that let them gaze over the roofs of the millionaires' homes on the Pacific Coast Highway to the beach and the ocean and the now-distant pier.

A gust came up. Odetta tested the wind with her fingers, decided to leave the shawl in her purse.

"Don't you ever get tired of worrying about your hair?"

She made a face, snapped a small twig she'd picked up and tossed the pieces over the short concrete fence guarding the bluff edge.

"I'm used to it. I don't think about it anymore."

"Rory won't let you go natural? I see black women with afros all over."

"Not as mall managers," said Odetta.

So they talked about that for awhile. As a matter of fact, Odetta said, Rory just might let her go natural. Two relatively hip retail tenants had signed leases; Rory thought they might nudge the mall's positioning as more 'Westside' and less 'Torrance,' and that a black assistant manager with natural hair could be a plus. But it would be a commitment, she'd do the big chop, practically go bald and wear wigs until her natural hair grew in. And if Rory didn't like it or they got a K-Mart type anchor store and he decided to go full-bore Torrance, she'd have to relax her hair all over again.

Plus Doris didn't think she'd look good with natural hair. Mark had already heard about Doris: Odetta's nemesis, a jealous assistant manager marginalized after Odetta's hiring.

"No matter what I do, she wants Rory to think I'm bad for the mall's image. She's practically told him I'm ugly."

"How can anyone call you ugly?!"

Odetta shrugged helplessly. "That's what she says."

"You know you're attractive."

"Come on, Mark. You don't need to ..."

"But you are. You're beautiful."

And if he'd stopped there, they might both have remembered only a short, awkward pause in the conversation, as an embarrassed Odetta grimaced and looked at the aloe and succulents garden. But he didn't stop. The pronunciation of the word's three syllables had cracked open a valve, and as emotion swelled and blood surged in his temples Mark added:

"Incredibly beautiful."

With still more emphasis on the three syllables. Much more.

And then it was out, spoken. There was no point in pretending that she hadn't heard or could have misinterpreted the emphasis. Mark's heart was pounding.

Odetta continued to stare at the leafy aloe, her expression shy, sad, embarrassed, resigned, but also unsurprised. At last she turned, and looked at him frankly.

"I'm married, Mark."

.   .   .

They talked about the finally-broached subject for the next hour, as cars droned by on the highway beneath the bluffs and park visitors strolled the path behind them. Odetta spoke patiently, sympathetically, directly, as if telling a valued mall employee why she couldn't approve a shift change. She obviously wasn't surprised. She had thought about this, Mark realized. Perhaps she had thought about it as much as he had.

If it gave him any satisfaction, and she hoped it didn't, her marriage might not even be technically valid much longer. Phillip had continued to deteriorate. The parents who had never liked Odetta had finally stepped in, taken Phillip home, installed their war-ruined son in his childhood bedroom. Odetta had maintained painful contact, had not mentioned the occasional phone calls to Mark because she knew how he would feel about them. Phillip was more paranoid than ever, had almost assaulted a police officer responding to his weeping parents' 911 call. The outlook was bad, very bad, and she was resigned to the fact that Mark and any professional she eventually might see would never accept her description of the loving, caring, Christian spouse she had lost to Vietnam, would always regard her as suspect for having remained with him as long as she had.

But Phillip was not her main reason for not wanting to be involved with Mark.

She had three reasons. Mark stared at her bewilderedly as she held up fingers, counted them off.

The first, the least important, was his color. If they could have secretly watched the people passing behind them, they would have seen that at least half were sneaking glances. Because she was black, because he was white, because they looked like a couple. And that was in Santa Monica. Maybe there wasn't a lot to see in Bakersfield, but she remembered what he'd said about not taking a ride anywhere near Route 99. Living with those obstacles was one thing short term, but another over a lifetime.

The second reason was that he wasn't ready to be a father. He was doing great now, but had he forgotten the Mark she'd first met only a few months ago? Who smoked marijuana several times every single day, even before his shift as a shopping mall Santa Claus? Wouldn't it be reasonable to give someone like that time and space to develop before becoming a parent?

The third reason was his looks.

"My looks," Mark repeated.

Odetta stood, faced him from the bluffs' guard wall in front of their bench, with her hips and hands on the waist-high top rail. Mark's cheeks felt flushed. His pulse hadn't settled down; he felt it in his temples as he stared at her, excitedly, incomprehendingly, unable to absorb or digest what she was saying to him. A list of reasons why he couldn't be in love with her.

"I've told you about my father," she said patiently. Now, today, in this moment, Mark had said she was beautiful, but what would he say when she was pregnant, fat, a mother with a changed body? Her father could get dates with a smile, a wink. A practical woman with an eye for the long term wasn't safe with such a handsome man. And Mark was better looking than her father.

"What you ought to do," Odetta said, "is think of me as your stick-in-the-mud roommate who's boring, and square, and goes to church, and wants to have a baby, and take up with one of those pretty white girls who's checking you out all the time. Then you'll forget about me."

"So I can only date a white woman."

Odetta managed a grim half-smile. "Then you can take up with one of those black, brown or yellow women who are checking you out all the time."

"So you're not attracted to me at all?"

She pursed her lips, bowed her head, frowned at the ground between the bench and the guard wall. Almost ten seconds passed before she raised her head to reply:

"I don't think I should answer that question."

CHAPTER FORTY-TWO

She got what she called a big chop only three days later. The salon cut off nearly all her hair; she was practically bald, would wear a wig at the mall until her natural hair was long enough to debut on the job. At home, however, she never wore the wig, and admitted that their conversation at the Palisades had motivated her to talk again to Rory about going natural.

"This way you'll stop having ideas about me," she said, and occasionally now held his eye with an amused, defiant expression, as if daring him to say that she was as attractive without hair.

And she wasn't. He thought she would look beautiful in the braided crown hairstyle she planned to wear eventually — she'd shown him photos in a magazine — but now, with almost no hair: no, she wasn't as pretty. But the impact was trivial, the change had come far, far too late to affect the evolution of his feeling for her, if it ever could have. He loved her, in his love felt helpless.

• • •

He had never been rejected this way before. Not like this. Women had refused sex to remain faithful to existing partners — 'I want to, Mark, but I promised Drake/Paul/Frank/Chuck' — and there had been others like Shirley, but no woman had refused to enter a real relationship. He didn't think he had ever felt smug or vain about his looks, but had known he had them. It had always been he who had had to say no.

How had this happened to him? Irrationally he wondered if he had been willingly ensnared in a kind of transcendental conspiracy, if he had been fated from or before birth to be paired with Odetta and ever since had unknowingly navigated a life landscape in which necessary events, circumstances had been cunningly set up, arranged in advance, like backdrops and furniture pushed into place behind curtains between acts by silent-moving stage hands. So that in the greater scheme of things their communication as Parker and Greta had been like early verses of a song or the caisson of a skyscraper or even, if he liked, if it mattered anymore, bars bolted successively into place on a cell to usher, shepherd, imprison, seduce him into tormented feeling.

How had this happened to him? If he had never lingered on any image suggesting black female beauty in any movie or magazine, if he had most frequently contemplated black women as token blacks in TV detergent commercials, bemoaning the horrors of ring-around-the-collar or stubborn stains. He was now attracted to Odetta specifically for her physical characteristics as a black woman: for her voluptuously full, generous lips; for her wider, flatter nose; for her sable brown skin and, especially, for her impossibly, almost scandalously deep, deep brown eyes, that seemed depthless, bottomless, of a hue that almost merged with the black of her pupils.

He had begun to react to her physically, erotically. He was twenty-three, like nearly any man his age could be frequently erect, of course if sexually excited but also without reason, through random ebbs and flows of testosterone. But his response to Odetta now entered a new territory. It was as if by throbbing rigidly stiff his cock demonstrated the naked yielding to feeling that he had not received her permission to state in words. She had explained her stance on the Palisades. He had to accept the boundaries she'd set if he cared about her in any decent way, especially as her roommate, but how much hope was there that this detached and antiseptic logic would persuade his unconscious mind? So he could talk with her about the mall, about Rory, about Doris, and smile in polite controlled response, even as his penis ached and groaned and pulsed with the pathetic sincerity of a dog howling in loneliness or snuffling to be forgiven for some unknown sin by its cherished human.

He sometimes became erect in this way as soon as Odetta entered a room. His overwrought thoughts of a transcendental conspiracy now sometimes included a faceless human agent as mastermind, string puller, puppeteer. Was he a pawn in a plan? Could there be an unborn soul in an immaterial ether between lives that had chosen Mark as its future father?

·   ·   ·

One evening he came close to telling her about the hotline.

They were in the living room. Odetta sat on their dilapidated sofa, next to a lamp shining on a stack of trade publications about shopping mall security. Mark lay on the floor in front of her, fingers clasped behind his neck, staring at the heavy palm fronds fronting one side of their window, the spiky leaves juxtaposed against the red-orange of the Los Angeles dusk sky.

He was in a good mood, even as he also felt bemusedly martyred, sorry for himself. They had shopped together that afternoon, and repeatedly as he had pushed the cart through the supermarket aisles Odetta had nodded at one woman or another and asked why he didn't date. "She's not your type?" "Didn't you see how she looked at you?" Maternally, solicitously, almost pityingly, as if the desire he had confessed on the Palisades amounted to nothing more than endearing, transient delusion, like a little boy's crush on his teacher.

And who was the man with whom Mark couldn't compete, to whom she would remain faithful, as a God-adoring Christian? Why, to Phillip, of course, her husband, who had beaten her and tortured her with a hot clothes iron.

"Is your back better?" Odetta asked. Mark had slid onto the living room floor to do some stretches.

"It's fine."

She tapped him with her toe. "Check this out."

Mark stretched out an arm to take the proffered magazine, held it over his face. The trade ad showed an evil-eyed shopping mall Santa flanked by bulky security cameras, with plastic EAS security tags clipped prominently to his red coat.

"In case one of the kids tried to steal your Santa cap," Odetta said.

Mark snorted, returned the magazine. Then Odetta thought of something.

"Mark, I never asked you. Why did you ever take that Santa job?"

Mark twisted his head on his clasped fingers to look up at her. Her hair had started to grow in. It wasn't yet long enough to part or comb, but she wasn't bald anymore. She would indeed be pretty with natural hair. So he would be as much as doomed to be attracted to that, too.

Her expression was innocent, merely curious, nothing else. Of course, she had no idea.

Chapter Forty-Two

Mark turned his head back, looked at the ceiling. He felt jaunty, reckless.

"I was obsessed with a woman," said Mark.

And with private smile continued his contemplation of the blank ceiling. A half-minute passed. He felt Odetta watching him.

"Obsessed with a woman," she said.

"Yep." Mark resumed the stretches, bent his left leg, tugged the knee toward his right shoulder.

"You never mentioned this before."

"You never asked."

He glanced at her a bit mischievously, repeated the stretch with the other leg. She was obviously surprised, interested, as he had expected her to be, hoped and wanted her to be. She had put down the magazine, was watching him intently.

Mark lay on his back, wriggled his clasped fingers at the nape of his neck.

"I had talked to her for months," said Mark, addressing the ceiling. "For hours, every week. I was worried about her. I thought about her all the time. I had to see her. Odetta, I quit my job and got that Santa gig just so I could look for her."

"She worked at the mall?"

Mark smiled. "She did, Odetta. She worked at the mall."

"Are you making this up?"

"No!" Mark laughed.

"Why didn't you tell me this before?"

"You didn't ask." Mark glanced at her again. "Odetta, you know what I did? This is going to freak you out. I was so obsessed, I snuck in one night and picked open a file cabinet to get her folder. I didn't steal anything. I just wanted to speak to her."

He crossed his ankles, squirmed comfortably on the floor. "Isn't that incredible? You never thought I could do anything like that, did you? Neither did I. It was a first."

"You're not making this up?"

"No, I'm not making it up."

"Did you find her?"

Mark thought of how to answer, laughed. "Yes, I did find her. Not how I expected to, but yes, I found her." He twisted his head, looked at her. "You're asking a lot of questions about her. Odetta, are you jealous?"

She didn't answer. She looked as if she still suspected a joke.

"A wee, tiny bit jealous? Just for me?"

Before she could speak he clambered to his feet, headed toward his bedroom, and while turned away from her in a wistful voice she couldn't hear added that if she were jealous, she didn't need to be.

CHAPTER FORTY-THREE

After work a few days later, again on impulse, Mark returned to the L.A.C.C. campus and asked the same sleepy-eyed, gum-chewing Latina clerk in the same administration office if they had any information on career choices.

"Like what fields have job openings, and the training you have to do. That kind of stuff."

The clerk paused mid-chew, flicked an index finger at a wall rack of brochures next to the counter.

"Help yourself."

Mark contemplated the selection (*Careers in Dentistry! Become a Cosmetologist!*), picked out a bundle, leafed through them while sitting on a bench in the L.A.C.C. quad.

He could be an EMT. Emergency Medical Technician. He flipped through the brochure pages, stared at the photos of blue-shirted EMTs kneeling beside prostrate patients, pushing stretchers into ambulances. Like the two guys he'd seen delivering the baby. When everyone had applauded. Mark thought he'd be good at it. He could handle stress, think on his feet. You had to have a GED, which he had now, and no serious priors. He *could* have had some choice priors, if he'd been caught in NorCal, but hadn't been.

Mark went back to ask questions. The sleepy-eyed clerk couldn't answer, sought help from a Mr. Kilber, a linebacker-sized black man who nodded at Mark pleasantly from the other side of the counter.

No, said Mr. Kilber, Mark couldn't do EMT course work there. L.A.C.C. hosted basic CPR classes, but for EMT he'd need to pass professional level training, which took longer. Then after he had the pro CPR cert he could enroll in EMT training.

Mark asked if the training was hard. Mr. Kilber looked ambivalent.

"It can be," he said. "A lot of people drop out."

"*Quien la sigue, la consigue*," interjected the clerk.

Mark blinked, stared. She was smiling.

"That's Spanish," she said, "'Who follows it, gets it.' Persistence pays. You can do it. Didn't you pass the GED on the first try?"

So he'd try this too. Mark felt excited, paused occasionally to look at the brochure photos as he walked to their apartment. A *career*. *Him*. He could become a paramedic. Or work in hospitals, alongside nurses, doctors. *With* them.

He'd tell Odetta, and Mark walked faster as he imagined her reaction, remembered how she had looked and spoken to him differently when he'd studied for the GED. But she wasn't home. Instead he found a handwritten note taped on the kitchen table.

She'd be out of town for a few days with Phillip's parents. Phillip was dead.

•   •   •

A grim, subdued Odetta provided details at the same kitchen table three evenings later.

Phillip had gone into a paranoid rage, yet again. His parents had called 911, yet again. The police had come, yet again. But this time Phillip had gone farther, had attacked one of the cops, and maybe if Phillip hadn't gotten the jump or grabbed the cop's gun the other cop wouldn't have had to do what he did. But he did do it, did shoot Phillip, and Phillip died in the ambulance.

"His mother stood up to yell at me in the funeral service," said Odetta. "His father shushed her, he knows I didn't do anything. But still. She blamed me."

Odetta smiled bitterly, stared at her fingers as she traced meditative circles on the table top.

"Do you know what our minister said a couple of weeks ago, Mark? If you want to do evil in this world, be sure to set things up so it won't get pinned on you. Any time Memorial Day or Veterans Day rolls around, you know who's going to pin the biggest flag on his tie and be first in the parade with the stiffest salute? Those war hawk politicians. Because maybe then the soldiers' families won't figure out who put their sons and husbands and brothers and daddies in their graves.

"She blamed me for Phillip. Not JFK or LBJ or Nixon. She blamed me."

CHAPTER FORTY-FOUR

So Phillip was out of the picture. Mark tried not to think that way, suppressed the thoughts when they came, felt embarrassed to imagine what Odetta would have thought if she could have seen inside his mind. Yet the thoughts returned repeatedly, when he showered or patrolled the mall or shuffled in the line boarding the bus back to East Hollywood: a pleasant, giddy, guilty surge of optimism, the knowledge that a barrier had been swept away, that perhaps his prospects had improved.

He was in love with Odetta. He wouldn't cross the limits she had set in the Palisades, not while calling himself her friend, not after what she had endured with Phillip. If he couldn't hold his emotions in check, he could be decent enough to leave, go back to the room at the Dobson's, sleep in Griffith Park, if he had to. But he could control himself now, and so patiently watched, and waited, and hoped. The patience was painful. He saw no alternative. He hadn't given up.

•   •   •

But the next Sunday afternoon Mark returned from a furniture hunting expedition in the F-85 to find Odetta standing in front of their apartment building with an unfamiliar man. He was about thirty, black — very black, Mark thought, almost like black onyx stone — crew cut, with a short, bristly mustache only a shade darker than his skin. He wore a blazer and dress slacks, and turned to smile affably as Mark walked up. Affably, Mark thought, but also appraisingly.

"Mark, I'd like you to meet Darrin," said Odetta, in a formal, self-conscious voice Mark hadn't heard since Knockers. "He was nice enough to drive me home from church today."

"So you're the famous roommate!" Darrin boomed, and shook hands.

They stood talking on the sidewalk for ten minutes. Darrin, Mark learned, was a CPA, worked as a senior financial analyst for the county and had a "little shack" in View Park, only a mile "up the hill" from their church. Did Mark know where that was?

No, no, said Mark; not his part of town. Odetta stood holding her purse primly in front of her church dress.

"So you *hitchhiked* from Northern California!" Darrin exclaimed. "My goodness, that's something I'd never dare to do."

Odetta said it was something she'd never dare to do again, either. Said it quickly, Mark thought, as if anxious that Darrin not see her as a hitchhiker. She held out a delicate hand.

"You're a gentleman for taking me home," she said. Darrin took the cue. Odetta waved as he drove off in a new Audi.

"Seems like a nice guy," Mark said.

"Very nice," said Odetta, as they entered the building.

But that was almost all. Mark asked if she'd known him long; 'I met him last week,' said Odetta, and then asked in the next breath how the hunt for kitchen chairs had gone. To change the subject. It hadn't gone well, said Mark; they'd have to keep making do; if one of the chairs collapsed he could eat at the counter.

I'm sure you'll find something soon, said Odetta. Lightly, insincerely, as if she were talking to a customer at the mall. A barrier already had risen between them; she had something she didn't want to talk about. And she was watching him, Mark realized. To see how he was reacting to Darrin.

Which was exactly what Mark didn't want her to see, so in a few minutes said that if she didn't need the car he thought he'd check out some more thrift stores that day after all. All yours, said Odetta, and Mark left, and only relaxed his guard and let his expression show worry after he shut the door behind him.

• • •

He drove to View Park. He knew that Darrin's neighborhood was one of the wealthier black communities in L.A., but had never been there. He tried to convince himself that he was only curious. He drove uphill along the wide, winding streets, watching out nervously for Darrin's Audi as he rounded every corner, admiring the palms and strawberry trees, the plush, manicured gardens and stately, set-back homes, and ignoring the occasional scandalized glance drawn by the battered Oldsmobile in such a posh part of town.

There wasn't much he could do now about the comparison, was there? He was much better looking than Darrin, who had acne scars and a head shaped like a cinder block, but he knew how little that mattered to Odetta. And other than his looks, what did he have? He was a high school dropout who'd been on the pipe almost every day from age fifteen to the night Odetta had made him chuck his stash north of Fort Bragg. He could make up some ground, but he wasn't going to compete for ready-to-start-a-family respectability with a senior financial analyst CPA who owned a "little shack" in a neighborhood like this. And no, it wasn't all his fault. He hadn't had a dad and his ditzy mom hadn't shown him thing one about growing up, managing life, becoming an adult, but at this point what difference did 'fault' make?

He left View Park, reminded himself that he was supposed to be visiting thrift stores. He felt depressed. For the first time in more than a month he felt a craving for weed, but suppressed it determinedly, instead reasoned with himself that he was making a mountain out of a mole hill. Darren had driven Odetta home from their church once. Once. So what?

He finally found the kitchen chairs he wanted in a cavernous thrift store in East Los Angeles, with the scraped, faded letters for SWAP MEET over the entrance and racks of used clothes identified with Spanish signage. The chairs were sturdy, rattan, foldable; he could cram them into the back of the F-85. Mark lugged them to the counter, asked the clerk the price for the pair, and when Mark raised eyebrows at the $5 price the clerk gave him an Honest Abe look, Mr. Sincerity, and said that "just for you" he'd let them go for $2.75 apiece, or even a fire sale $0.75 a chair leg. A comedian.

"Ha ha ha," said Mark, and dug out a fiver. Then fell into chat with him. He needed a distraction, and thought the clerk stood out, that he didn't go with the store. He was in his fifties, squat, short, with graying temples and a friendly, intelligent expression. Mark thought he looked French.

No, the clerk said, he wasn't the owner, and hadn't been there long. He was helping out. The store was a charity; their monthly take helped fund an orphanage. The clerk had helped set sales policy, and regarded Mark solemnly as he explained his policy "reforms." All items were now 100% guaranteed from the store interior to transaction completion, he said, and fully refundable. Even if he no longer had the chairs, Mark could be reimbursed for the full $5 price merely by bringing another $5 in cash to the counter for a currency exchange.

"Ha ha ha," said Mark, and asked as he hoisted the chairs if the clerk had at least been serious about the orphanage part. "That part, yes," the clerk admitted, and then became animated.

"If you need anything else, give us a call," he said. "We might have it." He plucked a business card from a small stack by the cash register, pointed to the name printed over the phone number. "That's me."

Mark took the card to be polite, glanced at it before shoving it in his pocket. It only had the first name.

"Thanks, Daniel," Mark said.

• • •

He told himself throughout the week that he was worrying without reason, that a one-time ride home from church and a chat on the sidewalk were meaningless. Even though their conversations in the apartment had changed. She didn't want to talk about Darrin. And she was still watching him, looking away quickly without comment when he caught her. She looked sad, he thought. Resigned. Perhaps even worried about him.

Then on Saturday afternoon Mark returned to the apartment from his shift at the mall to the sound of a ringing phone. The hallway was steamy, and he heard the water running behind the bathroom door. Odetta was showering.

"Mark! The famous roommate."

Mark clutched the receiver, answered in numb monosyllables as Darrin said why he was calling. A work meeting had run a bit late. Could Mark please tell Odetta that he would pick her up in front for their date at 7:15, and not at 7:00?

Mark stepped to the bathroom door. He started to speak, but his voice came out as a hoarse, choking sound. He bit his lip, waited until he could speak normally before calling Odetta's name.

"What?" she shouted. The sound of the water stopped.

Chapter Forty-Four

Mark gave her Darrin's message, then asked if he could use the car that night.

"Didn't you need it for the CPR class tomorrow?" Odetta asked.

He did, said Mark, but if she was going to be out with Darrin he thought he'd go out for the evening, too.

CHAPTER FORTY-FIVE

So he'd go out on a date, too. In his agitation and misery that was the one thought that registered with words, that dictated movement, action. He had thought it urgent to get out of the apartment before she left the bathroom, but had not been consciously aware of the reason: that it would have been unendurable to watch the woman he loved primp in make-up, earrings and night-on-the-town dress for an evening with the wealthy Darrin. He had only thought consciously that it was time for him to date, too.

He wheeled the F-85 onto Santa Monica Boulevard and headed west, pulling the sun visor down but still having to hold his hand over his eyes and squint as he drove toward the colossal orange sphere setting over the Pacific. It was summer now, warm, would be warm on the beach, too. He still had more than an hour of daylight left. He'd head out to Venice Beach, to the Boardwalk. There'd likely be something there, and as he tried to time the stoplights and robotically followed the tail lights of other drivers did not think consciously of what 'something' would entail.

In Venice he cruised stupidly from block to block on the labyrinth of streets west of Abbot Kinney, missing several obvious parking spots before finally berthing the F-85 in a slot sandwiched between trash bins in a near alley. Then he headed toward the Boardwalk, pausing once to inspect himself in a reflective window. He'd changed into a tank top. He looked muscly. A month ago he'd taken up an every-other-day routine to buff up, to bring out his upper body and arm muscles. He'd always had a good physique, although he'd done no more to deserve it than he'd done to be handsome, and now it was better. Of course, he'd started the calisthenics only to appeal to Odetta. Or to try to.

The Boardwalk was predictably crowded late on a summer Saturday afternoon, teemed with tourists, strollers, skaters, sun-worshippers; an improvisational, ever-changing parade shuffling past open sales stalls hawking tourist gear. Mark walked behind a plump, mini-skirted redhead wobbling on skates, side-stepped an Atlas-shouldered, stripped-to-the-waist weightlifter brandishing a pink stick of cotton candy. Grimly, resignedly, unhappily he began to eye approaching women, raked his gaze from figures to faces, tried to look seductive as he strove to hold the eye of candidates. Candidates there were; Venice Beach was a hook-up spot; he was hardly alone.

But his luck was dismal. One woman after another avoided his eyes; one even curled a lip in an 'Oh, gross!' expression, as if she'd been ogled by a pot-bellied senior. Mark ambled along, past buskers, a tarot card reader, fighting to hold depression at bay as the afternoon light faded steadily to diffuse, pearly twilight. He knew why he was striking out. It was because he didn't want to. Women could tell. Something in his face was giving him away. What he wanted was to not be alone while Odetta was out with Darrin.

When the light was closer to early evening than late afternoon he joined the loitering crowd at the counter of an open air food stand. Mark bought a soda, leaned with his back to the counter and his sad eyes on the still-steady procession on the boardwalk. Where would Odetta be now with Darrin? At the restaurant, Mark decided; bantering flirtatiously with Darrin across the table of a five star restaurant in Beverly Hills or Brentwood, a place that wouldn't allow the likes of Mark past the hostess stand.

"What a cute shirt," said a voice beside him.

The speaker was a short, stocky blonde in cowboy boots and a cherry red bikini. She stood beside Mark at the counter, looked up at him with glassy, lecherous eyes.

"Thanks," Mark said.

The woman slid closer, her tanned thighs brushing Mark's leg. She touched the bottom of his faded tank top, fingered the hem. Her nails were lacquered black, decorated with crude symbols. Zodiac signs.

"You're cute, too," she said.

Mark turned toward her, smiled, felt himself responding, getting hard. So she'd pick him up, and not the other way around.

She slid her hands up his torso, pressed her fingers onto his pectorals, squeezed. How old was she? Twenty-five, at least, maybe even thirty. Older than Mark. She looked okay.

"You've got nice tits," she said.

A bearded thirty something who had been standing on the other side of the woman issued a sudden, disgusted huff and moved away from the counter. Surprised, Mark watched him walk toward the Boardwalk. So they'd been together.

"All yours," said the thirty something, and waved a dismissive hand without looking back.

"Who was that?" Mark asked.

The woman shrugged, fondled his chest. "Some asshole."

•   •   •

They had sex in the Olds. He'd figured that they'd at least look for a motel on Lincoln or Washington, but she didn't want to wait, was all over him as soon as they got in the car, and by this time Mark mostly wanted to get it over with. The street was dark, quiet, secluded. They could get away with it. He was at least horny by then, sort of, kind of, a little bit, she'd done that much, but he didn't want to be with her and wasn't interested in chalking up a ridiculous first-ever screw in an automobile. Even if almost anything he did with her would be better than thinking about Odetta with Darrin and knowing that he was all alone.

She wanted to ball in the front passenger seat. Mark tried, but she didn't want to get on top and he couldn't push the seat back far enough. So they crawled into the back. She'd ripped off her bikini bottom. She was crazy, Mark had decided. Maybe crazier than usual because of whatever she was stoned on, but crazy when sober, too. He remembered something from one of the Rhaytana letters, that if you couldn't relate to someone you at least could remember that the other person already had accumulated a lifetime of experiences, just as you had, could name just as you could the life experiences that had been most fulfilling, painful, frightening, embarrassing. But how could this woman have survived even a single three hundred sixty-five day year as the person Mark was seeing now?

She sprawled on her back on the back seat with the nape of her neck on the rear seat armrest and her knees up and spread open, with one cowboy boot pressed against the rear window. She wanted him to take off his shirt. Or as much as ordered him to. Okay, fine, that was her thing, and he felt like an acrobat as he pulled down pants, shorts, angled hips between her thighs and entered her, started to stroke, thrust, grind, and even as the clasping pressure around his cock felt physically good he thought that it was as if he were punishing himself, masochistically, degrading himself as punishment for the helpless grief and misery he felt about Odetta.

She moaned, thrust, raked his back with the zodiac sign nails. Was the Olds bouncing on its springs? Could people hear her? Mark's knee ached, the position was ridiculous, but it had been a long time, he felt approaching orgasm. And then just as he was about to come he thought of what Rhaytana had written about nature's treachery, sex as delusion, necessities of the reproductive cycle hidden by a camo curtain of passing lust.

What if he impregnated her? Sired this crazy woman's baby?

In panic, Mark pulled out, orgasmed, spurted semen up to her bikini top, her hair.

"You fucking asshole!"

She pushed him off her, looked aghast at her white-spattered bikini and belly, swiped a disgusted hand through her wetted hair

"You COCKSUCKER! Jesus, what a fucking mess. My hair ..."

She grabbed his t-shirt, mopped up the semen, threw it at him, yanked on her bikini bottom.

"Fucking faggot!"

And then was out of the car. He heard the cowboy boot heels click-click-click on the asphalt as she stomped off, still swearing. He'd never asked her name.

•　　•　　•

For the next ten minutes he sat in the back, holding the soiled shirt on his lap, looking through the windshield and side windows at what he could see of the dark, secluded street. The windows in the closest bungalow were dark, too. Maybe no one had heard them. Not that it mattered.

He didn't have another shirt. He inspected it, thought of putting it on, knew that no one would know what the wet patches were, but decided to leave it crumpled on the floor. Mark hitched up his jeans, got out of the Olds, headed shirtless back down to the Boardwalk to look for some weed.

He couldn't make up the lost ground. Okay? He couldn't rate with someone like Darrin. Odetta was decent, clean, respectable, didn't have Mark's issues; there'd be other suitors at her church and Darrin wouldn't be the only eligible black man who'd climbed the straight and narrow ladder and established a career. What Mark was was a stoner. He'd never wanted to get high so badly in his life. He'd go back to the pipe, his medicine, and move out so Odetta wouldn't be embarrassed by him or wonder how she was going to get rid of him.

It was night; the crowd at the Boardwalk had thinned. Mark crossed to the coast side, away from the crowd, surveyed the benches as he walked under the palm trees toward the beach.

It didn't take long. Maybe there was some mysterious force that pitied him, knew he'd been out of his depth with Odetta, wanted to make it easy to go back to the life he understood. Mark caught the whiff of weed, turned toward a pair sitting in the dark on a bench under a palm tree. Two young dudes, passing a joint.

Mark asked them if they knew where he could score some pot.

One guy obviously didn't want to talk, kept his head turned, stared at the ground. The other regarded Mark warily. He had blond hair to his waist, a wispy mustache, sideburns. He might have been nineteen. If that.

"No idea, man."

Mark asked if they had any extra they could sell. The teenager snorted, "Come on, man," and curled his lip. As in, 'Why don't you get your own toke and leave us alone?' But in a shaky voice Mark said if they could sell him one decent joint he'd pay five dollars for it.

The teenager looked incredulous, amused. "You'll pay me five bucks for one joint?"

Mark nodded. The teenager shrugged, fished in his coat pocket.

"We're rich," he said to his companion, and showed Mark the joint. It was big enough. Mark paid him, asked if the kid had matches, got those, too.

"You must really want to get fucked up," said the teenager, as Mark was walking away.

Mark walked, told himself that he didn't want to be in sight of the two when he lit the joint but walked much, much farther than he had to walk to get away from them. Finally when he recognized that he was moving without purpose he stopped, dropped abruptly on the sand of the open beach and sat cross-legged facing the ocean. He flipped the match book on the sand between his legs and as he looked at the Pacific held the ends of the thick, zeppelin-shaped joint between his thumbs and fingers in front of his stomach, as reverently as he might have held prayer beads.

No one was close by. He was a little chilly without the shirt. Only a little. There wasn't a wind, he wouldn't have trouble lighting up. Mark twirled the joint between his fingers, listened to the now-distant carnival sounds of the Boardwalk behind him, mixed with the gentle, steady, rhythmic roar of the incoming surf.

He'd been looking at the ocean when Odetta had made him chuck his stash, hadn't he? No, that wasn't right; she'd handed him the bag and told him to throw it himself. To show himself that he could.

Over six months ago, that had been. He'd been straight for six months.

Mark put the joint between his lips and picked up the matchbook. He opened the cover and touched the matches, but didn't break off a match stick. Instead he sat holding the matchbook with the joint in his mouth for one minute, then two, then three, until he thought that he'd slobber on the tip if he kept sitting like that. So he put down the matchbook and took the joint out of his mouth and again now twirled it lightly between his thumbs and forefingers as he held it in front of his stomach and looked at the ocean.

If he lit up now, he'd lose all chance with Odetta. Period. If she found out, at least, and he didn't think he'd be able to keep it from her. Stone cold fact. It wasn't because she'd want to be a hard ass. She might even *tell* herself to give him a second chance. But she couldn't, wouldn't be able to. Because of her dad. With all the stories she'd told about him, all the times over years and years that Daddy had slipped, said he'd do one thing and then done another: if Mark slipped too, Odetta would never see him the same way. For now, still, tonight, in this moment, Mark was a man who'd said he'd stop and had kept his word. Not like her father. He'd stop being that man if he fired up.

Maybe he wasn't a CPA like Darrin and didn't own a ritzy house in View Park, or a house anywhere, but he wasn't that bad, was he? That horrible? He was a man; didn't twenty-three qualify as a full-grown man? Didn't a twenty-three year old have the right to be in love? And if she wouldn't, because he was white or because she didn't think he was ready to be a father, did he have to punish and degrade himself and shrivel himself back into an overgrown kid stoner who didn't deserve to live with her anymore? And chuck six months sober?

So he could take his medicine.

His medicine.

He looked at the joint, watched his thumb and fingers move as he twirled it. Round and round. Then he held it still. He stared at the joint as if he were watching a television show, as if there were nothing but a big fat joint showing on the screen, and then watched his left forefinger slide up to the center of the white cylinder. He'd clipped his fingernails carelessly; the fingernail had a jagged edge. He pressed the edge on the paper. Weird; so strange; suddenly he was curious, that was all, idly curious; would the edge of his fingernail puncture the rolling paper?

So he pushed, and his fingernail edge did go through, carved a slit, an opening, and when the slit was wide and the joint was ruined Mark twirled it again, and watched the marijuana flutter between his legs onto the sand.

CHAPTER FORTY-SIX

Mark's CPR class the next morning was at a community college miles east of downtown, practically to Pomona. His second day with the borrowed Olds. Mark hunted for the auditorium, parked when he saw a likely instructor toting plastic torso dummies into an open door.

Mark walked in. He felt groggy, had stayed out until 3:00 a.m. the night before so he wouldn't run into Odetta after the night with Darrin. Still, he didn't expect a hard time of it. Life wouldn't deal him two tough hands in a row.

· · ·

But life did.

The class was a near nightmare. Every single student in the session besides Mark was already working in healthcare. Every one. A respiratory therapist, or a nurse, or a cop. Some kind of professional role. Maybe it was just chance, his bad luck, the day, the place. Nobody had said anything about having a healthcare background to sign up.

All day long he felt like the village idiot. Everyone in the class besides him already knew how to do everything. The students would kneel on the mats beside the practice dummies, and every time he'd be the bonehead who got something wrong: who didn't tilt the head back far enough, or too far; put the heel of his hand too low or high on the chest for CPR, didn't pump hard enough.

The worst part was dealing with one other student. The nurse. She didn't mean any harm, Mark knew; she was a brassy, cheery Irish type who figured everyone else had armadillo-thick skin and wouldn't mind being pointed out as the class moron. But he did mind. He was shaky, stressed, about Odetta, Darrin, the close call the night before. And what was he supposed to do in a professional-level CPR class except suck it up? Break out crying? When he wanted to be an EMT, to speed to the hospital in an ambulance with gunshot victims? Could he cry in the ambulance, too?

"Oh, Ma-aark!" she'd call out, when he was the only one in the class to forget to do something. "Time to wake up, Mark!" To get the other students to laugh. So he did suck it up, made himself laugh along with the others. But it rattled him. It almost felt like something evil and malicious in life had it in for him. Like it was furious that he *hadn't* broken six months of sobriety the night before, like it wanted to drag him down, make him fail, put him back behind a liquor store cash register with his stash in his pocket. Keep him under its thumb.

Which bothered him too, and it must have shown, because finally at the mid-point another student discreetly moved his practice CPR dummy next to Mark's mat, and helped him out for the rest of the course. Ricardo. A working EMT. He was only a few years older than Mark, a short, thick-set dude with a wide jaw and a friendly expression. He seemed to know what Mark would have trouble with, coached him in a low voice while the instructor spoke.

The course wrapped up at 4:00 in the afternoon. Mark had his cert. He'd passed.

•   •   •

"EMT training's not going to be like today," Ricardo said later.

They were sitting in a shopping center cafe next to the freeway, drinking coffee and watching traffic drone past on the 10. Mark had asked if he could treat, to thank him for the help.

"Basic CPR is a whole 'nuther animal," said Ricardo. "Teachers, babysitters, John Q. Citizens who want to be Good Samaritans." He looked at Mark sympathetically. "How can you expect not to feel stupid if you're in a class with professionals who already know this stuff?"

Mark nodded. That was how he'd felt.

"When you start EMT training, everyone's going to be as green as you are."

Mark told about seeing the ambulance crew deliver the baby. Ricardo whistled lightly. That was unusual, he said; he'd never done it. "But you *will* use CPR," he added, and looked at Mark seriously. "No ifs, ands or buts, in an ambulance in L.A. Don't kid yourself."

And then Mark asked Ricardo about his toughest day on the job.

Ricardo leaned back in his chair, stared thoughtfully past Mark at the freeway. Seconds passed. Mark wondered if he'd accidentally touched a wound, reminded Ricardo of some horrible accident scene that he'd wanted to forget.

"For me personally, honestly," Ricardo said at last, "my hardest day was after the shift, when some son of a bitch of a waiter served me an Irish coffee. I'm an alcoholic. Maybe that shows what a heartless bastard I am for not feeling more for my patients, but that's the truth."

Mark stared, surprised. But Ricardo wasn't embarrassed. He told the story matter-of-factly, ruefully. He came from a family of drunks, was a chronic drunk by his late teens, but cleaned up, joined Alcoholics Anonymous, and had logged almost two sober years when he ordered a mocha while out with the crew, and the waiter brought the alcoholic coffee instead.

"One sip, I tasted the whiskey," Ricardo said. "I was going through personal shit, I'd broken up with my girlfriend. I wanted that whiskey bad. *Bad*." He grinned, shook his head. "All I had to do was keep drinking what he'd put in front of me. And then order a refill. Instead I got up, said I had the runs, went into the john, sat in a stall for a half-hour until I could get my act together. Easily my toughest night." He looked at Mark. "Maybe that doesn't make any sense to you."

No, Mark said, it did make sense.

And then he told Ricardo everything. Or almost everything. He felt that he was being reckless, he hardly knew Ricardo, but he badly, badly wanted to talk, and once he started he couldn't make himself stop. He told about Odetta, Darrin, the life he'd had in NorCal, the close call the night before.

"I don't want to go back on the pipe again. Okay? Everything I've got now is 'cause I'm not getting stoned. Last night scared the shit out of me."

Ricardo smiled, patted him on the shoulder, said Mark could come to his home AA meeting.

CHAPTER FORTY-SEVEN

At breakfast the next morning Mark decided to ask about the date with Darrin. Odetta smiled wryly.

"Darrin is married."

She looked at her bowl again, stirred pecans resignedly into her oatmeal. Mark had time to control his expression, to not look pleased.

"When did you find out?"

"When he wanted to kiss me."

She talked matter-of-factly about the date, between spoons of oatmeal, sips of orange juice. While watching him, still, as she had seemed to watch and study him ever since the encounter with Darrin on the sidewalk.

Yes, Darrin had taken her to a very nice restaurant, the fanciest restaurant she'd ever seen, as a matter of fact, but in the Valley, not Beverly Hills. Near Encino. Then to a ritzy club afterward, but by then she'd noticed a few details of his story that didn't add up, and when he slid close in the dark booth and went for the big smooch she dipped into harpy-at-the-mall mode to find out why.

He was planning to separate from his wife, Darrin told her. *Planning* to; hadn't yet.

"I told him I wouldn't tell the minister, but that I'd call his wife if I saw him trying to make time with any more women in the congregation. Aren't I a meanie?"

Mark shrugged.

"Where were you Saturday, Mark? Anything special? Out drag racing for pinks in my ugly car?"

"I hit the beach."

Odetta raised her eyebrows. "On a date?"

Mark grimaced. "If you want to call it that."

"Oh, Mark!"

Odetta sat up straight, started to beam at him, but bumped her glass in the process and needed a minute to sponge up the juice. She seemed flustered.

"That's wonderful! Finally! How was it?"

"Horrible. You don't want to hear about it. Trust me."

Odetta made a sympathetic face. Or tried to. Mark thought grimly that his interpretation of her expression was wishful thinking. He had thought she looked relieved.

• • •

Ricardo's Alcoholics Anonymous "home group" was in the back room of a church in West L.A.. Mark sat by Ricardo in a circle of fifteen folding chairs, with his back to a table supporting a coffee pot and AA brochures. The participants were nondescript, could have been chosen at random from a supermarket checking line. Mark recognized one portly businessman type he'd occasionally glimpsed at a desk behind the display window of a bank on Sunset.

It felt weird. Ricardo told the group that Mark's issue was with pot, but it was strange to listen to the others tell story after story of dealing with booze. And the "12 steps" felt weird, too. The third step was to "turn our will and our lives over to the care of God." What kind of crap was that?

But he still related to some of the alcohol stories, when the participants took turns "sharing" for five minutes about whatever they wanted to talk about. And his own five minutes to talk affected him. The others obviously understood what a trial he'd had on the beach with that joint. He'd never told anyone before what he was going through.

On the way out he picked up a list of other meetings in Los Angeles.

• • •

All Mark had told Odetta was that he was going to get together with a working EMT he'd met in the CPR class. Going to meetings regularly would be different; he thought he should tell her why, so she wouldn't wonder. They spent most of their free time together.

He talked to her in the evening, found her sitting as she often did with mall trade magazines on the living room couch. Her hair still wasn't long enough to part, but she wasn't bald anymore. Mark thought she looked unusually pretty.

He felt proud of her. Her job was completely secure; Rory didn't hide his admiration, had even talked about a promotion. She'd found her niche. Even in his Norcal stoner days he'd observed that people did way, way better in a profession that genuinely interested them. Odetta loved shopping malls. She called them oases.

Mark stood in front of the couch, said he might start going out a couple of evenings a week, and wanted to tell her why.

"Last weekend, I had kind of a close call. With weed."

Odetta's expression clouded. Mark felt suddenly hot, defensive, as if he'd actually slipped.

"I didn't take any. Okay? I am not like your father. I told you that I wouldn't, and I'm keeping my word. But on Saturday, I ... got pretty close. So ..."

He told her about the meetings. There wasn't a program for marijuana. AA was the best he could do.

She listened, looked sympathetic, unhappy. And something more, as if there were something she wanted to tell him that she wasn't ready to say.

"This was last Saturday?"

Mark nodded.

"When you were at the beach, and I was out with Darrin?"

Mark nodded.

"Did it have anything to do with me?"

At least ten seconds passed in silence. Mark pursed his lips, looked at her defiantly, didn't answer the question.

"You've got the right to be your own woman. Okay? You told me the score on the Palisades. It's not fair to lay some big trip on you when I'm your roommate. I just thought I should tell you that I'm going to be hitting the meetings. The rest is my problem."

⋅   ⋅   ⋅

Odetta now often looked preoccupied. She seemed to study him more often, would quickly avert her eyes if he looked at her. She seemed worried, ill at ease. His sense grew that she had something she wanted to say to him.

It was because of the near slip on the beach, Mark thought. Maybe he shouldn't have told her. Maybe now she expected to come home any day and find a young white version of her prom-ise-breaking father sitting red-eyed on the couch, full of slurred apologies, stinking of dope.

Finally he asked one morning if she wanted him to move out.

"No, Mark," she said quietly. She shook her head, winced, as if the idea were painful to think about. "No, no. Please. That's the last thing I want. The last thing." And kept saying 'no, no' under her breath for the next minute.

.   .   .

One Saturday they returned for breakfast to the hippyish restaurant that had treated them to the seed rolls after their hike to the Observatory. Mark thought it was too counter-culture for Odetta's tastes, but it was nice to go to a place where other diners didn't sneak glances.

The Mama Cass waitress recognized them, complimented Odetta on her hair as she showed them to a table. A few min-utes later they both stood briefly to allow a radiant-looking Asian mother in a tie-died dress to push her baby carriage to the rear of the restaurant. The baby responded to Odetta's coos with a merry, toothless smile.

They sat down, but now Odetta seemed preoccupied again. She didn't answer a question Mark had about Rory, sat staring at her plate and twisting her napkin around her finger. Then abruptly she asked:

"Mark, do you ever think about becoming a father?"

In a light, casual voice, but she was watching him, wanted to hear what he had to say.

"Well, no," Mark said. "Frankly. But I'm less than a year sober. I'm still getting adjusted to a new world."

"What if it happened, though? If she got pregnant and didn't want to have an abortion?"

Mark thought. He'd get by, he said. He'd already told her about the delay to start his EMT courses, but this time for sure he had a slot reserved for training that started in six weeks, and when he graduated he'd be in a real career, with better pay. And if he had a kid his mom would want to help out. Like Odetta had said her own mom would help, if she had a baby.

Odetta listened, twisting the napkin, sometimes lowering her eyes to the table when Mark looked at her. Mark wondered wearily if she was sizing him up as a potential future babysitter.

.   .   .

For two days Mark winced every time he had to take a leak. He figured that red bikini had given him gono, but the VD clinic offered unexpected good news a few days later. Maybe he'd had a urinary tract infection. What he didn't have was the clap; he was clean.

His main obstacle now in staying straight was how he felt about Odetta. She'd joined a group at her church for singles, had already had lunch with another man from the congregation: Reggie, divorced, twenty-nine, an attorney. Odetta had said that he'd spent the whole meal gabbing about himself, but how long would it be before she met a man who appealed to her? She was twenty-three. Women that age needed bear spray to chase off suitors, and there were lots of eligible men at her church.

Mark felt as if he'd been diagnosed with terminal cancer, that his days were numbered. Sooner or later — next week, next month, in three months — she'd break the news about another man, another CPA or attorney or, who knew?, an executive, banker, doctor, some responsible bachelor who wouldn't be a sneak-around like Darrin or a me-me-me like Reggie, and then for Mark it would be game over, he'd be like the cancer patient watching the doctor grimly shake his head and say there wasn't any point in more therapy. How could he compete with a man in that league?

He could vent about Odetta when he shared in AA, and that helped, but the meetings weren't perfect. He wasn't an alcoholic. He could have collected meeting recovery chips for six, seven, however many months of sobriety, but what was the point if alcohol for him was something he could take or leave?

Worse: a few of the regulars leaned on weed to help them stay off the bottle. Not many, but a few. It was tough to listen to an alkie share about how he'd stayed sober by rushing home to smoke a bowl.

· · ·

One night after a meeting he had a run-in with a pot-smoking newcomer. Mark had never seen the guy before, had learned by then that any kind of ding-a-ling could wander in from another galaxy and disrupt a meeting once or twice before rolling back into the gutter with his bottle. This newcomer's name was Shane. He reeked of weed. Mark deliberately sat on the other side of the circle, but noticed that Shane was staring at him intently when Mark talked about staying off pot.

Then after the meeting Shane wanted to talk to him. He stepped up while the meeting secretary Enzo was stacking brochures and the other alkies were filing out of the church.

"You've got it all wrong about marijuana," said Shane, and looked at Mark belligerently. Marijuana heals you, he said. Marijuana was used in ancient Assyria.

"If you want," said Shane, "we can go out and smoke a bowl right now."

"You flaming ASSHOLE!" shouted Enzo. "Out! Out now!"

Enzo looked like a hippified Al Capone, had regularly been cast as a TV cop show heavy in what he called a mercifully short acting career. Shane grumbled, but shuffled off, mumbling to himself. Mark figured he'd stay to help Enzo tidy up.

"Thanks."

Enzo shrugged. "These things happen."

Mark stacked the chairs while Enzo dealt with the coffee pot and finished collecting the AA lit. They left, stood together on the sidewalk in front of the church.

Enzo looked at Mark appraisingly. He was ten years sober.

"What you need is a sponsor," he said. "I mean, everybody in AA needs one, but especially if you're in a program that's not a perfect fit for you." He nodded at the church. "You laughed it off, but what that bozo did to you in there wasn't great therapy."

Mark half-smiled, stared at passing traffic. Enzo held up his hand, counted off fingers.

"One, a sponsor to help you work the program. You can take 'higher power' however you want, but you need someone to hear your inventory and help you do the steps. And two, maybe especially, a sponsor you can call and vent with if you hit a rough spot and want to go back on the weed. You could have some heavy sailing coming up with this what's-her-name you keep talking about."

"Odetta."

"There are people in program who've dealt with issues with weed. You can ask around."

Then Enzo thought of something. He snapped his fingers, thrust his hand in his coat pocket, pulled out a battered pocket address book.

"I think I know someone who could sponsor you. He's in AA, but he was heavy, heavy into weed, and gave that up, too. And he's long time sober." He hesitated, looked at Mark appraisingly. "His Higher Power is the group, though. He doesn't believe in God."

Mark said that was fine. Enzo flipped through the address book, then held it in front of Mark, pointed to an address in East L.A.

"It's for a thrift store," Enzo said. "He works there. Daniel."

Mark's eyes bulged. "I know that place! I bought chairs there! You mean the guy who works at the counter? French looking dude?"

"He's Spanish," corrected Enzo. "From the north coast of Spain. That's him, though."

Enzo pocketed the address book. He smiled broadly, pleased that he'd offered a good suggestion.

"Super nice guy," Enzo said. "You might even have heard of him. He had his fifteen minutes of fame awhile ago."

"Oh?"

"Do you remember when *White Rhino* published *Letters from Rhaytana*?"

CHAPTER FORTY-EIGHT

11/7

Don't laugh, Paul,

   but coincidence, fate or both today find
me within the municipal boundaries of a
comedian's punch line: notorious Barstow,
"America's armpit," too frequently regarded
as the homeliest city in the Southwest. We
passed it occasionally on the I-15, may have
ventured a disinterested glance from the
freeway, but never stopped in town. Do you
remember? A little burg, about a third of
the way northeast on the slog from L.A. to
Vegas? Barstow lures motorists from the I-15
with gas stations, motels, outlet stores
and, I'll admit, not a whole hey of a lot
more.

   You now likely gird loins for a torrent of Barstow jokes; I'm in town, after
all, must have collected plenty. Well, not
from these lips, Paul, never again! I may
even indignantly knock over the TV if Carson
includes another Barstow chestnut in his
Tonight Show monologue.

   To me, Barstow has become one of the
most attractive spots in California. It
is so beautified by the radiant soul of a
single individual: a gray, stooped, leathery-cheeked sixty year old, the indomitable
Valentina. While she is here, San Francisco,
Monterey and Carmel will seem shabby and
soulless in comparison.

I met her on arrival. A fellow friend of
Bill W. had given me a lift west from Nee-
dles. I spotted the no-longer-spry Valentina hobbling beside Route 66 as we motored
in, suggested that we offer a ride. Valentina insisted on repaying the favor with
a snack in her humble cottage on the city
periphery.

My friend liked Valentina, but that was
all; he soon bade a polite adieu. I, in
contrast, bonded strongly. I bed down in a
nearby motel (where I scribble these words),
but return to the cottage daily to spend
hours in platonic chat, and also to assist
in some simple chores and repairs she is too
infirm to comfortably handle unaided.

Valentina is my confessor. To her I can
describe not only my profound, abiding shame
for my partner Abby's death, but also my
more private and, I'll admit, less reasonable torment in knowing that I also failed
the two month old soul then growing inside
her, that could have come to term as my first
and only child.

11/8

Paul, dear Paul,

Valentina also lost a loved one: her son
Mateo, a UNAM undergraduate, killed among
dozens or hundreds of unarmed protesters
in the 1968 Tlatelolco massacre in Mexico
City.

Mexico would host the Summer Olympics that year, had spent profligately on preparations. Mateo and likely millions more thought that the funds should have been spent elsewhere. They protested. Demonstrations grew, spread. President Díaz Ordaz knew that the world's news crews would soon flock to the capital to cover the Olympics. He wanted them to point their cameras at the pricey re-do of the Estadio Olímpico Universitario, and not at slogan-chanting dissidents.

On October 2, troops were sent to surround ten thousand demonstrators in the Plaza de las Tres Culturas. A massacre ensued. The body count ranges from forty into the hundreds.

I knew embarrassingly little about Tlatelolco, which likely would have pleased Mexico's leaders. They have fought determinedly to whitewash and cover up the massacre ever since. Fortunately, a journalist published an oral history, *La noche de Tlatelolco*, which includes eyewitness accounts of the carnage. Poor Valentina's copy is falling apart. She has read it hundreds of times. Two of the interviewees knew her son.

About Mateo's death Valentina is surprisingly matter-of-fact, unbitter. Her son was an idealist in a grossly corrupt country, knew before Tlatelolco that Mexico had murdered, tortured, kidnapped. Only luck, she says, saves such idealists from martyrdom. Valentina seems resigned to life in a world led largely by evildoers.

Mateo was her only child. About her feeling for him Valentina is not stoic at all: she adores his memory, reveres it, pays an almost continuous homage. Five framed photos of the slim, delicate, boyish Mateo decorate her living room. Her coffee table creaks beneath an enormous Day of the Dead *ofrenda*, which she hasn't yet dismantled, nearly a week after the holiday's conclusion. It includes more photos, his high school graduation ring, his baseball glove, a straight A report card from fourth grade, more. I have spent hours with Valentina on the sofa behind this coffee table, her open photo albums balanced on our knees, listening to her wistful narrative as she leafs through the pages.

Valentina encourages me to talk not only about my shame and grief for my partner Abby, as others have encouraged me, but also about the two month old fetus that perished with her. Paul, why does this torment me so? Miscarriages are common before the ninety day mark. The fetus likely was the size of a kidney bean, looked like a tadpole. If she'd miscarried, the kidney bean probably would have disappeared in the West L.A. sewer system. And I am adamantly pro-choice (as is Valentina, although with greater reservations). Why such anguish?

Because it was my issue, sprang from the fertilization of her egg by my seed. Because at two months it had begun to develop lungs, ears, arms, legs, and perished in such an ignominious fashion, as rotting tissue, practically an abscess within the uterus of a partner who wouldn't have overdosed if I had attended to her decently. I wring hands, am embarrassed, struggle for words to describe my distress. I never even knew the little thing's gender. What might it have been? A baseball star, ballerina, Mafia hit man, human rights crusader?

Route 66 traffic drones past my motel room window; the walls shudder occasionally with the vibration of a passing eighteen wheeler. Far from perfect, but I don't think I'll ever make another joke about a place where people live. Even the shabbiest place might include a soul like Valentina's.

My eyes have begun to glaze. To be continued.

11/9

I don't stump for life, Paul. I say that our meat machine existence simply is, like the moon, dirt, Pluto, solar radiation, that its worthiness (and the worthiness of the eons-consuming evolution through which we developed intelligence, for both joy and frequent agony) is to be judged by the individual, that the only demonstrable alternative is nothingness, non-life. Life for some is an utter hell, a nightmare. For millions it is at least brutal and short. I'm not going to insist that they cherish what I wouldn't want to endure.

But Valentina does stump for life, seems to advocate for it unconditionally. She acknowledges horrors that are suffered, but still champions it, defiantly, adamantly, passionately, and flings my non-life argument back at me. How could anyone offer nothingness as an alternative? Life is all.

Valentina is a believer, as you might have guessed, is willing to think mystically. Her Mateo hungered and thirsted for righteousness, as described by his namesake in Matthew 5:6; he is thus blessed, she believes, and believes also that on some unknown plane of existence he is today present, intelligent, conscious. She says that she has felt his soul beside her when she has most grieved for him, comforting her with benevolent smile, reassuring her that he can return. Valentina's faith could be described as a customized Christianity. Christians generally don't believe in reincarnation, but Valentina is partial to the idea.

She shared a beautiful short story: *Las ruinas circulares*, by the Argentine literary giant, Borges. (As you would expect, given Valentina's heritage, all our chat is in Spanish. Your library likely stocks an English translation of the story, if I've piqued your curiosity.) *Circulares* tells the story of a shaman who ventures deep into the jungle to dream a man into life, to make the dreamed man as flesh-and-blood real and three-dimensional solely through effort expended in deep trance. In trance, the shaman communicates with a cosmic amphitheater of unborn souls, some centuries distant, each ready to be made corporeal. He must select only one to build, to sculpt, to transform into a living earthly son.

Valentina believes that her martyred, righteousness-longing Mateo would be first in line.

And I like to warmed by her belief, Paul, as I might warm my fingers over a candle in her *ofrenda*; that a similar incarnation might be possible for my unrealized, unconsummated child. Silly, I guess. Reincarnation is conjecture, a notion, unsupported by any convincing evidence. But it is a comforting notion, and as we sit together on that sofa before the *ofrenda* in the waning light of late afternoon I open my soul to Valentina as I have to few others, and yield to the tearful imagining that the incomplete little life arrested in Abby's womb might have another chance at life, to be born.

Valentina encourages me. My child's gender was never known, so she helped me pick out a unisex name, suitable for girl or boy. I adored it as soon as she suggested it. The name is a word for a color, always my favorite: the profound, fathomless, magical hue of the deepest, deepest blue, a color suggestive of a mystical gate between worlds, dimensions, and because we speak in Spanish the name for my longed-for child-to-be gets an acute accent over the first letter:

Índigo.

CHAPTER FORTY-NINE

The business card said that the thrift store was open until 10:00 p.m. At 8:30 the next evening Mark walked up from the nearest bus stop, his copy of *Letters* tucked in his back pocket. He felt calm. He knew he would have been freaked out if he'd never met Rhaytana, but he *had* met him, talked to him, even come close to haggling with him when he'd bought the chairs. He just hadn't known then who the guy at the counter was.

The thrift store looked more cavernous at night under the flickering ceiling lights than it had during the day. Customers milled quietly around racks of coats, dresses, shoes, browsed the aisles of the furniture section where Mark had found the rattan chairs.

Daniel — Rhaytana — stood by the cash register, hands on a turntable, arguing heatedly in Spanish with a thirtyish Latina on the other side of the counter. She was tall, angry, pretty, called Rhaytana or the turntable a 'chinga' something or other while repeatedly rubbing her fingertips with a contemptuous thumb.

Rhaytana stepped back, held up his hands in a 'What can I do?' gesture. The Latina flipped him off, stomped out. Mark stepped up to the counter as a sheepish-looking Rhaytana was moving the turntable to the floor.

Rhaytana recognized him.

"The young gentleman," he said. "What ware may we offer for your pleasure tonight, kind sir? A girdle, perhaps? A space suit?"

"I'm in program," Mark said. He described the conversation with Enzo, the recommendation to look for a sponsor who had also had problems with marijuana.

Rhaytana became serious.

"It's possible." he said. "I've got one sponsee now, but I could take two. We can set up a time to talk. I'd like to know who I'm dealing with."

"Also," Mark said, "I'd like an autograph."

Mark took out his rumpled, dog-eared, underlined, obviously read and re-read copy of *Letters*, put it on the counter.

Rhaytana shut his eyes, pressed his hands on the counter, lowered his head with an expression of enormous weariness.

"*Lo que faltaba*," he muttered.

"What?"

"Are you going to tell all your friends about me?"

Rhaytana regarded him with a defensive, vulnerable expression, as if he were a shopkeeper bargaining with gangsters running a protection racket.

"What?"

"I think I'm doing good work here. I can come every day. They don't have to pay me. This is a good charity. If you blast the news all over L.A. and I have to quit ..."

"I'm not going to blast the news about anything!" said Mark hotly.

To an obviously skeptical, unhappy Rhaytana, Mark provided background: his years-long interest in *Letters*, the move to L.A., the lucky coincidence of his encounter with Enzo.

"I'm going to tell my roommate Odetta, and that's it. I don't know anyone else here to tell, and neither does she. Can you give me a break? Jesus!"

Mark sensed someone behind him, stepped aside to allow a grandfatherly looking man to buy a sweater. Rhaytana shut the cash register drawer, regarded Mark again as the man hobbled out. He looked slightly mollified.

"You understand that I never expected those letters to be published. If I'd had any idea of what I'd go through, I would have told Paul 'no.' I am not a guru." He looked exasperated. "Half the planet over age fifty could have written a lot of what I wrote. You get older, you figure some things out."

Mark felt vaguely as if he were bargaining with a supervisor for a day off.

"Look," he said quietly. "You're not a guru. I get it. But I came all the way to Los Angeles to meet you, I sent a seven page letter to your pal Leonard ..."

Rhaytana looked surprised. "Leonard never told me anything about a letter."

Mark closed his eyes, exhaled a weary groan, continued. "In that case, I wasted my time writing a seven page letter that your wonderful friend Leonard likely never intended to forward and threw away. And now I'm here, after a long bus ride, and you've got more than an hour before the store closes, and the customers aren't exactly stampeding the cash register. So, do you mind if I keep talking to you awhile? Oh, Mr. Great Rhaytana, sir? Please?"

"If you put it that way." Rhaytana half-smiled, nodded at a stool behind the counter. "Have a seat."

Mark slid onto the stool. For the next half-hour he told his story: the whole story, from Greta's first call at the hotline to his stint as a mall Santa to his discovery of Odetta's identity near Pismo Beach and their life since in East Hollywood. Rhaytana listened, interrupted occasionally to ask for repetition or clarification, paused occasionally when a customer had a question or was ready to pay.

"So," he said at last, when Mark was done, "your greatest threat to your sobriety is how you feel about Odetta."

"I guess."

Rhaytana looked at him levelly. "You haven't made any overtures since the Palisades, because she set boundaries there and you don't want to be a royal pain as a roommate, and think she's been through enough grief with men with ... with ..."

"With Phillip."

Rhaytana nodded. "With Phillip. But! on the Palisades she also wouldn't answer your question about being attracted to you, and looked relieved when she found our your fling on the Boardwalk didn't work out, and has been mooning around and sneaking looks at you for the past month. And!" Rhaytana held up an emphatic forefinger. "And, she still hasn't seen the heavy artillery, which is that you're the great savior Parker from the hotline. You haven't told her."

Mark took a deep breath. "And I don't ever want to tell her. If I can go to my grave knowing ..."

"No! Forget it!" Rhaytana interrupted with a brisk wave of his hand. "If you want to work with me in any way at all, I mean at all: adios, Parker. Parker never existed. You pulled her through her crisis. You were a dropout stoner when you did it, but it was still you, and she's going to find out."

Mark swallowed, stared at the short, squat Spaniard who regarded him from the cash register. Rhaytana looked determined.

"What I think you ought to do is walk out of this thrift store, go home, talk to this Ms. Odetta and tell her what you just told me. You've been with this lady a long time. You've been trying to be a gentleman, but it's time to put your cards on the table, Parker hole card included, and make your big pitch. If Darrin and this other what's-his-face have the right to be suitors, you do, too."

"And if she says no ..." Rhaytana grimaced. "And if she says no, which she has every right to do: you've got to move out of there as soon as you can, and try to forget about her. If I'm going to be your sponsor, I won't bet on anyone with less than one year of sobriety trying to stay clean while she's being wined and dined by Mr. Wonderful right under your nose."

Mark squirmed, averted his eyes, felt his face getting hot.

"I hear you," he said. "Thank you. Seriously. Maybe this weekend, we can ..."

Rhaytana shook his head. "Unh unh. Not this weekend. You might lose your nerve."

He looked under the counter, pulled out a crumpled cap, stepped up to stand close to Mark's stool. Rhaytana looked suddenly ferocious, ferocious and cheerful.

"You want me to be a guru? Okay. Just once. I'll be a guru. I'll put on my guru hat."

Rhaytana tugged the cap onto his head. A beret.

He stepped closer still, until Mark could feel his breath on his neck. Rhaytana's eyes were merry, steely, set. He extended his forefinger, pressed it to Mark's chest.

"You get on that bus, you go home, you talk to Odetta, you tell her everything. *¿Estamos?* Parker included. Parker absolutely included.

"Tonight, pal. Not tomorrow, not this weekend. You tell her tonight."

CHAPTER FIFTY

An hour later Mark stood in the dark hallway before Odetta's closed bedroom door, trying to summon up the nerve to knock. He was trembling. His life wouldn't be the same after they spoke. If she wanted him to move out, he might never see her again.

Mark shut his eyes, cursed himself as a coward. He knocked.

No answer. He knocked harder.

"What is it?" Odetta mumbled sleepily.

"It's me. Can I come in?"

"I was sleeping."

"I'm sorry. I need to talk to you now."

"It's open."

Mark had only been in Odetta's bedroom a couple of times, to fix a sticking window and help set up the bed frame they'd dragged up from the basement. Odetta was sitting up in bed with her head bunched against pillows, yawning, her drowsy face and the top of her lacy yellow nightie lit from the window by the faint saffron light of a distant street lamp. The heavy fronds of a date palm shadowed part of the glass, whisked restlessly in the evening's light breeze.

"I have a meeting tomorrow morning," she said.

Mark took a deep breath. "It can't wait until tomorrow."

Odetta shrugged resignedly, sleepily, nodded at a wood chair at the wall. Mark pulled it to the bed. Odetta rubbed her eyes, looked at him, seemed to be realizing through sleepiness how upset he was.

"What's wrong?"

"I met Rhaytana."

Odetta was surprised. "He exists? A real person?"

Mark nodded. "I told him about you. He said I had to talk to you as soon as I got home. To tell you something." Mark clasped his hands, kneaded anxious fingers. "Odetta, I've been keeping a big secret from you."

She sat up straighter against the headboard, now regarded him intently, seriously, perhaps not still fully awake but far more awake than she'd been seconds earlier. Mark tried to control his breathing. He realized almost angrily that he was again responding physically to her. The response had almost disappeared during her interlude with Darrin, when any hope of intimacy had seemed lost, but now had returned with the giddy, terrifying prospect of confessing his true feeling.

"Odetta, why didn't you go to Saint Catherine's?"

"Excuse me?"

"Saint Catherine's. The women's shelter. Why didn't you go there to get away from Phillip?"

"Well ..."

Odetta glanced at him as she thought, as if she wanted to ask a question before answering.

"They wouldn't let me in," she said, finally. "I tried, but they said that they'd changed their policy, they were getting abused women who aren't Pentecostal and that I had to be Pentecostal to get emergency housing. And I'm not Pentecostal. I'm just not, so they wouldn't take me."

She paused, looked at him in a different way. "Mark, when did I ever tell you about Saint Catherine's?"

"You never told me about Saint Catherine's, Odetta." Mark said quietly. "In all the time you've known me since the mall, you never mentioned Saint Catherine's to me. I told you about it."

Odetta looked bewildered, obviously hadn't caught on. Mark started to speak, but his voice broke. He swallowed, turned his head to one side, found himself staring at two framed photos on her nightstand.

(Was that you who made me look, Índigo?)

The photos had to be of her parents. He'd never seen them before. Odetta's mother stared into the lens with resigned, weary eyes over a forced smile, as if unable to conceal the enduring trials of her life from the camera lens.

And there was the infamous father. Why did Odetta have the picture there? To be fair? To not exclude him, to acknowledge his role? Mark contemplated the photo of the great promise-breaker: a rugged, unquestionably handsome man, with Romeo eyes, a dazzling, insincere smile that seemed to apologize for its own insincerity.

"Odetta, can you try to pretend, for a second: what if you'd been a different kind of person? That you'd dropped out of school, and got high every day, and mostly just hung out being a stoner.

That you'd never really amounted to much. And you knew it, too, when you looked in the mirror."

Mark swallowed, bowed his head, fighting to control his voice. "And then somehow even though you're a piece of shit you manage to do something good and really important for someone who's way better than you. And that person doesn't know who you are, and gets all these crazy ideas about you as a big, respectable type hero, and is grateful. Wouldn't it make sense to want to keep it secret and not want that person to ever know what you really are? That as low and junky as you are you did something that helped in that way, that put you in another league?"

She'd slid back on the bed, holding the frilly top of her nightie, so that now only half of her face was lit in the wan light of the street lamp. Had she caught on? He couldn't tell. She stared at him fixedly, hardly seemed to breathe.

"Odetta, you never asked me who that woman was that I was so obsessed with at the mall. Did you?" Mark managed a small chuckle. "Odetta, would you believe, I'd never seen her. I didn't know what she looked like. I only knew her name. When she called me at the hotline. I volunteered there.

"When *you* called me, Odetta. You said your name was Greta. Greta."

Her face was frozen, lips set, the visible eye wide, unblinking, astonished. Mark breathed hoarsely, sat leaning forward with his forearms on his thighs, looked uncomprehendingly at wet drops on the back of one hand. He almost never cried.

"I'm afraid that's the truth. Parker the college professor was just old pothead dropout Mark the whole time. I got that job at the mall to try to find you, and couldn't even stay off the pipe long enough not to reek on the Santa throne. And then that night near Pismo I finally found out who you are.

"But I'm not on the pipe now. I've been clean every single day since you made me chuck my stash. I'm not like your father. I kept my word. I'm not a big Mr. Successful like Darrin or Reggie, but I'm going to be an EMT, and that's a respectable job. EMTs help people. That's the start of a real career. And I think it ought to count for something that we've been together all this time since that hitchhiking trip, and how I feel about you. I absolutely adore you, Odetta. I've never loved a woman as much as I love you."

That was as far as he got. For the next few minutes he wondered dizzily if she intended to rape him.

Suddenly he was on his back on the bed, Odetta straddling him, fingers in his hair, kissing him feverishly, thirstily. He touched her temple and the nape of her neck, far more tenderly than she touched him, slid his fingers adoringly into the short, natural hair that he had watched sprout, grow. Then she let him roll her onto her side, and their embrace changed, her kisses and caresses becoming more imploring, yielding, feminine as his own became hungrier, male, urgent, his adoring for her now also spurred, fueled by a furious, shackled lust, the crucial need to penetrate, to push deeply up and into her body, and even in this madness a tiny voice in the back of his brain told him that he was about to become a father.

(Which was you also, wasn't it, Índigo? That would be like you. You'd want to be fair.)

They struggled out of their clothes.

Her vagina was soaked, warm, swollen, ready. She hiked her knees up high, knees hovering over her shoulders, lips parted, eyes vulnerable, whispering his name. He pressed his fingers on the shaft of his cock to control the throbbing, shifted his knees on the sheets to change the angle of his hips to enter her, to push in, gently but urgently, completely, and clenching his buttocks and also whispering her name began to flex his hips, to rhythmically stroke.

And this was too much for her. She cried out, crossed her ankles high on his back, and, he was sure, orgasmed, violently, shudderingly, arching her back beneath him to push up his hips and then collapsing, panting, sobbing, and needing to push her hands on his chest for him to understand that she needed to recover. So he stopped, supporting his weight on his hands with his penis rigid and deep inside her, stiff now to a point of numbness, beyond any familiar physical sensation of pleasure, and the little voice *(Your voice, Índigo.)* reminded him again almost bemusedly that he was about to become a parent.

When she was ready he began to stroke again, to pump, thrust, supporting his torso on outstretched arms, not wanting to take his eyes off her. She tightened her jaw and urgently met the rhythm of his thrusts and looked at him almost defiantly as she did, as if to show boldly that the church-going Odetta who wouldn't swear could be as carnal and sexual and wild as was her image of the women he'd bedded before. But this also soon became too much for her, and with a moan and crying out of his name lay still and open, yielding and passive and overwhelmed, and now Mark bent his arms to rest weight on elbows to stroke more deeply, concentrating on her pleasure, and then Odetta managed to whisper *(you whispered, Índigo)* what he already knew: that she wasn't using birth control.

He drove on, determinedly. Always later in remembering the moment he knew that he could have stopped then. Did he seek selfishly and neurotically to bind her to him through child bearing, although he should have known that the Odetta willing to couple with him at all never thereafter could have treated him as dispensable, child or no child? Was it only to selfishly consummate pleasure? His penis had never been so stiff; he knew he would ejaculate violently, profusely.

No, he would decide later; not for any of those reasons. It was because he had accepted the message of that little voice; that the die already was cast, their fate sealed, that it would have been near blasphemy to turn away so late. He was being used, and as he shuddered, thrust to the hilt, felt himself beginning to come knew that this time he was being used willingly.

Certainly it was the most violent orgasm of his life. For years afterward he would dread having another like it. It was painful. Even as his penis throbbed and spurted repeatedly and copiously a part of him now also sensed the hidden, silent, aloof hand of the the agent that used him *(yours, Índigo)*, the string-pulling manipulator that drained him, emptied him, like a milking machine in a dairy, as a phlebotomist would with clinical detachment draw blood from a vein; intent only on the payload, the single predestined sperm cell among millions that would penetrate and fertilize the egg waiting in the fallopian tube.

Later when her pregnancy was confirmed he would admit that he could never prove that he had impregnated her that very first time. They wouldn't sleep for the rest of the night, would as much as devour each other in the days that followed. But in his heart he would always know that he had gotten her with child in their very first coupling, and knew it too as — satiated, spent, sweating — he now clung to the woman he loved, pressed tender fingertips to her cheeks, met her shy, vulnerable gaze, and with reassuring smile and whisper bent his lips to kiss ...

(What a coward I've always been about this. How much safer I've always felt to tell my story as if I were someone else. I couldn't admit to being me even in my diary. But now at the very end I'll force myself to stop pretending.)

CHAPTER FIFTY-ONE

... to kiss your mother, Índigo, your sacred, adored, beautiful mother.

Even in grade school we both knew how much smarter you'd be than either of us. How you'd dash about at Ferndell, Índigo, naming things: a koi, a button fern, an elephant ear plant, names neither of us knew. In a way we both preferred you when you were in early high school, when you were still juvenile enough to sometimes show how dumbfounded you felt with your parents' more ordinary minds. By eighteen you already were too well-mannered for such lapses, hid your incredulity behind a gracious smile, courteous beyond your years. By then you also were closer to the godparent who gave you your name. Maybe that's when you insisted on arriving when you did, Índigo, as ill-prepared as Odetta and I were then to be parents. You were in a hurry to meet him.

You always wanted the story. At last, it's ready for you.

This is how you were born, Índigo, how we conceived you. This is how your life began. I'll always wonder if you planned it all.

END

AFTERWORD

I just spent over two hundred sixty pages trying to seduce you into believing a make-believe story with made-up characters. Academics have a term for such seductions: narrative transportation.

Narrative transportation can be harmful. President Richard Nixon was likely inspired by the movie *Patton* to invade Cambodia. An adolescent who watches James Bond blast through road barriers in his Aston Martin may court disaster once set loose with provisional driving license in the family sedan. (See **https://pubmed.ncbi.nlm.nih.gov/25493323/**)

I'm too old to want to burden my conscience with any new unforced sins. I thus now seek to un-seduce, to puncture the bubble of any potentially harmful illusions I may have introduced in this story. As follows:

• In real life, we'd better acknowledge the so-frequently brutal hierarchy of appearance, especially when we are in the especially brutal prime years of the reproductive cycle.

Indigo's protagonist is described as a spectacularly handsome man. He eventually will judge his future partner as beautiful, but the novel never suggests that others regard her that way. He's the big looker; she isn't.

Those endowed with physical beauty regularly barter attractiveness to fatten wallets or advance careers. If such mercenary concerns aren't involved, however, we average-looking or homely folk are likely to be disappointed when mooning over the knockouts, sometimes tragically so.

I suggest a look into assortative mating. I don't like it, either.

• Don't hitchhike! Please!

Twenty-first century hitchhiking could be made reasonably safe, with an online database of vetted ride seekers and ride offerers, and a means of checking both driver and hitchhiker before the passenger door opens. But no such network exists, and I regard ride thumbing without it as prohibitively dangerous. I think of hitchhiking as something I was lucky to have gotten away with.

If you doubt me, read about the Toolbox Killers. The hitchhiker only has to get in the wrong car once.

• It certainly would have been more sensible for this novel's starry-eyed lovers to have used birth control and built a financial nest egg before having children.

• Feel free to call a hotline if in emotional need, but the volunteer is unlikely to be a dreamboat, will see you impersonally as a client, and may call the police if you become obsessive.

• I am not lobbying for anyone to have children. I don't have any, even had a vasectomy to insure that I wouldn't. A child's prospects for happiness in a presumably unasked-for life may depend on parenting, genetic patrimony, family finances and the environment into which the new life is introduced. (And, of course, dumb luck.) Would *you* have wanted to be sired by a slave with a strong predisposition to sickle cell disease in a Deep South plantation in the eighteenth century? Would you really have chosen such a life over no life at all?

•   •   •

I'll also feel better if I use this afterword to add:

• California's Route 99 in general and Bakersfield in particular were indeed regarded with dread by many hitchhikers in the 1970s. Old friend CG and I were marooned for *eleven hours* at a north Fresno on-ramp, which inspired Mark's reflections in Chapter Twenty-Four; on another hitchhiking trip, the only really rotten cop I've ever dealt with personally nearly railroaded me into the Fresno jail. (As for Bakersfield, I don't remember ever daring to hitchhike there.)

But: that was then, this is now. The real life, Route 99-centric Stanislaus Humanists let me hang out with them in 2016 while awaiting my Spain visa. I fondly remember the tranquil environs of the host's Modesto home, and also was impressed by Modesto while enjoying a social outing with the group at a Modesto coffee shop.

• Hollywood has improved since the 1970s, or at least had when I last visited in 2011. The now freeway-less Cloverdale probably has, too.

• The novel's suicide hotline is emphatically *not* modeled after the Santa Rosa suicide hotline where I volunteered in the late 1970s. Santa Rosa is mentioned specifically as a separate community in the second chapter. I remember the Santa Rosa service as well-run, with excellent phone lines and sober volunteers.

However, the Fishman was a real serial caller to the Santa Rosa hotline, and is accurately described in this novel. I spoke to him at least twice, and remember how abusive he became when I asked why he thought a suicide hotline would be interested in coastal fish farming. We volunteers did refer to him as "the Fishman," and did log his calls with sketches of fish in the office log book.